THE
HANGING
DOLLS

BOOKS BY RUHI CHOUDHARY

THE DETECTIVE MACKENZIE PRICE SERIES
Our Daughter's Bones
Their Frozen Graves
Little Boy Lost
The Taken Ones
The Lost Bones
Out of Sight

His Last Wife

RUHI CHOUDHARY

THE HANGING DOLLS

bookouture

Published by Bookouture in 2025

An imprint of Storyfire Ltd.
Carmelite House
50 Victoria Embankment
London EC4Y 0DZ

www.bookouture.com

The authorised representative in the EEA is Hachette Ireland
8 Castlecourt Centre
Dublin 15 D15 XTP3
Ireland
(email: info@hbgi.ie)

Copyright © Ruhi Choudhary, 2025

Ruhi Choudhary has asserted her right to be identified
as the author of this work.

All rights reserved. No part of this publication may be reproduced, stored in any retrieval system, or transmitted, in any form or by any means, electronic, mechanical, photocopying, recording or otherwise, without the prior written permission of the publishers.

ISBN: 978-1-83525-297-0
eBook ISBN: 978-1-83525-296-3

This book is a work of fiction. Names, characters, businesses, organizations, places and events other than those clearly in the public domain, are either the product of the author's imagination or are used fictitiously. Any resemblance to actual persons, living or dead, events or locales is entirely coincidental.

To my husband, Aditya, for always encouraging my imagination.

PROLOGUE
PAST

All Zoe saw was the motionless hand, hanging over the lip of the bathtub. A gold bracelet adorned the wrist.

And a broken, painted nail.

"Were you the one who found the body?" a balding man with a ruddy complexion asked, his voice devoid of any emotion, eyes glued to the notepad in his hands.

"Yes."

The man frowned at the innocent voice. His eyes tracked to the girl with thick glasses and high ponytail, wearing denim overalls. His face softened. "What's your name?"

She took a moment to reply. "Zoe."

"How old are you?"

"Fourteen years old."

"And who is that woman?" He hitched his thumb over his shoulder at the bathtub.

There was a crowd of people around the tub, and the sound of cameras clicking and people whispering did nothing to drown out the blaring silence in Zoe's ears.

"My mother."

The detective's face fell. He ushered her outside the bathroom, closing the door behind them. He ran his hand over his bald head, suddenly out of his element. Zoe figured he wasn't used to dealing with children. Maybe confronting evil was easier than shattering innocence. "What's your mother's name?"

"Rachel Sullivan."

"Where's your father?"

"I never knew him." She shrugged.

"Shit." He mumbled under his breath. "Sorry, kid." His eyes scanned the family room of the apartment; stuffed toys scattered around, a Tickle Me Elmo lay limply on the sofa. "There's another kid in the house? Younger than you?"

"My little sister, Gina. She's five years old and she's on a playdate. I have to pick her up in an hour."

"Is there anyone you can call? Grandparents? Aunts, uncles? Anyone?"

"No."

He scratched the back of his ear and narrowed his eyes. Zoe knew he was probably wondering if there was something wrong with her or if she was in shock. It was a mix of both. Tears wouldn't come—not yet anyway. She could feel them building behind her eyes, waiting to fall, in private.

But there was an energy crackling through her. A low vibration in the pit of her stomach. She crossed her arms and dug her nails into the palms of her skin.

"Are you okay to answer a few more questions?" he asked.

"Yes, of course."

"Okay... how did you get into the apartment?"

"I have a spare key. I was just getting back from dropping off Gina. The door was locked, and when I got in, I didn't see any sign of a struggle or anything different about the place. I knew Mom was supposed to be home. I was looking for her when I found her in the bathroom."

He stared at her, dumbfounded, before composing himself. "Can you think of anyone who might have wanted to hurt your mother? A boyfriend? A colleague?"

"No."

While the detective busied himself dispatching Child Protective Services, Zoe watched the scene in the bathroom unfold through the crack in the door. They were lifting her mother's body out of the bathtub and placing her into the body bag. When she glimpsed her mother's face, her throat closed, until she couldn't breathe.

She moved away and looked out the window into the gloomy skies. A flock of black birds formed like an arrow flew across. She heard her mother being taken away by the authorities. Something removed itself from her being and went out the door with her mother. But the tears still didn't come, just a feeling of suffocation like she was breathing through straws.

"Zoe." She turned around to find the detective solemn and sincere. "I'm sorry. I will find out what happened to your mother."

"Thank you. But I already know."

A frown. "What?"

"She was depressed. She killed herself." Her voice didn't crack at the lie.

He didn't answer. But she knew he would buy her theory eventually. Her clear-cut, logical explanation for her mother's death. This wasn't a simple case of breaking and entering, with her mother being in the wrong place at the wrong time. This was not a homicide. Months from now, the detective would eventually close the file, declaring that Rachel Sullivan did in fact commit suicide.

There were many things he wouldn't have known.

Like how the window to the fire escape was open and there were water marks on the floor outside the bathroom.

He would never know because before Zoe called 911, she

got rid of all evidence that someone else had been in the house. The person who killed her mother.

ONE
NOW

Detective Scott Cohen hadn't slept a wink in the last four days, and his pulsing headache was only amplified by the seagulls circling overhead, taunting him with their screeching, grating cries.

"Terri?" he said to his sturdy deputy in uniform. "Do you think I could shoot these little devils and get away with it?"

She pulled a face at the gulls as they swooped down to tussle over a piece of seaweed. "I wouldn't, boss. But aren't you vegetarian and against hunting?"

"Shush. I have a reputation to maintain." He fixed his tie. "Spread out the search pattern."

Terri instructed the rest of the officers as they continued to comb the sandy beach dotted with pebbles. The shoreline was jagged, with rocky outcrops jutting into the restless waves of the Pacific Ocean. Driftwood, bleached and weathered, scattered along the long, uneven expanse in artistic shapes.

Scott sat on driftwood, watching five of his officers disperse in all directions. Hope was a fickle thing. It could shrink to the size of an atom but it would never entirely desert you. As the likelihood of anyone finding anything began to dwindle, so too did Scott's optimism. He looked up at the heavy blanket of steel-gray clouds, mirroring the gloom blossoming behind his ribs. It wasn't the best day for a beach day, which was why there was only a small group of high schoolers watching them from a distance, instead of being in school.

Terri returned, shaking her head. "Sorry, boss. There's nothing here."

He stood up. "Another anonymous tip leads to nothing. Shocking."

"We'll find her." She swallowed. "How are the parents doing?"

"What do you think?" He sighed. "They were at the station early this morning."

"I heard the mother was hospitalized."

He nodded, his shoulders sagging. "She had an anxiety attack and had to be sedated. It's every parent's worst nightmare."

Seven-year-old Lily Baker had been missing for four days. Scott knew the statistics. The chances of her being alive were whittling down to zero every passing hour. That dreaded thought had been chewing at his sanity for the last few days.

"Let's pack up," he announced, inhaling the briny air. "I have to head to the station and talk to Travis."

The seagrass along the dunes swayed as he waded his way through to his car. In the distance, he spotted a woman with curly, red hair in a blue dress watching the scene at the beach unfold. When she noticed him watching her, she waved at him. He locked his jaw tight, got in the car and drove away.

* * *

Harborwood Police Station was situated at the edge of a dense forest, surrounded by towering evergreens and thick underbrush. The one-story building was clad in weathered, cedar shingles that had taken on a silvery-gray hue over the years, dark green trim around the windows and a rustic wooden sign above the door.

When Scott was a little kid, his father would bring him here late at night. While his father swept the floors, Scott would sit watching the police officers on night shift. He was so fascinated by their uniform and the power they emanated. It was a child's dream to be this close to real-life police officers. He'd only ever seen them on TV chasing the bad guys, and he loved the unexpected rush of adrenaline he experienced as he watched them hunt down murderers and get involved in high-speed car chases.

Upon entering the station, Scott ignored the few people sitting in the waiting area. He avoided everyone. There were too many eyes on him, being the lead investigator on the Lily Baker case. The prodding, piercing gazes had burned enough holes through him. They were loaded with accusing questions—*Why hasn't he found her yet? Isn't he looking hard enough?*

He was heading to the chief's office past the cubicles when he stopped at the bulletin board next to the television. Flyers were stapled all over it—the usual missing pets and the unusual case of a missing child. Lily Baker had long brown hair, parted in the middle, almond-shaped hazel eyes, and slightly crooked tiny teeth. In the photo, she smiled like she was up to no good.

"Cohen!" Travis appeared at the doorway to his office and beckoned him over with two fingers—like he always did.

Scott braced himself to give another disappointing update. Travis's office was the largest, with a window offering a view of the forest. Shafts of light filtered through the blinds. The desk was cluttered with paperwork, a couple of potted plants and a collection of maritime memorabilia. There was also a picture hanging on the wall of Travis graduating from the academy. The last thirty years had added several pounds to his waistline and snagged at the skin on his face. But the chief was proud that the hair on his head was thick like a "lion's mane" in his own words.

"We were following up on an anonymous tip—" Scott waltzed into the office and froze when he saw a slim man with a long neck, reddish orange hair in a blue suit that matched his eyes sitting across from Travis. "Mayor Hicks!"

"Detective Cohen." He offered his hand but did not stand up.

Scott shot Travis a questioning look. The chief subtly shook his head; the visit must have been a surprise to him too.

"You arrived just in time," Travis said by way of explanation. "The mayor wanted to discuss the case with you."

"Yes. Is there any progress?"

"There have been no ransom demands. We have rounded up everyone on the sex offender registry in town but there were no leads. We have entered her information on the NCIC and are getting assistance from the Washington State Police who are patrolling borders." Scott folded his arms, referring to the National Crime Information Center.

"Wasn't an Amber Alert issued?" Hicks asked in his deep voice.

"Not enough information on the abduction to meet the criteria."

Hicks released a sharp breath. "So now we are at the mercy of anonymous tips. We all know how those go. Why aren't the rangers helping?"

"She was taken nowhere near the woods," Travis pitched in, interlacing his fingers in front of him. "This is the first time we are dealing with a missing kid."

"I know." Hicks flattened his mouth. "Regina Warner is going to use this against me. Mayoral elections are in two months."

Scott stifled a scoff.

Travis gave him a side-eye. "We are pooling all our resources into this—"

"Make the call, Travis."

Travis stiffened. Scott's gaze bounced between them. "Call whom?"

"Mayor Hicks wants to involve the FBI." Travis twirled a pen between his fingers, clearly unhappy with the idea.

"Oh." Scott's eyebrows shot up. "Mayor, we have it—"

Hicks raised his hand. "Don't say you have it under control, Scott. Four days and absolutely *no* leads?"

Irritation crawled on Scott's skin like a serpent. His tongue sat heavy in his mouth like a chunk of iron. Hicks had a point. His words had twisted deep inside Scott, reminding him of his inadequacy. As if the entire thing was his fault.

"I'll call the Special Agent in Charge at the Seattle office," Travis conceded, still reluctant. Scott knew his chief. They were buddies more than anything. He could tell the chief's mood from the way his mustache wiggled when he spoke.

"Today." Hicks raised his eyebrows.

Travis sucked air through his teeth. "Today."

Hicks slapped the armrests of his chair and got to his feet. "Now that's a plan!" He shook hands with Travis and Scott. "Think of this as training. I'm sure you guys will learn a thing or two from the best in the field." With a swing in his step, he went out the flapping doors.

"Condescending bastard." Travis grunted and fell back on his squeaky chair once they were alone. "Someone that short shouldn't have this much attitude."

Scott smirked, used to Travis's controversial sense of humor. "He's more worried about the elections. He should be. He lost my vote."

"Regina is gaining momentum." Travis unlocked the bottom drawer on his desk and pulled out a bottle of bourbon and a glass.

"Have you met her?" Scott asked, shaking his head when Travis offered him a drink.

"Just in passing. I expect her campaign manager is going to want to set up a meeting soon." He inspected the color of his drink with thinned eyes. "She needs the cop vote. Will make big promises." He took a large swig. "Don't beat yourself up over this."

Scott recoiled. "Everyone should be beating themselves up over this."

"The biggest case this town has seen in recent years was that guy killed in a bar fight. Open and shut. The FBI can be helpful."

"I know." He nodded. He wasn't opposed to the help. His ego wasn't nearly as big as people perceived it to be, especially with a missing little girl whose life was hanging in the balance. But still he couldn't help feeling defeated that they had been searching for four days and not found a single clue. "I just hope it doesn't become a pissing contest."

TWO

Bop.
Bop.
Bop.

The sound of bullets flying out of the barrel blasted through the room, the noise dampened by her ear defenders. Dopamine pumped through Zoe's veins at the sound of the gunshots. The paper man at the end of the row now had three holes in his body. One through the head, one through the chest and one through the groin. Satisfaction spread through her.

In her mind, the paper man was very much real. But he was faceless and nameless. Often, she would picture a stocky man wearing a purple suit, his face concealed by a shadow. A leathery, viscous shadow of impenetrable darkness—so solid and unyielding, almost like a mask.

Sometimes in Zoe's nightmares, she would spend hours trying to rip that mask off the man's face. Her nails would pluck off and her fingers would bleed but there was always another layer of shadows behind the one she would manage to tear off. Infinite layers sluicing off each other until Zoe would wake up with a jolt and a racing heart.

"Do you have a vendetta against men, Zoe?" Simon whistled beside her.

Zoe removed her ear protection and clicked the button to draw the paper close. "I did spend two years undercover with a rapist," she said with an uncomfortable chuckle.

Simon's face fell. "Are you sure you don't want to take time off? I'm your boss, but I really don't want to force you."

"You can't force me. Your department will fall apart without me," she teased lightly.

He went to reply, but his phone vibrated in his pocket and he excused himself. Zoe watched his tall, muscular frame through the doorway. His golden locks crowded his forehead, but there was a ruddiness to his skin that came with age.

She still remembered how scruffy his jaw had felt under her fingers all those years ago when they'd foolishly spent a few nights together after she graduated from Quantico.

"I see. Yeah, I heard about that." Simon twisted the wedding ring on his finger. His eyes flicked to Zoe and she looked away. "You got it." He hung up and poked his head back inside the shooting range room. "Have you heard of Harborwood?"

"No." Zoe frowned.

"You'll love it there." He grinned.

"What?"

"The local PD wants assistance." Simon gestured for her to follow him. She had to sprint to keep up with his long strides as they made their way to his office. "They got a missing kid. Out of their depth on this one."

The office was unusually noisy today. Phones were ringing off the hook. All interrogation and conference rooms were packed with quarreling lawyers in stuffy suits arguing over charges and negotiating deals. Zoe had to strategically cut her way through the mass of bodies around her, trying to focus on the words coming out of Simon's mouth. "Missing kid? How old?"

"Seven-year-old girl. They don't deal with cases like these."

"How long has she been missing?"

"Four days."

Dread coiled like a rope around Zoe's throat, squeezing it tight. She stopped dead in her tracks at the same time as Simon. "Well, that kid is probably not ali—"

Simon raised his hand. "Zoe, I have known you since Quantico. I know you use dark humor as a coping mechanism. But Harborwood PD don't. Be careful, okay?"

She bit her tongue, holding back another cheeky comment as she rocked on her heels. "Yes, boss."

He released a breath and muttered, "I hope I don't regret this." He spun on his heel when Zoe interrupted.

"Why me then? There are others."

His face pinched in thought. "Because once you solved a homicide with no other clues but a torn up parking ticket. *And* you need this. I can tell that you've been... looking for something to do. Though, I won't send you alone. There's a missing kid and I got a feeling about this one."

"Why so? Kids go missing all the time."

"There it is. The brashness." He sighed. "Harborwood is a small town with no reports of any violent crimes in the past decade. I'll get a profiler to partner up with you."

She felt her face turn hot. "Okay. Give me what you got on this."

"I'm waiting for—" Simon swung open the door to his office with Zoe tailing him when he halted, causing her to almost crash into the back of him. "Nancy!"

A slender, tall woman with a narrow, heart-shaped face, doe-like eyes and wavy dirty blonde hair. "Simon." She smiled but when her eyes fell on Zoe, they lingered for longer than necessary on the closed distance between her and Simon.

Simon rushed up to her. "What a surprise."

"I was in the area so I thought we could go and grab some lunch together." She smiled tightly at Zoe as she asked, "How's it going?"

"Great." Zoe beamed. "Your husband's shipping me off to Harborwood on a case."

"Harborwood? Never heard of it."

"Always trying to get rid of me."

"I'm not trying to get rid of you. You're the best agent I got," Simon said. "Despite your tendencies to put your foot in your mouth."

Zoe stuck out her tongue, making him chuckle. When their laughter dissolved, Zoe noticed Nancy's fallen face forcing a smile.

A blade of guilt twisted inside Zoe. "Send me the files when you get them. Enjoy your lunch!"

As soon as she closed the door behind her, she could hear them bickering again. Something about Nancy questioning why Simon and Zoe spent so much time together. As she walked away, Zoe's ears burned and her eyes grew heavy.

A few hours later, Zoe was perched on the vanity countertop, whistling and swinging her legs. Outside the window was glittering blackness. No one used this washroom, especially at nine in the evening. It was quiet here, which she liked. Since she didn't have anyone to go home to, she'd stayed behind. Simon had sent her the information he had received from Harborwood PD.

Lily Baker disappeared from a playground halfway between her house and her school four days ago at 4:30 p.m. According to the sister, she had looked away only for a minute to finish paying for an ice cream for Lily but when she turned back Lily was nowhere to be seen.

Four days. The prospects were bleak. Hope was a thing of cruelty in her line of work, but it was a necessity. It was the glue that held together sanity of minds that could too easily be ravaged by violence and betrayal. It held Zoe together too.

It had been over twenty years since she'd nearly lost all hope. And still, a glimmer of it remained.

She memorized the basics quickly, but Chief Travis Hunter hadn't sent a lot of information. Maybe Simon was right. This was exactly what she needed because digging into her mother's past had hit a brick wall. It had sent her thoughts wayward. And she was thinking too much about the last time she went undercover. It was not only the longest undercover assignment, but also the hardest one she'd ever been on. No matter how much time had passed since and no matter how many countless showers she had, the remnants of the leader of the cult she'd infiltrated still lingered on her skin. He was like poisonous air she had inhaled that was taking forever to detox.

Zoe put the file away and stared at her reflection.

She was short but sculpted. Her dark hair, frizzy and curly, framed a squarish face with pillowy lips and dark brown eyes that were just a little far apart. Her skin was glassy, a light shade of brown. She searched for similarities between her and her mother Rachel. Other than the small nose and slightly protruding ears, they had nothing in common. It was her sister, Gina, who had inherited her mother's green eyes and thin lips and silky, brown hair.

Zoe could only assume she took after her father—whoever that was. She washed her face and braced herself. Her eyes landed on a picture of the girl. Razor-sharp fear twisted in her stomach.

What had happened to Lily?

Her phone buzzed. It was a message from Simon.

Dr. Aiden Wesley is on the case with you.

Her eyes ballooned at the name. *Aiden Wesley*. A groan escaped her throat and she slammed her head against the concrete wall.

THREE

"I'll have two Belgian waffles, two pork sausages, two eggs sunny side up and one chocolate milkshake." Zoe placed her order with a bright smile.

The bony, tattooed waitress with piercings in her eyebrows and lips asked sarcastically, "Not two milkshakes?"

"I'm avoiding sugar." Zoe joked as she tapped her tummy.

The waitress wasn't amused. "I'll be back."

Zoe wiped her sunglasses and scanned her surroundings. The drive from Seattle was over three hours long. This was the first diner she came across when she entered the town, a small shed-like structure that was being encroached on by moss. Rain tapped incessantly on the windows, the outside view a green blur. Wind howled like it was traveling through a tunnel. There were only three other patrons at the diner. A burly man at the counter having a Coke. An elderly couple sitting at the other end of the diner, eating their meal with a polished refinedness that almost seemed out of place in the diner.

The door opened with a ting and a tall man wearing a raincoat over his black suit entered. As soon as he turned, Zoe's lungs deflated. He was tall with a body too hard and honed to be a shrink. A light stubble dotted his scruffy jaw, and his heavy-lidded, calculating eyes that always looked down on the rest of the world would gleam with fascination when he found a challenging specimen. When he spotted Zoe, he pushed his thick glasses up his aristocratic, Roman nose.

"Agent Storm." He gave her a curt nod before sitting across from her.

"Dr. Wesley." She mimicked his deep voice, which only made him glare at her. "Sorry, I thought I should lighten the mood."

His thick lips twitched like he was trying not to smile as he shed his raincoat. "Perhaps we should prepare for our meeting with the detective. I tried contacting you, but you ignored my calls and emails."

Zoe drummed her fingers on the table. "My phone's dead."

"You couldn't charge it?"

"A dog ate my charger." Right then, her phone pinged with a notification. Their eyes remained locked in a silent battle.

"You want to check that?" He clicked his tongue.

With pursed lips, she stole a glance at her phone. "He'll be here in five minutes."

Zoe was well-liked at work. Back in the Seattle office, she was in charge of all the holidays—from decorating the Christmas tree and organizing Secret Santa to the Fourth of July barbeque. She knew what everyone liked—that child-like quality of carefree innocence. A mind which had not been withered or eroded by years of stumbling across bodies of all ages and watching trust crack. The nitty-gritty machinations of Zoe's brain slipped right through to her mouth.

That's what everyone believed. Everyone but Dr. Aiden Wesley. The genius shrink who watched her like she was a Christmas tree blinking out of sync, never once buying the show she was putting on.

"Anything in the case files stand out to you?" Zoe asked, unable to bear the thick silence between them.

His long fingers flicked the pages of a file, leisurely. "This is a rare occurrence. The last time someone went missing in Harborwood was around two decades ago. A small-knit community with low crime rates. My first thought was to consider the environmental factors."

"What do you mean?"

"Floods and storms are a common occurrence here." He pointed outside the window where the rain was battering against the glass. "There was no ransom or obvious crime scene since Lily Baker just wandered away. So I considered the possibility of her getting trapped or injured but the weather was perfect that day and the locals searched the woods. Which brings me to the second possibility—an outsider."

Zoe nodded. "Not a townie."

He shrugged. "This town barely sees any violent crimes and everyone knows each other. At this stage, the possibility of a transient individual, some recent arrival or someone passing through, is more likely."

She took a shuddery breath. An external perpetrator would be harder to track down. She peered out the window into the blur of green. There was a quiet fear that lurked beneath the beauty of the wilderness of Washington.

The door to the diner opened again and a man came in. His jawline stretched to a pointy chin, his dark hair shaven almost to the scalp and a large forehead.

He spotted Zoe and approached her. "Special Agent Zoe Storm?"

"And you must be Detective Scott Cohen." She shook his hand. "Thank you for meeting me here. This is my associate, Dr. Aiden Wesley. He's a criminal psychologist."

They shook hands and just then the waitress arrived with the food and placed it in front of them.

Scott frowned. "You guys had a long drive?"

"This is just for me." Zoe pulled the plates toward her and began tearing into the food with renewed hunger.

"Can I get you anything?" Scott turned to Aiden.

"I'll order a coffee."

"So hit me with it. What happened to Lily?" Zoe asked.

Scott stared at her, puzzled, and then shook his head vigorously. "Right." He retrieved a case file from his raincoat. "Lily's sister, Bella, reported her missing at around 4:30 p.m. four days ago on October 3. She was getting Lily an ice cream and when she turned around Lily was gone. There were no reliable eyewitnesses."

"What about surveillance?" Zoe asked with a stuffed mouth. "These waffles are good. Do you want some?"

"Uh... no, thanks. We rounded up sex offenders in the area. There are barely any. We put up missing person posters and we shared information with the sheriff's office and WSP. There have been no sightings." Scott conveyed the information in a monotonous, matter-of-fact tone as if he had repeated it many times before.

Zoe let it percolate when she noticed the burly man by the counter raise his arm to answer his phone, revealing a tattoo on his arm.

"What about family? Any disputes?" Aiden asked.

"Both parents work at the fish processing plant and can't think of anyone who would want to hurt them." His impatient eyes tracked the food as it slowly disappeared from Zoe's plate.

"And I'm guessing this is your first missing child case?"

Scott's face hardened as he gave a curt nod. "For me, yes. The last missing person case in the town was in the eighties."

Zoe chewed her food slowly, realizing she had inadvertently poked a raw wound. She knew how these things worked. No one appreciated an outsider waltzing in and taking the reins on an operation. But that is what the FBI often did. Before her deep undercover mission, she had hopped from one place to another, stepping on toes and bruising egos all over the country.

"We'll start again." She swallowed down her milkshake. "With the playground where she went missing from."

"Look, I don't mean to be an asshole but why did they send *you?*" Scott asked flatly, his patience finally worn out.

Aiden explained. "In seven to nine percent of the cases, the perpetrator is someone known to the child, but not a family member—a babysitter, a family friend, a neighbor—"

Scott shook his head, irritation flaring on his face. "The family doesn't have any enemies. There have been no reports of suspicious neighbors. This is a safe community—"

"And in one percent of cases, the abductor is a stranger. If that's the case, this might not be their first time or last time. We need to build a psychological profile."

A fleeting look of resignation before he turned to Zoe. "And what about you? Why you?"

"My sunny personality." She bit her tongue, Simon's warning ringing fresh in her ears. The two men watched her grimly. One puzzled and the other with a tinge of amusement.

She blinked, slurping the dregs of her milkshake. "That couple behind you?" She tipped her chin and he followed suit. "They don't appear to be from Harborwood because they're dressed in a completely different style. Where most people around here have some kind of waterproof coat with them to shield them from the Washington weather, he has a wool coat. He can't be from the South, that would be much too warm, and the cut is expensive, so he's likely from a big city with designer shops. But they have been coming here for a very long time because the waitress knew their order. So I am guessing that this diner means something to them. It's their little tradition. That man at the counter..." Scott's eyes followed. "He isn't just some trucker passing by. He likes the waitress because she ignores him and he keeps staring at her and tries to make conversation.

She's upset with him, though, and that might be because he was involved in something illegal. He has a tattoo on the left side of his torso. It was a serpent design with a trident, which is a gang's signage, but it's been covered with a tattoo of a date. Perhaps he has left the gang and is trying to make an honest living, and the date indicates when he left prison." Zoe's eyes swept over Scott. "*You* were in AA or still are. That bronze plastic chip in your keychain. You get that when you finish one year of sobriety."

Scott put the keys back in his pocket. "Fine. You notice things."

Zoe bit her tongue. Her reflection was distorted in everyone's eyes, even her sister Gina's. They saw a chatty, effervescent woman who just *noticed* things. Reduced to an aspiring Sherlock with a badge and a gun.

"We should draw up a list of anyone who is new in town. Even if it's some family member visiting," Aiden said. "You think you can help with that?"

"Yeah, yeah. Chief Hunter at the station sure can. He's involved with the community and can point you to the right resources."

Zoe slammed her hands on the table. "Great. Why don't Detective Cohen and I head to the playground, and, Dr. Wesley, you can go to the station?"

Aiden opened his mouth as if to protest but his shoulders fell as he nodded. "Sure. I'll just finish my coffee and head over."

Scott's eyes bounced between them. "Weather's going to get worse if we don't hurry."

Zoe left a bill on the table. On her way out, she looked over her shoulder, catching the interaction between the waitress and the man. As the waitress walked past him, he gripped her wrist, forcing her to face him. Her expression switched from defiant to fearful. He whispered something through gritted teeth and the waitress wrenched her hand free—an angry red bruise marring her pale skin. Her other hand mindlessly flew to her neck and Zoe noticed purple fingerprints on the sides of her throat. The waitress lifted the collar of her shirt to hide them and nodded at the man.

The man's smile was satisfying and cruel.

Zoe clenched her jaw. A hot swoop of rage flicked over her stomach. Her vision tunneled on the man.

"Agent Storm? You ready?" Scott asked.

"Yes." Zoe beamed, making a mental note of the man's license plate number as they left.

FOUR

"How do you do it?" Aiden had asked, twirling a pen between his long fingers.

"Do what?" she asked, arching one eyebrow.

"Mold all that gunk into your brain so easily."

"Gunk?"

"The violence, Storm. The violence you see every day." His eyes sparkled with fascination.

Zoe scoffed. "Compartmentalization. Thought psychologists knew that concept."

Aiden's eyes softened, his mouth set in a grim line as he scribbled in his notepad.

* * *

Harborwood was a small town, nestled between two Native American Reservations, Hoh and Quinault tribes, just a stone's throw from La Push beach. Zoe followed Scott's car as he led the way to the playground where Lily was last seen. The car glided smoothly on vast country roads with the Pacific Ocean stretching into infinity on one side. A thick layer of fog lingered on the horizon; the path was sprinkled with gas stations and casinos, sprawling farmlands with warehouses and billboards advertising services that Zoe deemed to be fraudulent.

Lose 100 pounds in 10 days! Zoe snickered.

She had never stayed in one place for long. Even when she was a child, Rachel was always packing them up and moving them on every few years. Zoe didn't understand the loyalty people felt to their surroundings—how could a home be sacred if it was just bricks and mortar? What joy was there in getting coffee from the same place every day? Her roots were deeply entrenched in Gina and memories of Rachel. People, not places.

"Promise me. Promise me if anything happens, you will forget about it and move on."

Zoe swallowed hard. It was one promise she had no intention of keeping.

The car twisted into muddier, bumpier roads, weaving through blocks of gray, bleak apartment buildings. Zoe tried to commit the town to memory, but it was clear they were far from the core. Scott found a parking spot and Zoe parked right behind him.

As she got out of the car, a shiver rolled through her. She was used to the wind, having worked out of the Chicago office for years before transferring to Washington. But while Chicago winds were cutting and brutal, blowing her hair in a tangled rope and looking to stir chaos, the ocean breeze had a silent power to it. It seeped through her pores and chilled her to the bone.

A slow killer.

"You should buy some appropriate clothes." Scott noted her shudder. "I thought you'd been in Washington for a while."

She fell into step next to him. "Lakemore. Heard of it?"

He chuckled. "Yeah, anyone who follows football has. Were you on the Sharks case?"

"No. But I worked with the people who cracked that one. Only there for the summer though. It was warm."

"Summers are getting drier."

They came to the edge of the empty playground enclosed by a barbed fence. It was misting lightly, and the ominous gray skies overhead threatened more showers. The park looked deserted like it hadn't been used in years—rusty swing sets, lopsided seesaws, dulled slides and a faded merry-go-round. The sandbox was a bed of scattered leaves and dirt.

"When was the last time this was inspected?" Zoe wondered out loud.

"It's a low-income area but everything's solid," Scott said defensively. "How long have you and Dr. Wesley known each other?"

"We worked closely on a case five years ago and since then our paths have crossed here and there." She gave a nonchalant shrug but a sharp thread of unease pulled through her.

Zoe cleared her throat and that memory. She had looked at the surrounding area beforehand so that she was familiar. Behind the playground was a labyrinth of ancient trees. It was fall—other than the evergreens, the rest of the trees had a feathery barrenness to them. The vegetation on the ground was sparse and spiny, looking half-dead. In the distance, the mountain range was visible with snowy tips.

She pulled out a map from her backpack. She couldn't rely on Google Maps as her cell phone didn't always get reception out here. "So tell me where the ice cream truck was parked."

Scott pinpointed a spot on the map, only ten feet from where they were standing.

Zoe looked around. "And one minute Lily was next to her and the next she disappeared?"

"It was a sunny day so a lot of kids and parents were around."

"Playgrounds attract pedophiles too."

"I looked into the registered sex offenders. But I don't know how many closeted ones are hiding in plain sight." Something in his own words disturbed him.

"What?"

A look of horror flashed across his face. "I just realized I might have come across whoever did this, maybe even exchanged words. It's a small town, everyone knows everyone."

Zoe cleared her throat. Behind her was the entrance to an apartment building and next to it a little coffee shop. "It might not necessarily be a townie like Aiden suggested. Did you check for surveillance in there?"

"Yeah, the café's camera was set to stream so does not record, and the apartment building's camera faces the building —not the street."

Zoe rolled up the map and tucked it into the back pocket of her jeans. Her eyes narrowed to slits as she noticed something about the building.

"What do you see?" He saw the look on her face.

She hurried over to the building without replying. She threw a swift glance around the street. There was no one lurking around. Overhead, the clouds were beginning to circle. It was about to pour *again*.

She swung open the exterior door and entered the vestibule. The camera faced the interior door, not the exterior.

"See? It doesn't offer a view of the street," Scott said.

"No. It faces the interior door. Which is made of *mirrored glass*."

Realization dawned and he squeezed his eyes close. "Damn. Reflection. All right. Let's see what they have."

He banged on the inner door until the security guard who was busy scrolling on his phone and bobbing his head to music suddenly looked up. With a scowl, the guard pressed a button to open the door. When Scott flashed his badge, his demeanor shifted and he wriggled on his squeaky chair.

"This is my associate from the FBI, Zoe Storm," Scott said sternly. "Do you keep recordings of the security camera over there?"

"Yes." He blinked wildly. "Why? What's happened?"

"How long do you keep them for?"

"Two weeks."

"We need to see the recording for the evening of October 3. Right now." He placed an elbow on the reception desk.

"I... Maybe I should call my manag—" His hand hovered over the phone when Scott interrupted.

"This is regarding the disappearance of Lily Baker."

The security guard's face fell. His eyebrows pulled together and he nodded. "Of course. Follow me through to the back."

Zoe and Scott exchanged a satisfied look. The guard led them to a dimly lit room with two monitors and a stack of files on a steel rack. He sat down at a computer and pulled up a file from the date. "Here you go. You can fast-forward or rewind it." He wheeled himself out of the way.

Scott fast-forwarded the video to 4:30 p.m. and hit play. One corner of the parked ice cream truck was visible in the reflection. Zoe waited for a glimpse of the little girl and a few minutes later, she spotted Lily holding her sister's hand.

Zoe held her breath—she didn't know what to expect, what they would discover—but watching Lily in action, giggling and frolicking, thickened the saliva in her throat. While Bella, her teenage sister, searched for cash in her purse, Lily left her side.

They watched her run to the street, reaching the edge of the camera's view, where only the trunk and taillights of a black car were visible.

Zoe held her breath. Within seconds, the car rolled away and Lily had vanished.

"Did she get in the car?" Scott said, his eyebrows pulling together.

"Possibly. We only have a partial view. But this means that she knew who it was. She willingly went to them."

Scott kept replaying the video and clicked his tongue. "Damn it. It's a reflection so the quality isn't good enough to read the license plate. Wait, the FBI has software that can help, right?"

"The FBI has got everything," Zoe boasted. "Let's get a copy of this and I'll send it over to my guys."

"How long will it take?" he said, a hint of impatience in his voice.

"It's a missing kid. I'll make sure this gets priority," she said. Butterflies swarmed in her stomach at the anticipation. They had traced who had pulled Lily away from her sister and this person obviously hadn't come forward.

Maybe this was the abductor they were looking for.

Or the killer.

FIVE

"We are back and I'm joined by Regina Warner, a former schoolteacher and businesswoman, now running for mayor of Harborwood." The journalist with dirty blonde hair and a squeaky, high-pitched voice beamed at Regina. "Ms. Warner, you have no experience in politics or being in public office, so what makes you a better candidate than Mayor Hicks?"

Regina snapped back her shoulders, her lips spreading in that easy, confident smile that she had spent weeks mastering in front of the mirror every morning. "Sometimes you need someone on the outside to stick their neck in and get the job done. I think Mayor Hicks has been too cushy in his job and far too removed from the daily lives of voters." Her fierce gaze never wavered as she looked directly into the camera. "But *I* am one of them. I know what it is like to be a hardworking citizen in this town. I understand the frustrations and anxieties of the people who live here because these are my frustrations and anxieties too."

Behind the journalist stood a short man in a sharp suit, with a chalky, pale complexion and slick, black hair. He gave Regina

THE HANGING DOLLS

a thumbs-up. There were too many cameras around her to gloat at her delivery—slick and effective.

"Is the disappearance of Lily Baker a cause of distress for you?"

Regina looked down briefly before spotting a missing person poster—under the stack of papers on the table. Her lungs deflated, expelling all the air from them. The corners of her lips quivered and turned downward. Lily Baker—a little girl with a mischievous grin, unaware of what this world could do to her. Below her photo were the haunting words: *Have you seen me?*

"Y-yes... Lily." Regina's voice softened around the edges. "It infuriates me. The fact that this has happened is unacceptable. If our kids aren't safe in this town, then we are doomed."

The journalist nodded solemnly and then turned to the camera. "We'll be back after a short break." As soon as the cameraman confirmed that they weren't rolling, she sat back and sighed dramatically. "Someone get me water! I'm parched!"

Regina turned around with a sharp jerk of her head and pulled him aside. Her house was full of people, from the local news crew with all their sprawling equipment to her small team of makeup artists and interns. She pinched the side of her waist, flustered.

"That was epic!" The man gripped her shoulders, his energy almost infectious. "You're doing great."

She clenched her teeth. "Connor, what was that?"

"What do you mean?" He dropped his arms.

"You said all the questions were planted. Did you know she was going to ask about Lily Baker?" Regina said, glaring at him.

His eyes twitched and he lowered his voice. "I did but—"

"*What?*" Her voice piqued and Connor took her by the elbow and guided her toward the kitchen away from prying eyes and ears.

"Like I mentioned before, you're not polling well with a

certain demographic. Hicks is attacking you for failing to represent family values because you're single and childless—"

Regina rolled her eyes and blew a frustrated grunt. It wasn't the first time this was held against her. Like she was somehow incapable of empathy and basic decency without a husband and a child. "This is the twenty-first century—"

"I know." He raised his hands in surrender. "But get real, Regina. You need those conservative votes, too."

She wavered. "You could have given me a heads-up."

"I needed a genuine reaction. And you gave one. You looked positively disturbed. That will resonate with the voters."

"Weren't *you* disturbed exploiting that for votes?"

Connor shoved his hands in his pockets, a mask of indifference on his young face. "Anything to get you elected. That's my priority. That and not wasting my time on children I don't know."

Connor brushed past her to discuss more questions with the journalist, who had been eyeing him with interest. Regina blinked at his harsh words ringing in her head. She didn't realize that the piece of paper with the missing girl information was crumpled in her fist. She smoothened it out, the sight of Lily like a slap across her face.

* * *

On. Off. On. Off. On. Off.

Zoe flicked the lamp on her bedside table. The motel room smelled funny. Not quite like something had died there, but she was convinced someone had left food behind which was rotting. She was planning on switching rooms first thing in the morning. Tonight, somehow, she was going to survive and hope that no bed bugs surprised her.

Aiden was staying somewhere in this motel too. She wondered how his room was. It probably smelled better or he had brought scented candles with him. She remembered how polished his office always was—gleaming surfaces devoid of water rings or even a fleck of dust, curtains with perfectly spaced pleats, and pens in holders arranged in ROYGBIV order. Zoe chuckled at the time she had made the grave mistake of not using a coaster and how his eyes had popped out in horror as he scribbled furiously in his notepad.

She got out of bed and pulled open the curtains to view the night sky shrouded in thick, rolling clouds that blotted out the moon and stars. Wind raced through the trees in the distance, whipping branches and sending leaves spiraling in the air. Thunder rumbled ominously in the distance, growing louder with each passing moment, as if the sky itself was growling. Lightning cracked, illuminating the landscape in brief, blinding flashes, casting jagged shadows across the ground. And then the rain began to fall, first as a light drizzle, then intensifying into a torrential downpour, each drop striking the ground like a drumbeat.

Zoe tied her frizzy hair in a tight bun and put on her black hoodie. She'd received a message from a colleague at the FBI, sharing the location she needed. Her tepid gaze hardened and she stepped out into the rainy night.

She jogged to her destination, having memorized the layout of the town. A chill tightened her skin. Drops of water hung off her eyelashes, making her vision blurry, but she plowed on. By the time she rounded into the street lined with single-story homes, her heart was thumping and her legs were seizing up. She remembered the address. It was the little house at the end of the street.

And there was the truck she had seen earlier in the day at the diner.

Her pace slowed as she made her way to the house. It was past midnight so all the lights were out, and the sheets of rain obscured her vision even further.

She reached the modest house and gave it the once-over. The tattooed man from the diner was probably asleep. She could key his car but that would wake up the neighbors. A quick scan revealed no cameras at the door. She took the simplest approach.

She rang the bell. Twice.

Then she stood around the corner, her back pressed to the side of the house. After a minute, the front door opened with a creak. She slowly peered around the corner, careful not to be seen. It was the man, in his pajamas. He glanced around, squinting in the rain. He mumbled something under his breath, spun on his heel and stomped back inside.

When the door slammed shut, she crept around to the front of the house and rang the bell again.

This time he swung open the door with a growl. Zoe slithered further around the corner of the house, her jacket sweeping the wet plywood. His boots squelched in the pools of water as he walked down the steps of the porch, his eyes scouring the area.

But the storm had knocked out most of the lights on the streets. Shadows slanted and rippled on the street, occasionally fractured by lightning.

He might not be able to see clearly, but Zoe could see everything.

But darkness was a friend. At least when she was like *this*. It was at night when she came alive, when some parts of her that were otherwise dormant suddenly reared their heads. She slipped easily into the folds of the velvety night, not in the least bit afraid of the monsters that lurked in the shadows.

She lurked in the shadows. *She* was that danger people feared. And in the dead of night when the rest of the world slept, Zoe shed the sugary, sweet layers that most people knew. She became that angry girl whose mother was murdered, and *she* had to clean up the evidence because of a promise she'd made.

She imagined unleashing all her pent-up rage on this man—the man who was hurting the waitress from the diner. How satisfying it would be to feel his bones break under her pounding fists; how gratifying it would be to see his blood on her skin. He would absorb the blows; his body would convulse. And he would know—deep down, he would know that he deserved this, to feel pain like he made the waitress feel pain. Because justice mattered to Zoe. And justice wasn't always served.

The sound of the rain amplified as she slowly let the rest of the world back in. Her senses began to wake up and the red hot rage reduced to a simmer.

The man went back inside the house, cursing. Zoe contemplated ringing the bell again but stopped herself. She was new to this town; she couldn't afford to get into trouble.

With whitened knuckles and quivering fingers, she shot a text message.

Z: How soon can you put me on the books?

The reply was instantaneous.

Unknown: Are you sure?

She knew that if she slipped once, she wasn't going to be able to stop.

Z: Yes.

SIX

"If you had the chance to hurt them without any consequences, would you?" Aiden asked.

Another dreadful day with the shrink and Zoe was striving hard to maintain her professionalism. "Them?"

"The people you were undercover with. They did horrible things and you had to pretend to be a part of their group. What would you have done if there were no laws?"

She leaned forward. "I'm supposed to say that I wouldn't hurt them, right? So that you don't mark me down as some red flag?"

"Now, I'll know that you're lying."

She chewed her lips, thinking hard. "I would have. And I think most people would."

"So you think it's fear of punishment that makes people do the right thing?"

"Why is hurting killers and drug peddlers the wrong thing?"

"So you believe in vigilante justice?"

Zoe could feel the irritation climbing up her skin like an itchy blanket. These sessions were going to be brutal. And Dr. Wesley had no idea what kind of justice Zoe believed in.

"Yes, I'm Batman," she growled.

Aiden smirked.

* * *

The next morning, when Zoe arrived at Harborwood Police Station, she wasn't sure if it was the right address. But the faded sign hanging above the door confirmed it.

The station's entrance was flanked by two lantern-style lights, their soft glow barely penetrating the fog that often rolled in from the coast. A narrow gravel path led to the front steps. The scent of pine and damp earth hung in the air, mixing with the salty tang of the ocean. She carried a tray of coffee she'd bought from the local shop on the way. Too used to big buildings made of steel and glass, the sight before her was jarring.

A large wooden desk dominated the reception area, behind which a wall of outdated filing cabinets stood in neat rows, each drawer labeled with handwritten tags. The walls were paneled in knotty pine. A few framed photos of the town in its earlier days hung crookedly on the walls, alongside a faded map of the surrounding forest. A small cluster of desks occupied the center of the room, each one cluttered with papers, radio equipment, and personal items—mugs, photos, and old police memorabilia.

A narrow hallway led to the back, where the cells were located—two small holding rooms with thick metal bars. The back door opened out onto a small clearing in the forest, where the patrol cars were parked under a makeshift carport, their roofs often covered in a layer of pine needles.

"Special Agent Zoe Storm?" a voice said from behind her. A man with thick hair, a thick mustache, and a thick belly. "Travis Hunter."

"Chief!" She did a little salute. "Coffee?" she said, holding out the tray.

He paused and blinked. "S-sure." He took a cup. "Your partner is here already."

Behind him, Aiden was leaning against a doorway, his ankles crossed and his face screaming boredom. When he saw her, his eyes twinkled and he waggled his fingers in a wave. She gave him a forced smile.

"How was your first day?"

"It was *great*." Then backtracked. "I mean... upsetting, of course. Which reminds me, where is Detective Cohen? I got something for him."

"Let's take this to my office."

As they walked through the station, Zoe drew a lot of attention. Curious eyes, even hesitant ones, flocked to her. She smiled brightly and waved at them, introducing herself to some passing patrol officers. When they reached his office, Scott was already present, thumbing his phone.

"Good morning, Detective Cohen!" She held out a cup of coffee. "Two milks and no sugar, just how you like it."

He stared at the cup before taking it. "How did you know?"

"I saw it scribbled on your empty coffee cup yesterday in the car."

"Christ, you're scary."

"You have no idea," she whispered under her breath.

"Based on my discussion with Dr. Wesley yesterday, we have started looking into any new arrivals or tourists," Travis said. "You have something for us? Scott was telling me about the video."

"I do. My tech guy got back to me early this morning. The license plate of the black car is registered to an Andy McMaster. Do you know him?"

Scott and Travis immediately locked eyes.

"Who is he?" Zoe said, intrigued.

"He works with Lily's dad at the fish processing plant. He's his supervisor," Scott said.

"Did you interview him?" she asked.

He shook his head. "There was no reason to. His name didn't come up when we talked to the parents and teachers."

"Then how do you know who he is?"

"It's Harborwood. Everyone knows everyone." Travis sighed. "Okay, go talk to him. I'll see if he has any priors. Dr. Wesley and I will continue digging at our end."

* * *

"Has this guy ever been in trouble?" she asked Scott as they pulled into the parking lot.

"Nope. No one really gets into trouble in this town. Until now."

The building was a large, industrial structure with corrugated metal walls streaked with rust and patches of peeling paint. The faint hum of machinery emanated from within, mingling with the distant cries of seagulls that circled above, hoping to scavenge scraps. As they stepped out of the car, the sound of the ocean waves crashing against the rocky shore echoed in the distance.

Zoe plugged her nose as the smell of fish overwhelmed her.

"How's your motel?" Scott asked.

She shrugged. "I've had better... and worse. How long have you been a detective for?"

"Four years. It's just me and two other guys. One of them is close to retirement. We never felt the need for more. Until now."

They made their way to the entrance, passing rows of stacked crates filled with freshly caught fish, still glistening with seawater. Workers in rubber boots hauled crates, loaded trucks, and tended to the conveyor belts that carried the fish into the plant.

Zoe shuddered at the sudden drop in temperature inside—necessary to preserve the catch—and the smell of disinfectant and chemicals, laced with fish.

They were directed to the supervisor's office where a burly man in his fifties, wearing a stained apron and a baseball cap, was leaning over a desk cluttered with paperwork and charts. A multitude of schedules and safety notices were pinned to a bulletin board behind him.

"That him?" she asked.

Scott nodded and knocked the doorframe. "Andy McMaster?"

The man looked up, his face lined and hands calloused. "Yes?"

"We have some questions for you. This is Special Agent Zoe Storm from the FBI."

He glanced at the clock behind him. "What is this about?"

"Lily Baker," Scott said. "You know her father, Tim Baker?"

"He's a good worker," he replied in a gruff voice. "I promoted him to manager last year. He's on leave right now... understandably."

Zoe read the safety protocols on the board behind him and studied his minimalistic office. Andy seemed comfortable talking to the police. It didn't seem like he had anything to hide.

"We have you on tape talking to Lily at the playground the day she disappeared. In fact, technically, you're the last person she was seen with."

Andy's stiff expression crumbled. He unfolded his arms, his eyes bouncing from Zoe to Scott. "What?"

"We have your car on video," Scott said. "So don't deny it."

He looked around at his messy desk as if searching for something. "I... I didn't do anything!"

"Well, then why didn't you come forward?" Scott retorted.

"I didn't think... it was so brief. I was just driving by and saw her and she recognized me from the times Tim would bring her to work... I just wanted to say hello. Please believe me. I didn't hurt her. I wouldn't do that. I got kids of my own!"

As if that ever stopped anyone, thought Zoe. She sat down and swung one leg over the other, invested more in the confrontation.

"You got problems with Tim?" Scott asked.

Andy's mouth fell open. "I just told you I promoted him. He's a solid guy. Very dependable. Come on, man!"

"What did you and Lily talk about?" Zoe asked.

He fumbled for words, scratching the back of his neck. "I... I don't know. I just said hi and asked if she was feeling better. I asked her who she was with, she said her sister, and I told her to say hi to her parents from me. That was it."

"She was sick?" Zoe didn't recall seeing anything about that in the statements from the family.

"Tim said she'd been throwing up a few days before. Food poisoning, I suppose. But it was just chitchat."

"And where did Lily go from there? Which direction?"

He gave it some thought. "She said something about how *he's* calling her so she has to go and say hi."

A zing of surprise pulsed through Zoe. She jerked upright and drew a sharp breath, her eyes catching Scott's.

"*He?*" Scott arched an eyebrow.

"Yeah, I don't know. I didn't see. She just ran off and there were so many people—"

"You didn't see who she met?" Zoe pressed.

"No! I thought she was referring to a friend. It was a sunny day. We don't get many of those here, and the park was teeming with people."

"So which direction did she run off in?"

"The opposite direction to the one she came from. I had to get home so I thought nothing of it and drove away..." Andy licked his lips. "Am I in trouble? Should I have done something else?"

They didn't answer. Zoe was preoccupied trying to trap the gloom that was cresting inside of her. *He.* Could be a boy. But could just as likely be a man. Lily must know him and that's why she went to say hi to him. Unfortunately, Zoe had come across one too many cases of children being groomed and lured by adults. And the possibility of worst-case scenarios skyrocketed when the adult was a male.

After asking him for his alibi, they emerged from the building to a windy day. Zoe's curls whipped around in all directions in a frenzy and she almost slipped on the weathered boards slick with rain and sea spray.

"This doesn't bode well," Scott finally said, huddling further into his coat. "If a man took her. Literally calls her over and then she goes missing for five days."

Zoe's gaze drifted to the boats moored along the sides, bobbing gently on the waves, their hulls scuffed and battered. "Okay, we should confirm Andy's alibi and do a preliminary dig into his financials. Maybe spare a patrol officer or two to interview the coworkers to confirm that Andy and Tim weren't on bad terms."

Scott nodded. "Already on it."

She tried to focus on the sound of water slapping against the dock piles. The likelihood of the grim outcome they dreaded lay quietly between them.

SEVEN

Zoe's eyes darted across the wall adorned with nautical memorabilia—faded maps, old fishing nets, and a large, mounted fish that had seen better days. She sat at the long, polished bar that ran along one side of the room, behind which shelves lined with bottles of whiskey, rum, and a few local brews stood in neat rows.

She connected to the VPN on her laptop and was busy going through all the reports from the sheriff's office and WSP. Lily's details had been recorded on NCIC, but nothing. Frustration clawed at her. An information net was pointless without information. She looked out the window at the harbor.

How did a little girl go missing in a small town like this and no one knew anything?

"Here you go." The waitress placed a hot chocolate in front of her.

She was guzzling it down when she heard a deep, throaty voice say to the waitress, "When you get a chance, check the stock in the back, we're running low on the local brew. Thanks, kiddo!" It was the bartender, a grizzled man with a weathered, narrow face and long, straggly, gray hair.

"Sure thing, Keith."

Zoe's heart dropped to her stomach like a thick boulder rolling down a hill. The bartender looked like he was in his sixties. She stared at him as he wiped down some glasses at the other end of the bar with a rag, trying to find cracks in her memory where he would fit. But she was coming up with nothing. And yet there was something about him.

She pulled out a faded picture from her wallet; one of the few things she had found among her mother's belongings and kept all these years. A picture of Rachel and the man who was tending the bar across from her. It was taken in 1977. The two of them, much younger and barefoot, sitting on a beach and smiling against the sun. His arm was around her shoulders.

Her heart did a little flip. Slightly unsteadily, she approached him. Why was she trembling?

"Can I get you anything, miss?" Keith asked, not really looking at her.

She bit her lip and then decided to just rip off the Band-Aid. She placed the picture in front of him when his back was turned.

Keith turned around to repeat the question but his eyes fell on the picture. He didn't say anything. Zoe wondered if it meant nothing, but then why would Rachel have kept it all these years?

The color drained from his face. Slowly, he lifted his head and narrowed his eyes. "Who are you?"

"I'm Zoe Storm. Her daughter."

His eyebrows almost touched his hairline. "*Daughter?* Wow... I didn't know she had a kid."

"Two kids. My sister lives in Vermont."

"Right..." He leaned on a hand and touched his lips with the other, as he stared at the photograph. "Well, where is she?" Before Zoe could form the words, her face gave it away. Fear registered on his face. His eyes widened a fraction and his lips parted. But it was gone in the blink of an eye, replaced by a crumpled forehead. "I'm so sorry... what happened?"

"She killed herself." A lie.

"Suicide? Rachel?" He wrestled with the words, finally shaking his head. "I guess you don't know what goes on in anyone's head, right?"

"How did you know her?"

"I just met her at a concert in 1977. We spent two weeks together. I was just passing through the Midwest. It was a fling," he added bashfully. "We never saw each other again. I had to go back to California and get my shit together. I even forgot about this picture."

Something was amiss. "She kept the photo all these years."

His eye twitched. "She did, huh? That's sweet of her, lady. Look, I got some work to do—"

"Do you remember anything she told you about her past or anyone else in her life?" Zoe pressed. "Parents, cousins, siblings, boyfriends, anything?"

Keith stared at her dumbfounded. "No. I frankly don't remember. It was forty years ago."

Before she could probe further, he went back to the kitchen.

Zoe's hands curled into fists. Another dead end. She slammed her laptop shut and marched out of the bar, fighting back tears. Sometimes she wondered if this was all Rachel's doing. How she must be influencing the events in her life to ensure that Zoe was as far from the truth as possible. How was it that an FBI agent was unable to find out *anything* about her own past?

Thin clouds stretched across the horizon, their edges tinged with the faintest traces of pink and lavender, remnants of the sun's last rays struggling to hold on. The sky over the town was a soft, muted gray, the color deepening as the day slowly gave way to evening.

Zoe was heading to her car when she decided to sneak a last

peek at the only person she had found who was in some way connected to Rachel. Through the window, she spotted Keith back at the bar. His hands rested on the counter, his head hanging low. As he raised his head, he wiped away a stray tear racing down his cheek.

Alarm bells went off in Zoe's head. She thought back to his reaction to learning about Rachel's death and how she had died. He'd looked positively shaken, disturbed. Why would he cry over someone he knew for just two weeks forty years ago? Why would Rachel keep this photo?

He was lying.

But why did he lie to her?

She was contemplating going back in and confronting him again when her phone trilled. "Hello?" She answered without checking the caller ID.

"Agent Storm, it's Scott." His voice was low and measured. "We found Lily."

EIGHT

Zoe's heart was in her mouth. The only light came from the screen of her phone, its soft glow illuminating the brown carpet of soft earth under her boots. She hated the woods—always had. Ever since she was a kid, there was something about so much *green* that unnerved her. And then there was the constant fear of someone jumping out of those tangled branches.

It was some karmic debt she must have owed that made her go deep undercover for two years, living as part of a cult in such a place. Now the woods reminded her of *him*—the sick man who often got high and chased her in the woods.

"Your heart is racing, Zoe," Aiden said. He was right next to her. For a second she had forgotten he was there. But that's how he always was—a quiet but formidable presence.

"How would you know that?"

"Your breaths are deliberate and your face is turning red," he said dryly.

She ignored him and focused on her surroundings.

The woods were draped in a shroud of dark gray, shadows deepening under the towering evergreens that loomed overhead. The trees were massive, their rough bark and thick trunks barely visible in the low light, blending into the inky darkness. A faint, almost ghostly green hue lingered at the edges of Zoe's vision, from the moss and ferns that carpeted the forest floor. The path beneath her feet was uneven, a mix of damp earth, twisted roots, and scattered pine needles that muffled her footsteps. She inhaled the cool air with the scent of wet leaves, earth, and the distant tang of the ocean, a comforting reminder that the coast was nearby.

Her breaths *were* deliberate—she knew exactly what she was going to find. The question was how bad it was going to be, so she wanted to prepare herself. The closer they got to the green dot on her phone, the raspier her breaths became. Every now and then, she'd hear the rustle of leaves or the snap of a twig.

"Zoe," Aiden said, lightly touching her arm, making her stop in her tracks. "We have to get along if we are to work together." His face was earnest and chiseled. The first time she met him, he had reminded her of Clark Kent. "And I can tell you're nervous."

Every time she blinked she saw Lily's face on that missing child poster. It still didn't feel real.

"We would get along if you'd stop *shrinking* me all the time. Just be normal."

A frown appeared between his thick eyebrows. "Do I do that?"

"Yes. It's annoying."

Then a scene came into view. A crowd of people stood huddled around a space. The woods were too thick for any car to get through. By Zoe's count there were around six people—three patrol officers, one ranger, and two in casual clothes. She recognized the back of Scott's head at the front. As she got closer, the crowd parted and the sight before her shattered all her thoughts.

A towering Douglas fir, with an ancient, gnarled trunk. The rough bark was a mottled gray-brown, covered in patches of soft, velvety moss that clung to its surface. Lower branches, thick with needles, hung heavy, dripping with moisture from the recent rain. The base of the tree was surrounded by a tangle of roots that twisted and turned, and propped against it was Lily.

She was wearing a red dress, with a strawberry hair clip in her hair. Her body rested against the trunk, motionless, eyes closed and hands on her lap. It looked like she was peacefully sleeping against the tree. But there was a faint smell—something rotten under the overwhelming smell of pine and damp earth.

From the branches hung three ropes. The empty nooses swayed slightly in the breeze. Pinned to the left noose was a small, faded photograph, its edges curled and damp.

A photograph of Lily.

"What the hell is this?" Zoe strode up to Scott, who looked like he was about to explode.

"A ranger made the call. He was out here monitoring the wildlife when he stumbled across this." He gestured to a man sitting on a big rock, who was being offered a bottle of water. "He sounded messed up when he called."

"Where is the CSU?"

"Travis is escorting them. They should be here any minute now," he said, without tearing his wide, fierce eyes from the scene.

Her eyes darted to Aiden. His statuesque figure was stiff and rigid, but his face gave nothing away. It never did.

"What do you think?" she asked him, pulling him aside.

Aiden blew out a breath. "I need a moment..."

"No obvious signs of assault from what I could see," Zoe recounted, unable to look at Lily again. Too soon. The scene was scraping against her eyeballs. "The rope. Why is there a rope there? Why are there three of them?"

He blinked hard. "He didn't hang her from one of them, but

he could have. The deliberate placement of empty nooses indicates two things—an organized offender and someone who intends to strike again."

"Are you sure?"

"One-time offenders don't stage a crime scene, Storm."

Her stomach tightened. She went to Scott, who was heaving. "Shit." Zoe patted his back. "You okay?"

"Yeah. Have you seen anything like this before?"

The lump in her throat hardened. It was right behind her. A dead little girl. Travis arrived, leading a small team dressed in white coveralls. He introduced Zoe to a wiry man with thick glasses—the coroner. The coroner's face tightened at the sight of Lily, but he quickly pressed on. Travis hung back, his hands buried deep in his pockets, his body subtly angled away, as if trying to distance himself from the scene unfolding before him. His eyes, however, remained fixed on the spot where Lily lay. The air was thick with mist and gloom, swirling together as the CSU team moved in slow, deliberate motions, setting up lights in the dark soil.

Aiden's warning was screaming at her. This was not going to be a one-time offender. But maybe he was wrong. The thought subsided as quickly as it had surfaced. She knew he wasn't often wrong; this wasn't the first case they'd worked on together. He had earned his doctoral degree in criminal psychology from UPenn. And he had written several seminal books on the mind of a killer.

Zoe covered her shoes with plastic bags and put on some gloves. She plucked Lily's picture from the noose, wanting to take a look before it went into the evidence bag.

What did this rope and noose mean? Why didn't the killer just hang the body? Questions clamored in the back of her skull. And why were there *three* nooses?

When she turned the picture over, her lungs collapsed. Aiden was right. There was a note scribbled on the back.

I'm sorry. I've already plucked a flower, please stop me from climbing a hill and stealing a star.

NINE

Regina woke up with a headache. The last few days were a blur of numbers and regurgitation of the same words over and over again. Yesterday, she had spent the day at a soup kitchen and she was convinced the smell of broth and garlic was seeping from her pores. Downstairs, the camp was already set up—her team engaging in strategy discussions and making calls for votes. She wasn't ready to go out. Not yet.

She ran a comb through her short, shoulder-length dark hair, trying to disentangle her thoughts. Their campaign was gaining some momentum, but Hicks still had a good hold. She stared at her reflection—almond-shaped, piercing dark eyes, plump, red lips, and caterpillar-like eyebrows. A bold face with a dazzling smile and a penchant for sharp words. But her shoulders drooped from the weight of carrying the hopes of so many people. The stress pressed on her chest like a heavy brick. But she decided to deal with that later. Right now, she needed to go downstairs and be a part of the circus.

"Polling has shown that you are closing the gap, but we need more." Connor stood next to her, smelling of too much body spray. She wondered if he ever showered or slept. "What did you think of that speech for the blind school?"

"I want to read it again." She gestured to an intern to bring her more coffee. Unlike Connor, she had blood running through her veins, not caffeine.

"The governor met with Hicks today, while I've been trying to set up a meeting with him for over a month." He scowled. When an intern approached him with some papers, he snatched them and waved him away dismissively.

"Give me a minute, Connor." She raised her hand, her tone tight and controlled. "Just give me a minute."

He twisted his mouth like he wanted to say something, but when his phone rang he scurried away to answer it. She took a deep breath, free from his intense scrutiny. She barely recognized her house. The furniture had been pushed against the walls to make room for a haphazard array of folding tables and chairs, where team members sat, hunched over laptops and stacks of paperwork. Papers were scattered everywhere—across tables, the floor, and even draped over the backs of chairs—many of them covered in highlighted notes, scribbled reminders, and printouts of poll data.

The large flat-screen TV mounted on the wall played a 24-hour news channel. On one side of the room, a whiteboard was covered in a mess of numbers, names, and key dates, with dry-erase markers in various colors strewn around its base.

When Connor returned, a jittery energy clung to him. He was gripping his phone so tightly that his knuckles had whitened. "I just got a call from my source at the Harborwood PD. Remember Lily Baker?"

"As if anyone wouldn't." She frowned. "What happened?"

"She was found dead in the woods. Murdered."

The murmurs around her drowned into a keening silence. Blood roared in her ears. "Murdered?"

He nodded and pinned her with a look. "Do you know what this means?"

"No."

"We can use this against Hicks. Crime rate is high." Connor rambled on animatedly. "Kids aren't safe anymore. You will put money toward police—"

"Are you insane? You want to use this?" She searched his eyes. "How insensitive are you?"

"You are right. We should meet the parents first. Beat Hicks to it. I'll leak the meeting to the news."

Regina dug her nails into her skin, suppressing the urge to whack him. "Connor, can we just take a moment to absorb the news?"

He huffed. "You need an ace up your sleeve to close the gap. Time is running out, Regina. The dead are going to stay dead."

"Lower your voice, Connor." She placed a hand on her waist and puffed out her chest. "You don't want anyone finding out what an asshole you are."

He let out a mirthless laugh and rocked back on his heels. "You're the politician so you have to care what people think. I don't care about who I offend. And this is your golden ticket."

She knew Connor was laser-focused on his goal. But his rough edges were getting a little too sharp for her liking. "Connor, I need to remind you that you work for *me*—"

"Yes, I do. I've done a lot for you," Connor said casually, but there was a tilt of a threat in his voice. "Don't you think I've done a lot for you, Regina? That if it weren't for me, you'd be in prison?"

Regina swallowed hard.

The corner of Connor's mouth lifted in a cocky smirk. "That's what I thought. Why don't you focus on winning and I focus on making sure you win?" He gave her a wink that made her stomach recoil.

Regina was standing near the whiteboard, her mind half on the conversation with Connor, half on the numbers scrawled in bright marker, when suddenly, someone turned up the volume on the TV.

Conversations trailed off, the rustling of papers ceased, and the clattering of keyboards stopped. One by one, heads turned toward the screen.

The room fell silent, the only sound in the room the voice of Chief of Police Travis Hunter. The camera zoomed in on Hunter, his face framed by a thick, graying mustache, clearly shaken. He stood at a podium, flanked by officers, the seal of the police department visible behind him.

His eyes, sober and tired, scanned the room of reporters before he spoke. "It is with great sadness that I inform you we have found the body of the missing girl, Lily Baker, in the woods just outside of town. At this time, we don't have much information to share, but I can tell you that the FBI is assisting with the investigation. We are doing everything in our power to find out what happened to Lily. I want to extend my deepest condolences to Lily's family and friends during this unimaginably difficult time. I also want to ask the public to come forward if they have any information that could help us. Even the smallest detail could be crucial. We need your help to ensure that justice is served."

The camera lingered on Hunter's face for a moment longer before cutting back to the newsroom.

Regina's eyes darted to Connor who was leaning against the wall. She sensed a sly plan was forming in his head.

TEN

Zoe drummed her fingers on the steering wheel. It was a bleak morning—sky painted with a dull gray and clouds lazily gliding. She sipped on her coffee with three sugars, hoping for the caffeine to kick in after a sleepless night. But her brain was too foggy after the discovery in the woods. It was refusing to wake up and begin solving that puzzle. She was getting used to the perpetual grimness of the Pacific Northwest. The cold she could tolerate. She had spent years in the windy city. But the lack of people and noise in this town grated on her nerves at times. The silence and vast stretches of empty land was agonizing, making it harder to be her regular chirpy self. But she couldn't afford to let the depressing nature of her job drag her down.

When Scott's car pulled up next to hers, she climbed out. He emerged, looking as tired as she felt, his hair disheveled and tie askew. "Morning."

"Morning." She handed him a cup. "We need some working neurons."

"Where's Dr. Wesley?"

"He's going through the archives to check if this MO matches any old or cold case."

He grumbled something and took the cup and led her to the chalky white block of building that Zoe thought was the hub of drug deals before finding out it was the coroner's office.

The space was stark and clinical, walls tiled in white, giving the room a sterile and antiseptic feel. A harsh fluorescent lighting buzzed faintly overhead. The smell of disinfectant hung heavy in the air.

The coroner, with thick glasses, a stubble, and gloved hands, came up to them. "Detective Cohen and Agent Storm. Please follow me."

Zoe's footsteps echoed in the hallway as they rounded into a room with a steel autopsy table in the center, gleaming under the bright lights. The body of Lily Baker lay on a stretcher beside the autopsy table, covered with a crisp, white sheet. Zoe almost tripped over her feet but steadied herself against the frame. Currents ran up and down her skin like little snakes. Next to her, Scott stilled, his jaw locked so tight that it looked like it would break if he released the pressure.

She decided to distract herself with the details of the room. The table was slightly tilted, with a drainage system at one end. Nearby, a stainless-steel cart was lined with various surgical instruments, meticulously arranged in neat rows: scalpels, forceps, scissors, all cleaned and ready for use.

"Do you know the cause of death?" Scott asked, his voice thick.

The coroner stood on the other side of the table. He turned on a monitor which displayed a detailed scan of Lily's body. "An X-ray of her neck confirms that she was strangled. The hyoid bone was broken." He spoke with an odd melody in his tone.

"What was used to strangle her?" Zoe asked.

"The ligature marks on the neck of the victim match the texture of the rope. The rope has been sent to the crime lab to lift any DNA or prints. The marks were slightly angled and the bruising on the neck was more pronounced on the sides of the neck, suggesting that the assailant most likely strangled the victim from behind."

"Did she struggle?" Zoe tried not to look at the body, albeit covered, just a foot away from her. Somehow its small size was taking up the entire room.

"No defensive wounds found anywhere. We have collected samples from under the fingernails. We'll have the results by this evening but I don't think we'll find anything there."

"Were there any signs of... assault?" Scott rubbed his forehead.

The coroner crossed his arms. "There was no injury indicating sexual assault. Protocol dictates to swab it anyway, which we did, but I'm ruling it a negative."

Zoe's mind ticked over the note that was found with the rope. "Okay. Anything on the tox screen?"

"Yes." He pulled up the tox screen results on the monitor. "We found high levels of chloroform and trace amounts of Loratadine, which is the active ingredient in Claritin."

"Chloroform has a short half-life in the body. One to three hours," Scott said. "If it was found in large quantities that would suggest recent exposure prior to death."

"That's why the victim didn't struggle. Killer knocked her out and then strangled her," the coroner agreed.

"And what about the Claritin?" Zoe asked. "When do you think that was administered?"

"If we extrapolate based on her weight, age, and the contents of her stomach, I would say around two days ago."

"Two days ago, when she was in captivity. Do we know what she's allergic to?" She turned to Scott.

"The parents would be able to shed light on that one." Scott scratched his ear. "Travis visited them last night, but we still need to go and talk to them."

Zoe remembered the first time she had informed a parent their child had been found dead. The mother had gone into an erratic shock episode, unleashing a barrage of slaps and punches at Zoe. She absorbed them all and didn't let anyone stop her. She knew what grief felt like.

"We're also checking the contents of the stomach. Will send the report as soon as it's available." The coroner pressed his lips in a thin line and escorted them out of the room before disappearing around the corner into one of the laboratories.

Zoe slumped against the wall, her eyes catching the covered body of Lily all alone in the room. There was something so uncouth and immoral about how they had got to the truth. The town of Harborwood had spent days and nights searching for a little girl, and now here she was lying on a stretcher in an autopsy room.

"In the two days that I've known you, this is the longest you've been quiet," Scott said gently.

"Yeah, it feels wrong to have a light conversation right now but it's the only way I seem to compartmentalize."

He nodded. "So what do you think?"

She didn't respond and instead dialed Aiden. "You're on speaker. It's me."

"Yes, I have your number saved." His dry voice filtered through. "How did the autopsy go?"

"He gave her Claritin, Aiden." A beat of silence. She bit her lip. "Well?"

"Were there signs of any other kind of assault?"

"None at all. She wasn't even dehydrated or malnourished for someone who was in captivity for four days."

"That would suggest two things—either this is the killer's first kill or it's someone who knows her well. We aren't looking at a sadist. Were there any other signs that he hesitated?"

"Yeah!" Scott's eyes widened at the thought. "He strangled her from behind."

"Avoiding seeing her face. Suggests a guilty conscious."

"I plucked a flower. Please stop me from stealing a star," Scott recited from memory as he paced the small hallway. "He sounded apologetic. Think he's being forced by someone?"

"No. If he was he wouldn't have left the note like that so out in the open for us to find," Zoe said.

"It appears that the killer is experiencing an intrapsychic conflict. There's a struggle between his primal urges and his Superego, which is moral conscious. Their *Ego*, which mediates the two, has broken down, manifesting as a plea for intervention. They are unable to self-regulate."

"So we're dealing with an insane killer?" Scott muttered.

"It takes some kind of insanity to kill someone," she whispered.

A memory surfaced in the back of her mind.

It was a balmy day in Frisco, a suburb of Dallas, when Zoe was in the backyard, watering the yellow, dying grass. Texas heat was dry and abrasive. She was convinced that her skin would start shedding. Gina spent all her time inside even though she was cranky about being unable to run around. Beads of sweat trickled down her back as she hosed the little backyard in wide sweeps. Rachel came outside carrying a basket of washing to hang out.

The piercing sound of sirens punctured the air. Zoe's head whipped to Rachel. Rachel's back straightened like a stiff arrow. Her rattled eyes met hers and then they both sprinted to the front of the house, following the noise.

"What's happening?" Zoe asked her.

Rachel was in a state of panic, breathing hard, her face cinched with worry. She held Zoe close as other neighbors started coming out of their houses to see what was going on. There were two cop cars parked in front of a house at the end of the row.

"Mom, what is it?" she asked.

Rachel's eyes narrowed when the cops escorted a man out of the house. She assessed the thickset man with a sneer, wearing a wifebeater. Behind him a woman was crying and being comforted by another cop. "It's okay... we're okay." Rachel sighed in relief and crushed Zoe against her. "We're okay..."

"What are you talking about?"

"Nothing." She wiped the tears running down her face. "I just got worried. I need you girls to be safe."

"Why would we be unsafe?"

Rachel never replied.

ELEVEN

Zoe watched Aiden climb out of his sedan. After days of thick moisture choking the air, the sun was finally blazing in the sky. But still Zoe felt a chill clinging to her skin like gum. Aiden's reflection mushroomed up and out in the glass of the cars lined along the street as he crossed the distance between them.

"Waiting for Scott?" he asked.

"Yeah." Her voice croaked as she stifled a yawn.

"Didn't sleep last night?"

"I don't know about you, but that motel mattress sucks."

"I ordered a new mattress."

"*What?*" She gasped. "Who orders a new mattress, Aiden? Is the FBI paying for that?"

He shrugged, innocently. "I don't know how long we're here for. I'm paying out of my pocket. We do spend more than a third of our lives sleeping." He retrieved a yogurt bar from his coat and handed it to her. "It's got extra sugar and is strawberry flavored."

She eyed it with suspicion before taking it. "Why?"

"It's going to be a tough conversation." He jutted his chin toward the house in front of them. The only one in the neighborhood that didn't have Halloween decorations, and it still managed to be the spookiest one. A house that echoed deep sadness.

"So a new mattress." The sight of the house had taken her last bit of breath so she changed the topic. "That's weird, Aiden. Were you picked on in school? Or were you homeschooled?"

He chuckled, pushing his glasses up. "Homeschooled until middle school. You'll be fine, Zoe. You've done this many times before. We can talk about it, if you're struggling."

"We can't talk, Aiden. Because you hide behind control and I hide behind chaos." She flashed him a smile that didn't reach her eyes, while he stared at her with a mix of hurt and disapproval. This wasn't the first time Aiden had tried talking to her in an attempt to peel away the layers to understand what lay underneath.

* * *

Zoe felt a flare of anger. "Listen, I don't need to be here."

"Actually, you do." Aiden sighed and stood up, sauntering over to a sleek table to pour himself a coffee. "Your boss mandated this."

Zoe curled her hands into fists under her thighs. The desperation to crack a joke or roll her eyes or scurry away to find more sugar rose inside her. "Simon? Why would Simon think I need an evaluation?"

He shrugged, bringing the cup to his lips. Every movement he made was so measured, every word that came out of his mouth deliberate. "Deep undercover missions leave wounds, Agent Storm. I'm the doctor who has to diagnose just how deep those scars run."

"I'm different. I don't bruise easily."

* * *

"Mr. and Mrs. Baker, this is Special Agent Zoe Storm and Dr. Aiden Wesley from the FBI. They are consulting on the case," Scott said in a gentle, rehearsed voice.

Zoe sat next to him on the faint pink couch in a living room cluttered with cat figurines. The walls were painted a soft, faded yellow, their surfaces almost entirely covered with framed photographs of Lily right from the time she was a newborn in the hospital to her seventh birthday party. With a sinking feeling, Zoe realized that that's where the pictures would stop.

The cat figurines were everywhere—lined up on the mantel above the brick fireplace, perched on the windowsills, and arranged in neat rows on the shelves that flanked the room.

"I'm sorry for your loss," Zoe mumbled. She hated saying those words because she knew they weren't *really* listening. They were just empty words that washed over them like water.

Tim and Mary Baker sat across the sturdy coffee table. Their faces were identical—hanging low like their facial muscles had loosened all elasticity since they learned the news. Their eyes stared into the distance, perhaps searching for Lily. The clothes on their muscled bodies, from years of hard labor in the processing plant, looked musty and worn out.

Bella stood in a corner of the room with her arms crossed and slender body slightly curved into the wall. Her face was hidden behind her dark hair, like she didn't want to be there. From the corner of her eye, Zoe noticed Aiden watching Bella.

"We have some questions to ask you." Scott rubbed his hands in front of him, excessively. "Were there any men or boys in Lily's life?"

"What do you mean?" Tim asked, almost sleepily.

"Lily left Bella to go say hi to your boss who was driving by. But then she told him she had to go to some man who was calling her over."

Mary's face lifted and she blinked vehemently. "Man? What man?"

"That's what we are asking. Was there any man she was in contact with? A teacher she mentioned, a neighbor who was extra friendly or an uncle who visited often..." Scott asked. "Can you think of—?"

"No!" Mary cried, and looked at Bella. "What are they saying? Did you see anyone?"

"I didn't," Bella pleaded. "I swear. It was a regular day. I often take Lily to that park. I never noticed any pervert. Lily never mentioned any man to me."

"You should have been more careful, Bella," Mary said through gritted teeth. "Why did you look away? What have you done?"

"Now, now..." Tim said, making a half-hearted attempt to pacify her. Then she broke down and sobbed into his chest. He just sat stock-still, making no attempts to hold her or soothe her. "We didn't notice anything like that."

Bella was horrified. She looked at Mary somewhere between hope and yearning, as if waiting for words of comfort. Aiden opened his mouth but she ran into the hallway, banging a door closed behind her.

"She's been taking it very badly," Tim explained.

"Was Lily allergic to anything?" Zoe asked.

"Why?"

She didn't have the stomach to tell him the killer had offered their daughter Claritin before killing her. "It's relevant to our investigation."

Mary continued to sob into his shoulder. His face tightened in irritation and he pushed her away sharply. But she didn't seem to notice, instead burying her face in her hands.

Zoe and Aiden exchanged a glance. What was all that about?

"Devil's club," Tim answered. "We went camping last year and she got hives on her skin when she brushed against it."

While Scott continued to tactfully gather more information,

Zoe stared at her boots on the thick, slightly worn carpet with a floral pattern that had faded from years of use. While Mary had folded her body in half, Tim was barely holding it together. His patience was wearing thin. He wanted to be alone in his grief. Perhaps he wanted to mourn in silence.

"Mind if we see Lily's bedroom?" Aiden asked.

Tim led them to the back of the house to Lily's room—the door slightly ajar. When Zoe entered the space, a chill coated her skin, raising goosebumps on her arms. There was a single bed against one wall, covered with a thin, slightly worn quilt featuring cartoon characters—Elsa from *Frozen*, Rapunzel, and *Looney Tunes* characters. The bed sheet was plain and white and crumpled.

A shelf housed a few toys—dolls, puzzles, and a couple of board games—but they were almost untouched, gathering dust as if playtime had become less frequent. Next to the toys was a small, neatly organized basket with medical supplies: bandages, ointments, and a few small bottles of over-the-counter medications.

Aiden picked up a cough syrup bottle sitting on the small nightstand and turned it over in his hand. Andy, Tim's boss, had mentioned that Lily hadn't been well a few days before she went missing.

"She hated that syrup." Tim's voice came from behind them. He stood at the doorway; his eyes haunted. "I would promise her that she could watch TV in return. Of course, Mary didn't know that. She was strict about things."

"I can see that." Zoe looked pointedly at the basket of medicines. What an odd thing to keep in a child's room. It was something Rachel kept in her room, but Zoe and Gina had had a very unusual upbringing.

"Did Lily fall sick often?" Aiden asked.

"Past two years, yeah. But Bella was the same. She grew out of it. Can I ask you something?" His eyes pinned them with a desperate look. For the first time, tears welled up in his eyes and the tip of his nose turned red. "Was she... was she in pain? Please be honest."

There it was. That first uncorking of questions. It always started with shock and then melted into *"Was she in pain?"*. It didn't take long for *"Why would anyone do this?"* to come.

Zoe picked up a stuffed animal from the bed. A gray elephant. She threw a glance at Aiden, who nodded at her. "No. He was gentle in his approach."

Tim nodded, releasing a breath. "Have you worked on cases like this before?"

"Yes." She kept stroking the soft toy.

"What do the parents do?" His voice was small.

Zoe didn't usually hang around once her job was done. She caught the bad guy, put them behind bars, and moved on with her life. It wasn't callousness; it was self-preservation. She took a choppy breath, afraid she might say the wrong thing to a weak man.

"I'm sorry, Mr. Baker. We can tell you the truth," Aiden said. "We are also here to offer you support—I can put you in touch with resources."

"Does the truth matter if it can't bring my kid back?"

Truth was a double-edged sword. It didn't offer any closure but the lack of it ravaged the mind. Festering lies was like a death by a million paper cuts, drawn out and never-ending. The truth killed you swiftly.

"Yes. The truth always matters. You'll realize just how much if you have to live without it."

TWELVE

The next day, Travis Hunter rubbed his chest to ease the pressure blooming behind his ribs. He rummaged through his bag for his medicine. Finding the bottle, he flicked open the lid and popped a pill in his mouth. He turned on the faucet and sprayed cold water on his face over and over again.

He heard the front door open and close, followed by the sound of heavy footsteps.

He checked his watch. It was only 1 p.m. He went out of the restroom and saw his tall, gangly son with a messy mop of hair in the kitchen. "Why are you home early?"

Ryan stirred in surprise. "Uhm... what are *you* doing here?"

"I was at the station all night so came to take a nap before I go back. Don't you have school?"

Ryan avoided his gaze as he took out a root beer from the fridge. "Yeah, but I had a free period so I came home early."

Travis eyed him. "How's... how's school going?"

Ryan paused and sighed. His lips pressed in a tight, hard line. With a jolt, he threw the can in the trash. "I have schoolwork to do." He tried to shoulder past him, but Travis blocked his way.

"Ryan, what's been going on with you? We don't talk anymore," he said, avoiding his son's eyes. For someone who had spent his lifetime interrogating criminals and boring into their eyes until they fessed up their crime, he was shockingly bad at speaking to his own son. The words that he wanted to form with his tongue always seem to get lodged in his throat. The air between them swelled with tension before Ryan spoke.

"We never talked. Let's keep it that way," he said, his tone curt and dismissive. He pushed past Travis and marched to his room, slamming the door shut behind him.

Travis fell heavily onto one of the chairs around the dining table. The air in the kitchen was still thick, a witness to his failing relationship with his son. Ryan was right, they didn't talk much, but Travis always felt a lot was said in those snippets of strained conversations. He stared at an old picture hanging on the wall—of him, a newborn Ryan in his arms and his late wife.

Somehow during all those years spent analyzing and breaking down strangers, he had lost track of his own son. The pain in his chest increased, like a sharp object growing bigger. His thoughts flew to Lily. In the periphery of his vision, he saw a young girl with pigtails.

He didn't look at her. It was the ghost that always followed him.

* * *

"Say hi to Aunty Zoe!" Gina shoved the phone in the face of a little boy who was too busy making a Pac-Man with Lego. "Davey! If you don't say hi, I'm taking that away."

Davey's head snapped to the camera with a wide toothless grin that was forced. "Hi, Aunty Zoe!"

"Hello, Davey." Zoe blew him a kiss. "I heard you're kicking ass in school."

He chortled at her use of the word *ass* and Gina took back the phone. "Zoe! You can't use such language in front of kids!"

"Aunty said *ass*! Aunty said *ass*!" Davey sang as he danced in the background.

"Thanks, Z. Thanks." Gina sighed, her hair haywire. "I'm going to be listening to this for days now. Where are you, by the way?"

Zoe was sitting on the bonnet of her car, munching on a sandwich. "I'm on a case in a small town."

"What kind of case?"

"You don't want to know," Zoe replied with her mouth full.

Gina's lips puckered. "Oh God, it involves kids, doesn't it? How do you do this, Z?"

Zoe gave a watery smile. "Someone's gotta do it."

Zoe and Gina were polar opposites. Gina, harebrained and erratic, had somehow found her groove in motherhood. But Zoe knew her baby sister lived a sheltered life and was too young to really remember anything. That ignorance gave her the superpower to infuse lightness into everything. Unlike Zoe who was only good at painting a bright, sunny varnish. But Zoe was hellbent on trying to scratch that itch of truth. There was a gaping hole in her life, her own mother a big question mark, and she had made promises she was too young to make.

She sucked on the straw, drinking more pop when Gina's face dropped. "What is it, Z?"

"What do you mean?"

"You're drinking pop. Is something upsetting you?"

"It's just the case." Zoe shrugged. "And you know my policy. Sugar fixes everything."

"Sugar fixes everything," Gina repeated, smiling. "Oh God, I gotta go, catch you later, okay?"

Zoe hung up but continued to stare at Gina's name on the screen. She grazed her thumb over it. Guilt reared its ugly head as she thought of the secrets she was keeping from Gina about what really happened with Rachel. Shreds of clouds chased each other overhead, casting a bleak shadow over town, the mist forming a thin film on her face.

"Yeah... yeah... okay." There was the sound of gravel crunching as Aiden walked toward her with a bag of taco bell in one hand and his phone in the other. "We'll look at it when we get back. Thanks, Scott."

"What happened?" Zoe asked when he disconnected. "Oh! Is that taco bell!"

"Yes..." He stared at her like she had two heads. "It's just a bean burrito." Zoe snatched it from him and began ripping into it, silencing those pangs of hunger. "Which was for me."

"Huh?" she asked with a mouthful.

"Nothing." An amused smile tugged on his lips—and suddenly, Zoe realized that she had never noticed how handsome his smile was. "Anyway, patrol officers found a toy around thirty feet from the crime scene. They bagged it. It's back at the station."

"A toy?" Zoe's eyebrows shot up. "But Lily didn't have a toy when she went missing, right?"

The wheels in Aiden's head began to move at full speed. "She didn't. Now, I highly doubt that the killer went to her place and picked up one of her own toys—though you should look into that anyway, just in case. Most likely, it was his way of trying to make her feel comfortable. The lack of evidence pointing to a struggle suggests that Lily wasn't scared of him."

After wolfing down the burrito, she continued sucking at the pop even though there were only bubbles left.

"Are you thirsty?" He frowned.

"No. Oh, how rude of me! Would you like some?"

"N-no." He scratched his ear. "He could be engaging in grooming. The juxtaposition of the kindness followed by violence aligns with psychopathic tendencies—"

"But you said before he might not be a sadistic psychopath."

A fleeting grimace. "*Might*. Not all sadistic psychopaths will torture and maim. Though, the toy might be an indication of something else."

"What?"

"Unresolved childhood trauma. The act of giving toys could symbolize a regression to their own childhood, representing a transference of their unmet needs onto the victims."

"Have there been any instances like this before? In the archives?" Zoe asked.

"I didn't find anything, but of course not everything is reported. What did you think of Bella?"

Zoe hadn't given her much thought. "Regular teenager plagued with guilt. By the way, I was thinking about the message he left in the woods." She pulled up the picture on her phone. "I think we are focusing too much on his tone and we should pay attention to the words he uses too."

"Okay..." He leaned against the side of the door and crossed his ankles.

"I plucked a flower. Lily is a flower," she began.

His eyes widened. "Stop me from stealing a *star*."

She nodded. "I think we need to find a girl whose name means 'star'."

Zoe had known the moment she saw Lily's body in the woods, the rope hanging ominously above her, and the picture pinned to it. There was a deliberate, almost ceremonial arrangement to the scene. This wasn't a crime of impulse—it was calculated, ritualistic.

"This just confirms it. There were three nooses—one for each victim," Aiden said quietly.

THIRTEEN

Scott stood outside the crowded bar, the neon sign above flickering in the evening mist casting a dull, red glow onto the wet pavement. Through the large, fogged-up windows, he could see the throngs of people packed inside, their voices rising and falling with laughter, shouts, and the clinking of glasses.

It was too damn tempting. He wanted in, wanted to get lost, wanted to feel like he was floating and flying and laughing again.

The door swung open every few seconds, letting out bursts of music and the warm, intoxicating scent of alcohol. He could feel the pull, the familiar ache gnawing at him, as he fidgeted on the sidewalk, shifting his weight from foot to foot, his hands clenching and unclenching at his sides.

Scott knew he shouldn't go in. He'd been clean for months now, but guilt was a relentless weight on his chest, pressing down harder with every passing day. Lily's face flashed before him, her lifeless body in the woods, the rope, the picture—it was all he could think about. The thought that he hadn't done enough, that he had missed something, was tearing him apart. The need for relief, for something to take the edge off, was overwhelming. He swallowed hard, his throat dry and tight, and before he could stop himself, he found himself pushing open the door.

Inside, the air was thick with the smell of spilled beer, whiskey, and sweat, mingling with the faint scent of old cigarettes that clung to the walls. People crowded around the polished wood bar, their elbows jostling for space as they ordered drinks, laughing and leaning into each other's conversations.

Scott slipped through the crowd, his heart pounding in his chest. Just one drink, he told himself. Just one to quieten the thoughts that wouldn't stop racing through his mind. He found an empty spot at the bar and sank onto the stool, his fingers drumming on the worn wood surface.

The bartender, a burly man with a beard that seemed to take over his face, approached him. "What'll it be?" he asked, his voice gruff.

Scott hesitated for a split second, the words sticking in his throat. Then, almost too quickly, he said, "Whiskey. Neat."

The bartender raised an eyebrow, as if sizing him up, then nodded. "Coming right up." He turned to grab a bottle from the shelf. Scott's heart raced as he watched the bartender pour the amber liquid into the glass, the sound of it seeming to fill the room and drown out every other noise around him. "Here you go," the bartender said, sliding it across the bar with a knowing nod. "Rough night?"

When the glass was set in front of him, he stared at it for a long moment, his reflection distorted in its depths. His hand trembled slightly as he picked it up, the cool glass feeling familiar and yet alien in his grip.

Scott forced a smile, the corners of his mouth barely lifting. "Something like that." He brought the glass to his lips but didn't take a sip. He just sniffed it, inhaled deeply. The smoky scent slid up his nose and he closed his eyes, warmth spreading through his chest and sinking into his bones. He knew how it would taste—like sin. It felt like coming home, like waking up a part of him that had been asleep for too long. The edges of the world softened, the noise of the bar faded to a distant hum, and for the first time in what felt like forever, the turmoil inside him stilled.

But he couldn't do it. He had come too far. He pushed the glass away.

"Look what the cat dragged in," a throaty, unkind voice said next to him.

He knew exactly who it was from just the smell of her perfume. "Get lost, Carly."

"Back to your dirty old habits?" she mocked him.

He looked at her gaunt face plastered with tacky makeup and her curly, red hair that made her stand out in the bar. "You picking up clients at the bar now? This place is a little too classy for you, don't you think?"

Her expression hardened. "It was a mistake to come here and offer you a few words of kindness after that girl was found dead in the woods."

"I don't need anything from you. Especially not your fake sympathy."

"It's not fake. I'm a mother too, in case you've forgotten," she retorted, her voice cold.

He didn't need alcohol to loosen his tongue. "Yeah, I can imagine what kind of mother a coked-up hooker is."

Even as the words left his mouth, guilt twisted in his gut. She inhaled sharply, tears welling in her eyes as she turned to leave.

"Wait."

She turned back to face him, lips pursed and eyebrow raised, waiting for him to grovel. That's how it always went between them. She'd push, he'd snap, and then he'd apologize. The same cycle, every single time.

He steadied himself. "I'm sorry. I shouldn't have said that."

A slow, satisfied grin spread across her face, and he instantly regretted the apology. She leaned in, her voice dripping with that familiar, cutting sweetness. "I understand, Scott. Maybe if you'd done your job right, that girl would still be alive."

Speechless, he watched as she walked away, her hips swaying with deliberate confidence. His vision narrowed, the room closing in on him like crinkling, burning paper.

"Another?" the bartender asked, eyeing him carefully.

"No." *Yes.*

FOURTEEN

The morning sky outside was a burst of peach and pink, shifting quickly to deep orange as the sun climbed higher in the sky. Light seeped through the thin curtains, painting the space in a warm glow.

Inside the gym, Zoe's fists slammed into the punching bag, the thud of each hit steady and relentless. The gym across the motel was bare—equipment that looked rusty and squeaky, and a punching bag. But Zoe only needed the latter. Her breath came in sharp bursts, matching the rhythm of her punches.

As the sky outside deepened to gold, the room filled with a sharp, warm light. Sweat plastered her forehead and collected on her upper lip.

Keith didn't want to talk to her. She knew he was lying about knowing Rachel but she had no idea why. Could he have had something to do with her death? The thought made her freeze. She ran through his reaction when she told him Rachel was dead—the palpable shock and resigned grief. His reaction seemed authentic. But there was that pesky doubt knocking on her brain. She was good at noticing things that slipped through the cracks. But this time it was about *her*. It was hard to study people like specimen without that distance.

But why would he lie about their relationship?

She opened her wallet and looked at the old, faded picture. Rachel and Keith in Santa Barbara. They were leaning into each other, his arm around her shoulders. There was an ease between them, an intimacy that came with time and not with lust.

A two-week fling, my ass, she thought. It was not a coincidence that she had been sent to Harborwood where Keith happened to be; it was a sign. Her eyes zeroed in on something in the picture. The sleeve of Keith's shirt had risen up, revealing the lower half of a tattoo. It looked like the letter *R*.

Zoe landed a final, hard punch, sending the bag swinging wildly. She stepped back, breathing hard, her gaze shifting to the bright morning sky through the window.

She was making her way across the street back to the motel's parking lot when her phone rang.

It was the number on her phone saved as "Unknown".

"Tell me you have something for me," she said.

The throaty voice damaged by years of smoking chuckled on the other side, sounding like an engine that wouldn't start. "Straight to the point. I like that."

It was one of the few people who didn't see the chirpy, wonky Zoe who apologized to the objects she bumped into. He probably wouldn't recognize her in the real world. He knew the *other* side—the one hidden under layers of sugar, spice, and everything nice.

"Well?" she pushed.

"I got an opening. It's with Bruiser. It's a tough one, Z. You sure?"

She had heard about Bruiser. Had seen him in action too. But this was exactly what she needed.

"I'm in."

"Great. I'll send the details," the voice said, before hanging up.

The coroner had sent over some reports that they needed to go over. The cool morning air hit her skin, refreshing after her intense workout. As she turned to walk down the motel's narrow outdoor corridor, she noticed a man and a young woman emerging from a room a few doors down.

The man was in his mid-thirties, dressed in a rumpled business suit that looked like it had been slept in. He ran a hand through his thinning hair, straightening his tie as he glanced nervously around the empty parking lot. The woman beside him was barely out of her teens, dressed in a tight, short skirt and a low-cut top that screamed last night's work not this morning's casual wear. Her makeup was smudged, and she looked both tired and satisfied, a sly smile playing on her lips.

Zoe slowed her pace, keeping her eyes forward but her ears tuned to their conversation as they fumbled with the door.

Right at that moment, she bumped into a wall of muscle. "Ouch."

"Did you really not see me?" Aiden cocked a thick eyebrow.

"I have bad peripheral vision." She rubbed her forehead, still focused on the couple.

"You might have a tumor in that case." His tone was flat and dry.

"Can't believe I'm doing this before work," the man muttered, half to himself as he glanced at his watch.

The young woman laughed, a light, teasing sound. "Relax, handsome. No one's gonna know. Your wife's not gonna show up here, is she?"

Zoe grabbed Aiden's elbow and nudged him forward, while maintaining a distance from the couple.

"What are you—?" He was horrified at the touch.

"Shush!" She pinched him.

The man chuckled, though it sounded more nervous than

amused. "God, no. She's gotten fat and boring since having the baby. She doesn't have a clue."

The woman smirked, adjusting her purse strap on her shoulder. "Well, that's why I'm here. To keep things interesting for you."

"That's right, babe," he said, dropping his voice. "I'll be back tonight. Same room, same time."

"Looking forward to it," she purred, leaning in to plant a quick, almost casual kiss on his lips.

"Still into spying, Storm?" Aiden muttered, half-amused, as they walked past the couple and out of earshot.

"What do you mean?" She resisted the urge to glance back. Her mind raced, her stomach churning at the man's brazen infidelity, the casual way he betrayed his wife without a second thought. The young woman sauntered off, heels clicking on the pavement, while the man pulled out his phone, probably to call his wife and lie about his morning.

"You did this at Quantico too. Watching people like you were trying to catch them."

She froze. "No, I wasn't. And you weren't at Quantico."

"I was there for a seminar for a few weeks." He avoided her gaze and fixed his glasses. Was that a nervous tick? "Anyway, I returned my car so we should carpool."

"Why did you return your car?" She crossed her arms.

"So that we could carpool. And save FBI money."

"Sure," Zoe agreed nonchalantly, but her skin prickled at how astute Aiden was. He was always poking and prodding, looking for something in her to shake off. While Zoe walked with a skip in her step and muscles in her face hanging loose, Aiden was the opposite.

Statuesque and stoic.

* * *

"Did you ever have thoughts about wanting to kill him?" Aiden had asked, his long legs crossed.

"What?" It was their fourth session. Why wasn't he signing her off to say she was fit to return to duty?

"He was a rapist and a master manipulator. Surely, you had violent thoughts about him?"

Zoe did. Every night. Every night she bottled the thoughts about wanting to break his bones one by one and slit his throat. That rancid rage clotted in her throat.

"Never," she snapped.

Aiden stared at her blankly. "I don't believe you."

FIFTEEN

Harborwood Police Station was a whirl of activity. In the two days since Zoe had arrived, she'd quickly realized this level of chaos wasn't normal. The phones rang off the hook, with concerned residents eager for updates, curious callers fishing for details, and amateur sleuths offering their latest theories. Local reporters, starved for a story more compelling than the ongoing mayoral race, had finally found something to sink their teeth into.

As Zoe and Aiden approached the entrance, she noticed a "Vote for Me" poster for Regina Warner stapled haphazardly to the wooden siding. She'd heard snippets of conversation hinting at something brewing, but nothing concrete. A patrol officer passed by, tearing the poster down with a quick, practiced motion. Catching Zoe's eye, he muttered something about keeping the station a politics-free zone.

As if any place truly was.

"Do you think it's a coincidence that something so out of character has happened in this town in the run-up to the elections?" she asked Aiden.

"It's a drastic step."

"Did you come across any new visitor or passersby?"

"We had two leads but none of them have any history and both have alibis." His face fell. "It looks more likely to be a townie."

They made their way to a small room just ahead of the lockup that was their assigned working space. The room was cramped and sparsely furnished, with a single, old desk cluttered with files and a flickering computer monitor that cast a dim, uneven light across the space. The air was heavy with the scent of stale coffee and the faint mustiness of papers left untouched for too long. Her mind was still absorbed by thoughts of Lily. She had stayed up all night going through Violent Criminal Apprehension Program and N-Dex for any similarities between Lily's case and any other. But she found nothing.

"Hey." Scott came up in a crinkled suit. "Jesus, it's so bright in here. I got this toy from the evidence locker." He placed the bagged teddy bear on the table between them. "I sent a picture to Lily's parents. They confirmed it's not hers."

Zoe picked it up and turned it around. The fabric was worn, with threads fraying and one of its glass eyes cracked. "This is really old," she murmured, her brow furrowing. "Could it belong to the killer?"

"Or he picked it up from some donation site or the dumpster." Scott blinked forcefully and fished for something in his coat. He took out a bottle of eye drops and squirted some in his eyes.

"Either way, it means something to the killer," Aiden added.

"Did you find anything on your end?" Scott asked.

"Nothing on ViCAP or N-Dex. But we got more reports from the coroner." She powered up her laptop. "No DNA under her fingernails. And we can definitely rule out assault."

"The crime lab will be slower because of the backlog. Can you make some calls?"

"Yeah, I'll see what I can do," Zoe said, her tone measured as she studied him with a pointed look. His eyes were slightly bloodshot, and there was a sluggishness in his movements that hadn't been there before.

He hadn't slept.

He shifted under her gaze, running a hand through his hair. "If there were no ligature marks on Lily anywhere, does that mean she was drugged throughout her ordeal?"

"It's possible..." Zoe skimmed through the reports, trying to catch anything relevant. "But a child that age being drugged for four days would do some damage. Wouldn't it?"

"The kidneys were mildly damaged. Evidence of tubular necrosis and interstitial nephritis," Scott read from the report. "Suggestive of exposure to some nephrotoxin."

"What about her stomach contents? Her body weight hadn't changed significantly so she was being fed well." Aiden drummed a pen on the table, digesting the information. "Food was found in her stomach which means she ate two to four hours before she was killed. But something isn't adding up."

"What do you mean?"

Zoe's eyes narrowed as she scanned the chromatograms included in the report. The detailed chemical analysis of the stomach contents had been included as an appendix, raw data that required a careful eye to interpret.

Scott straightened up, noticing her shift in focus. "What is it?"

She pointed to a series of peaks on the chromatogram. "These spikes here? They indicate the presence of certain organic compounds—vanillin, among others."

"Vanillin?" Scott repeated, leaning in closer. "Like vanilla?"

"Exactly." She was on the cusp of discovering something that could help; she could feel it in her fingertips. "But look at the concentration. It's unusually high, and there's something else... see this minor peak here? This isn't just any vanilla. It's a much purer form, almost certainly from natural sources, and not the synthetic stuff."

Scott frowned, trying to piece it all together. "So, what are we saying? This isn't just any chocolate—this is high-end, gourmet stuff."

"That's what I'm thinking! The presence of natural vanillin, in this concentration, suggests it came from something rare, like a high-quality ingredient. This could very well be Tahitian vanilla bean."

Aiden took a sip of his coffee, as he reflected. "And how many chocolatiers around here are likely to use something that specific?"

"Not many," Zoe said, flipping back to the summary in the report. "The ME found remnants of chocolate truffle in her stomach, but they didn't go into detail about the ingredients. It could be in that truffle." She glanced back at the chromatogram, her mind working through the possibilities, her heart beginning to race as a path forward became clearer and more defined. "I think we need to check with some local high-end chocolatiers, the ones who might source rare ingredients. If this is Tahitian vanilla, it could lead us straight to the person who gave her that truffle."

"I'll start compiling a list. We can hit up the boutiques, see if anyone's been buying truffles like this recently," Scott said.

Zoe glanced up as he headed for the door. "Also, Detective Cohen... take care yourself."

Scott stopped, catching the implication in her words. He lingered at the doorway, turning red.

"Sugar solves most problems," she said.

He gave her a brief, tight-lipped smile, but didn't say anything. "Thanks. Also... call me Scott."

SIXTEEN

Regina gripped the steering wheel tightly, her knuckles white against the leather, as she drove through the winding streets of Harborwood. The town felt oppressive today. The coastal mist clung to the air, blurring the edges of the tree-lined roads and shrouding the small houses in a gray, eerie veil. It was as if the town itself was closing in on her.

Her thoughts swirled like the fog outside, thick and suffocating. The election was looming closer, and with it, a relentless barrage of interviews, debates, and the constant need to present a perfect image. Every word, every gesture was scrutinized, and she was suffocating under the pressure. But it wasn't just the election. Connor had made it clear that he intended to use Lily's death to their advantage, a tactic that left a bitter taste in her mouth. And he had threatened her.

She could still hear his words, dripping with menace, as he threatened to go public with information that could ruin her if she didn't fall in line. That sick bastard. She ground her jaw, imagining how good it would feel for her fist to meet his jaw.

Morality. It's one lesson her father had tried to instill in her as his father had done before him. The Warners came from a long line of public workers. They all died with no money but with lots of integrity. The two didn't go hand in hand when working for the government. She could feel her father's disappointment—it followed her like a shadow.

How Regina had slipped. How she had gone against her principles. How he was maybe right to think that she just wasn't strong enough.

She had canceled her afternoon appointment. Instead, she was following Connor.

The car's engine hummed softly as she trailed him through the twisting roads of Harborwood. The town's familiar landmarks passed by in a blur—The Harborwood Diner, its neon sign flickering in the mist; the old library with its towering stone facade; and the docks, barely visible through the thickening fog. But Regina's focus was entirely on Connor's car, a few car lengths ahead.

They left the main roads behind, turning onto a narrower, less traveled street. The houses here were older, more spread out, with large yards that bordered the thick woods. Regina's heartbeat quickened as she realized they were heading toward the outskirts of town, a place she barely knew.

Connor's car slowed, then turned into the driveway of a house set back from the road, partially obscured by tall, overgrown trees. Regina eased her foot off the gas, stopping her car a good distance away, hidden behind a large oak tree. She killed the engine, the sudden silence deafening in her ears. She watched as Connor got out of his car, glancing around before striding up to the front door. The house was nondescript, with peeling paint and a sagging porch that hinted at years of neglect. Regina's pulse raced as she leaned forward, trying to get a better view without revealing herself.

Connor knocked on the door, his movements confident, almost rehearsed. A few tense seconds passed before the door creaked open. Regina's breath caught in her throat as a man stepped into view.

The shock hit her like a physical blow, her mind reeling.

"What the hell is Connor up to?" she whispered to herself, her voice trembling as she watched the two men exchange words. The man glanced around, his gaze sweeping the surroundings, and Regina slid down lower in her seat, her heart pounding in her chest. She watched, paralyzed by fear and confusion, as Connor and the man disappeared inside the house, the door closing behind them with a finality that made her shudder.

It was a face she recognized instantly, though she wished she didn't. The man was someone she had hoped never to see again—someone tied to the darkest parts of her past, parts she had worked tirelessly to bury.

* * *

If Zoe was anything, it was adamant. She found a corner in Keith's bar and got on her phone to check how to retrieve a list of kids registered in the school system in Harborwood. There was another target—there had to be. She knew killers like this one. Despite the pathetic apology in his note, he wanted attention. The crime scene was staged. He liked drama.

Or he was making a statement.

She had applied for a court order to access that information. But it still hadn't arrived. *Damn it*. She chewed on the pad of her thumb. Who knew how long it would take for him to take his next victim?

Stop me from stealing a star.

Her skin felt porous and raw, like she was slipping off a ledge. She decided to work back through the initial reports. Lily knew a man who had come to the park to say hi to her. And kids talked. Girls told each other things. Had Lily's friends been interviewed? Restlessness brewed in her chest as she leafed through the reports.

"You don't have to keep coming here, kid," a gruff voice said, interrupting her thoughts. Her eyes tracked Keith standing with his arms folded. "Unless you're here for today's special."

She looked at the arm where she had spotted a tattoo—a potential R. But with his arms crossed, she couldn't make it out. "Sure, I'll take a coffee."

He pulled a face while she smiled. A few minutes later, he placed a coffee in front of her. As he turned to go, she said firmly, "I won't stop, you know. Until you stop lying to me."

His arms dropped to his side. "Why would I lie to you?"

"I don't know. But unfortunately for you, I'm an FBI agent. It's my job to spot liars." The tattoo on his arm was visible now. A definitive R. "Who is R?" she asked.

Instinctively, he lowered his sleeve. "I had a wife. Ruth. She's dead now. Anything else?"

"Tell me, do you usually cry for women you only knew for two weeks thirty years ago?" She tilted her head.

"I'm a sensitive guy."

"You're going to make this difficult, aren't you?"

He sighed. "Kid, I'm sorry you feel like you need closure. But really... you can't make up stuff that didn't happen."

She could make him. One sweep of her eyes and she already saw two violations of the health code. But the defiance in his eyes stemmed from pain and distrust. She was willing to give him one more chance. She was willing to do this the right way.

"I think I'll have today's special. What is it?"

He frowned, annoyed she'd changed the subject, but composed himself. "Chocolate fudge cake."

An idea came to her. "Do you have truffles?"

He shook his head.

"Do you know where I can find any? Tahitian bean?"

"No... that's some fancy shit. Only one bakery can afford that supplier. Seaside Sweets. If anyone has Tahitian bean variety, it's them."

Zoe was already on her feet, gathering her things and calling Scott. She fished for her wallet but Keith told her it was on him. She patted him on his shoulder. "I'll be back."

"Great," he mumbled under his breath. "Stubborn, just like her mother."

* * *

The bell above the door chimed softly as Zoe and Scott stepped into the small bakery nestled on the corner of Harborwood's main street. The warm scent of freshly baked bread and sweet pastries assaulted her senses. The bakery was quaint, with a rustic charm—wooden shelves lined with baskets of pastries, a glass display case filled with beautifully decorated cakes and cookies, and a chalkboard menu with the day's specials written in looping script.

Behind the counter, a young woman with flour-dusted hands and a friendly smile looked up from arranging a tray of croissants. "Good morning! What can I get you?" she asked cheerfully.

Zoe exchanged a quick glance with Scott before stepping forward. "We're here about your Tahitian vanilla bean truffles. We understand you sell them here?"

The woman's smile faltered slightly, replaced by a hint of curiosity. "Oh, yes, we do. They're one of our specialties—made with real Tahitian vanilla. We get the beans from a special supplier in Seattle."

Scott nodded, his eyes scanning the display case, noticing the empty spot where the truffles should have been. "We need to know if anyone's been trying to buy them lately," he said.

The woman's brow furrowed as she thought for a moment. "I'm sorry. I don't think I can give out that information—"

Scott flashed his badge. "We're from Harborwood PD."

The woman's eyes widened. "Oh! You're here about the theft! Finally! I called it in five days ago but with the young girl that went missing and then found dead, I thought you'd be busy."

"What are you talking about?" Zoe said.

The woman hesitated, her gaze flicking between them. "Well, about a week ago, we had a break-in. Someone stole a bunch of desserts, including some of the truffles. That's why we are out of them until our next delivery, which is two weeks from now. We thought it was just a homeless person looking for food. We reported it, but honestly, we didn't think much of it after that."

Zoe's eyes narrowed, the pieces starting to fall into place. "A break-in?"

"Yeah," the woman confirmed, nodding. "They didn't take any money or valuables, just the desserts—truffles, cookies, croissants. We were a little shaken up, but we figured it was just someone desperate for food. Like I said, we reported it to the police, but they didn't find much."

Scott frowned, his mind already working through the implications. "How much was taken?"

"A few dozen of each, I think," she replied, glancing back at the display case. "We had just restocked them that day. Whoever took them knew what they were looking for."

Zoe exchanged another look with Scott, a silent understanding passing between them. This was no coincidence. "Do you have any security cameras?" she asked, her mind racing.

"Yes, but we only keep recordings for a week. Though, we did send a copy to the Harborwood PD. So you should have it... what is this about?"

"Thank you for your help. We might need to come back if we have any more questions," Scott said.

"Of course," she replied, a little less cheerfully.

As they turned to leave, Zoe stopped at the door and turned back to the woman. "If anything else comes to mind, anything at all, please let us know."

As they stepped outside, the chilly air hitting them, Zoe turned to Scott. "Did you not hear about this break-in? It's a small department."

"I've been focused on Lily's abduction. Travis assigned all low-priority cases to patrol."

"This can't be a coincidence. You know this town better than me."

"It's not." His tie whipped in the wind like it was trying to get away from him. "But we can head to the station and see if there was anything in that surveillance. It must have been logged."

"Why didn't anyone follow up on that?"

"Probably because of Lily. All cases were put on a backburner and resources directed at her."

"But now we might have the footage of the killer. And this could all come to an end."

SEVENTEEN

Zoe climbed the narrow stairs to the attic, her small feet making the old wood creak under her weight. The dim light bulb barely cut through the dust and shadows as she pushed open the heavy door. The air was thick with the smell of aged wood and forgotten things, and she wrinkled her nose, brushing a stray cobweb from her face.

"Come on, come on," she muttered to herself, her eyes scanning the cluttered space. Boxes were stacked haphazardly, old furniture covered in sheets, and stacks of yellowed newspapers sat in a corner. Gina's wails echoed faintly from downstairs, a high-pitched cry that made Zoe's heart race. Her baby sister had been inconsolable, demanding her favorite doll that seemed to have vanished into thin air.

Zoe sighed, determined. "It's gotta be here somewhere..."

She pushed aside a box labeled "Christmas Decorations" and then another marked "Rachel's Stuff," but there was no sign of the doll. Her eyes fell on a small, worn box in the corner, half-covered by an old blanket. It didn't look like it had been touched in years. Curiosity piqued, she knelt down and pulled the box toward her, the blanket slipping off to reveal its faded surface.

The box creaked as she opened it, revealing a jumble of papers and... passports? Zoe frowned, pulling out the small, navy blue booklets. Three of them were in her mother Rachel's name, but each had a different last name. Her heart pounded as she flipped through the passports. Different photos, different names, but all of them Rachel. And then there were three more, all with Zoe's picture, but none with her real name.

"What the...?" Zoe whispered, her fingers trembling as she held the passports.

Confusion churned in her gut. Why would they have so many passports? And why with different names?

Gina's cries brought her back to the moment, snapping her out of her thoughts. Shoving the passports back into the box, she closed it hastily and pushed it back into the corner, covering it with the blanket. She grabbed the old, dusty doll that had been sitting nearby, almost hidden, and hurried back downstairs.

When she reached the living room, Rachel was trying to soothe Gina, who was red-faced and sobbing. Zoe hesitated for a moment, then stepped forward, holding out the doll.

"I found it," she said, her voice softer than usual.

Gina's eyes lit up, and she snatched the doll from Zoe's hands, the tantrum immediately subsiding.

Rachel offered Zoe a relieved smile. "Thank you, honey."

But Zoe didn't smile back. "Mom," she began, her voice low, "I found something... upstairs. In the attic."

Rachel's smile faltered. "What do you mean?"

"There was this box... with passports. A bunch of them. They had your picture and mine, but with different names. What's that about?"

Rachel's expression instantly changed, the warmth draining away to be replaced by a guarded, almost panicked look. She stood up straighter, her eyes narrowing. "Zoe, that's nothing you need to worry about. Forget you saw it."

"But—"

"Zoe." Rachel's voice was firm now, almost sharp. "I said forget it. It's nothing. Go and do your homework!"

Zoe flinched at her mother's sudden coldness. Tears bubbled in her eyes. What was she hiding? Rachel called after her but Zoe ran to her room and shut the door behind her. She threw herself on the bed and cried into her pillow, deciding that she was going to uncover Rachel's secret.

A drop of sweat slid down Zoe's nose and landed on her cracked, lower lip. She blinked through the pulses of heat unfurling from the baseboards lining the room. The man in front of her *was* huge—easily over six feet tall, glistening pale skin covered with curly hair, and muscles like ropes twisting down arms that were as big as her thighs.

He could easily squish her head between his legs. For a moment, she could hear the sound of her skull cracking and brain squelching.

"Bruiser! Bruiser! Bruiser!" the rowdy crowd chanted, thirsty for blood, *her* blood.

She kept her arms raised in tight fists, circling him in the makeshift ring, with chalk marking the boundaries and corners by sturdy chairs.

She dashed forward to take a swipe at him. He dodged her with a smirk on his face, not taking any of this seriously.

But he was favoring his left leg. There was a mild swelling on his right knee cap. The unruly shouting and egging on dipped into silence as she lunged forward, her leg hitting that swollen knee cap.

"Argh!" A scream ripped out of his throat and he lost his

balance. The crowd fell silent. No one was expecting this. But Zoe didn't waste any time, and with her bare hands, she landed brutal punches under his ribs.

One. Two. Three.

It took one fling of his arm to the side of her head to send her to the other side of the ring.

Pain ricocheted through her body as she rolled away, blinding her for a moment. She was on her back, her eyes adjusting to the sharp beam of white light overhead.

The crowd erupted in delight. She knew Benny was making money off of this. Who would bet on her against *Bruiser?* As her brain tried to settle down in her skull, a memory surfaced and suddenly she found herself in another place, another time when she went undercover for two years to take down a sick man.

"I see it inside you," he had said, twirling a strand of her hair around his forefinger as they lay in bed. The bulb overhead flickered, engulfing the lower half of his face in the shadows until only his eyes remained—glowing with a sickening reverence.

"Darkness?" Zoe ventured a guess, waiting for the drug to take effect.

"Cruelty." His finger grazed the side of her face before his eyes closed and the rest of him slackened on the bed.

Zoe covered his nude body with a blanket, her heart thundering against her chest. It was another night she had managed to get away from his touch. But it wasn't the close call that had left her nerves crackling.

It was what he had said. How did he know? Her vision melted into Bruiser standing over her, sneering that a woman had got one up on him. As he began kicking her down, her body curved into a ball, absorbing the blows into her back. But when she peered at him, she didn't see Bruiser—she saw *him.*

She blinked. And her sight was bathed in hues of red. With a guttural grunt that sounded like an animal, she crawled out from between his legs, her arm smacking him right between the legs.

Someone yelled foul. It was against the rules. But there were no rules in the real world. The real world was unfair.

Bruiser dropped to his knees, holding his junk, his neck straining and turning red. Zoe fitted his fat head in a deadlock and dragged him down to the ground with her. The rage that had been simmering inside her all day now boiled over, and she gripped him tighter, despite the fact he could barely breathe.

It seared her how unfair everything was. How that man from the motel was driving an expensive car, minting money and getting action, all the while betraying his wife. How that man from the diner was walking free while potentially abusing that waitress. And how that monster she had slept next to for two years as part of her undercover assignment never got to see the inside of a prison cell.

Cold nights when the fear that the sedatives she slipped him wouldn't work held her in a tight wrench.

Thwack.

When she felt his leery gaze sliding over her skin like snake.

Thwack.

The defeated and blank faces of the other innocent women she was unable to protect from him.

Thwack.

She carried the weight of the collateral damage inside her. Two years of an assignment to nail the bastard—he was dead, but he still infiltrated her mind, his voice and *scent* embedded deep inside her.

Thwack.

"It's done! It's done!" She felt arms loop around her, pulling her away from Bruiser who had tapped out and was fading away. "What's wrong with you, Z? You wanna kill him?" Benny's face was twisted in panic.

Her breath came in ragged grasps. "Sorry."

"You're not supposed to strike between the legs." Benny gritted his teeth. "Now all these folks want their money back!"

The crowd was angry, looking at her in disgust.

"I'll get you your money back." Her body suddenly felt too heavy. A dull pain stretched on the side of her face where she had been struck. She dragged her feet away from the fighting arena, relishing the pain, feeling it course through every fiber of her being. There was a burning tightness that resided under every nerve, muscle, and organ. At least this sore, aching pain was better than *that*. She threw one last glance over her shoulder at Bruiser.

But she didn't see Bruiser. She saw a thick, impenetrable, velvety mass of black that had killed Rachel.

EIGHTEEN

"Do you have any fears or phobias?" Aiden read from a booklet in his lap.

"Who cares if I'm scared of spiders?" Zoe asked, exasperated. "Does that mean I would fail my psych evaluation? Get kicked off the FBI?"

His brows furrowed. "Yes, of course. Fear of spiders is a dealbreaker."

Zoe stared at him. "Oh, you were trying to make a joke. I didn't catch it because of your dull delivery."

The corners of his mouth twitched as he adjusted his glasses. "So? Phobias?"

"Darkness."

"That's a common one."

"And shadows," she blurted without thinking.

That made him pause. "Shadows? What is it about shadows that you fear?"

A shiver rolled through her. "That they follow you. You can't get rid of them."

"Unless you're standing directly under the sun."

Her gaze collided with his and she understood the meaning behind his words.

* * *

Pain radiated down Zoe's jaw as she opened her mouth to stuff it with pasta. It was too al dente and the sauce wasn't spicy enough. But what else could she expect at the only diner that was open this late?

She observed her fellow late-night patrons in the dingy space with yellow-tiled walls and circular wooden tables with scratches and wobbly legs. Most of them were just truckers taking a break from being on the road too long. Bulky and rough-looking.

One shabbily dressed man with graying dreadlocks and a scarred face lingered at the entrance. He swayed like he was having trouble standing. Zoe noticed the waiter eyeing him suspiciously from behind the counter. From the state of his bedraggled clothes, she guessed he was homeless. There was an embarrassment on his face that twisted something inside her chest. He knew he was being watched, he was expecting to be thrown out. But his eyes kept flying to the food on people's tables.

"Excuse me!" Zoe called the waiter.

"How can I help you?"

"Can you charge whatever that man over there eats to my card? I'll cover for him."

The waiter blinked in surprise and then smiled. "Sure thing."

She peered out the window into the dark night. Small towns in this damn state. What she wouldn't give to be back in a big city with twinkling lights. She didn't understand the appeal at all. As her eyes bore into the swirling blackness, she realized how such towns were a manifestation of the darkest parts of her.

"What happened to you?" Aiden appeared out of nowhere, sliding across from her.

She recoiled. "What the hell are you doing here?"

"I was hungry and saw you." His eyes thinned, lingering on her face. "Did you hurt yourself?"

Zoe pulled her hoodie closer and pulled her thick hair across the side of her face where Bruiser had punched her. She hadn't had time to apply any makeup. Luckily, there was no swelling since she had managed to get an icepack after the fight. "I fell down some stairs."

"It doesn't look like that." His eyes were ablaze as he leaned forward to get a closer look, but she raised her hand.

"Not tonight. Please." She was too tired. She could tell he wanted to prod further but acquiesced. It irked her that while she was in a hoodie that needed a wash and her hair was in a state, Aiden had somehow managed to present himself with immaculate hair and a smooth suit. "Do you sleep in a suit?"

He repeated her question. "Why would you ask me that?"

"It's midnight, Aiden. Do you wear pajamas or sweatpants?"

The waiter arrived to take his order. "Just a cheeseburger. Thanks. Yes, Storm. I sleep in pajamas and my UPenn hoodie."

"Show-off. I expected you to be in bed by ten. What's keeping you up?"

He placed his elbows on the table and sighed. "The case. Children. It's always a hard one."

"We have seen worse," she said softly.

"Unfortunately, we have." He looked out the window. "I keep thinking about who the next victim might be. Did you find any leads?"

She squirted a generous amount of Tabasco on her pasta. "I have been using the school website to look into other kids with names that could mean a star or constellation. At least in Lily's year, there were none. There are a bunch of kids who are home-schooled or go to the school on the reservation..."

"What makes you think that the next victim is Lily's age?" he challenged.

Zoe's mind reeled. "I... I don't know. I guess I just assumed. But how is he selecting his next victim? On what basis? Just someone whose name means star?"

Aiden blew out a frustrated breath as his cheeseburger arrived. He scowled at the bun soaked in butter and dabbed it with a tissue paper. "What if it's some poem or a piece of literature?"

"Huh? Poem? You think he's artistic?"

He shrugged. "There is a disturbing creativity to the crime scene. Empty nooses arranged to indicate the number of victims. A photograph of Lily neatly tied to the rope with a lyrical prose on the reverse."

Blasts of images of the crime scene invaded her mind. "Right. It's possible. Every detail is significant to him..." The light in the diner dimmed, casting a softer glow on them, and suddenly they were the only patrons left other than the homeless man who was eating his food in a corner, keeping his head down to avoid attracting any attention.

"Why are you staring at him?" Aiden followed her gaze.

"He's homeless."

He frowned. "And staring at him will not make him homeless?"

"No, Aiden, I was having a moment of empathy. Which you wouldn't understand," she chirped, digging into her pasta.

"I'm a psychologist, you know that, right?"

"And you might be more psychotic than your patients. You know what they say," she said, teasing him.

Aiden laughed, dimples denting his cheeks. Zoe's phone buzzed. It was a message from Scott.

S: *We need you both at the station.*

"We've been summoned." She wiped her mouth and pulled a bill from her wallet to leave on the table.

"At this hour?" Aiden checked his watch.

"Maybe they found something."

They were rushing out of the diner, when Zoe turned back and saw Aiden handing a hundred-dollar bill to the homeless man. Fuzziness swarmed her chest but when Scott sent another message, the muscles in her stomach went rigid.

S: *Another girl just went missing.*

The rain pounded against the windshield as Zoe and Aiden pulled into the station's parking lot, the wipers struggling to keep up with the deluge. She was soaked by the time she sprinted from her car to the station entrance, her hoodie stuck to her skin, dripping water onto the floor as she burst through the door.

Inside, the station was humming with activity despite the late hour. The fluorescent lights buzzed overhead, casting harsh shadows as a handful of patrol officers huddled near the main desk, their faces tense. Scott was leaning over a table scattered with maps and reports, his brow furrowed in concentration. As Zoe strode toward him, an angry voice cut through the room.

"What the hell is going on here?"

She noticed a lean, short man, pacing back and forth, his face flushed with anger. Mayor Hicks.

"Another girl goes missing, and you're telling me you've got nothing? This is a disaster! Do you have any idea what this is doing to the election? To my chances?"

"Great," Aiden muttered.

Scott barely looked up as he spoke, his voice steady but strained. "We're doing everything we can, Mayor Hicks. We've got patrols out, and we're coordinating with every available resource—"

"Not good enough!" Hicks cut him off, his eyes blazing. "This town is in a panic! If we don't find her—if we don't get the situation under control—there won't be an election to worry about because there won't be a town left to govern!"

Zoe found it difficult not to judge Hicks, when the first thing he mentioned were the elections. Scott's nostrils were flaring and his features drawn tight. Aiden seemed to be the only one not upset by Hicks' outburst—Zoe chalked it up to nothing really surprising him anymore about people.

She approached Scott, water still dripping from her clothes, cutting through the charged moment between them.

Scott looked relieved. "Good, you're here. You guys need a change of clothes?"

"Doesn't matter," she replied, her voice tight with urgency. "What's the situation?"

Scott gestured to the table, where a map of Harborwood was spread out, various locations marked with red circles. "Eight-year-old Tara Bennett went missing about an hour ago from her bedroom. We've got officers combing the area, but the rain's making it difficult. And I've been making calls to WSP."

"Who reported her missing?" Aiden asked.

"Her dad." Scott gestured at a heavy man with a double chin, sitting in a corner, staring at an empty space, panic-stricken. "He's a single father. Lives alone with the daughter."

"He didn't hear anything?" Aiden's eyes narrowed at the man.

"The storm was well underway and it was way past Tara's bedtime. He went to check on her to see if the sound of thunder had woken her up and that's when he realized she was missing and the window was open."

Zoe's jaw clenched, her mind racing. "She must have been taken while she was asleep. This can't be a coincidence. She's almost the same age as Lily. Did they know each other?"

Hicks rounded on her. "What have you been doing since you got here? I thought the FBI knew what they were doing!"

"Mayor Hicks, why don't you worry about your elections and let us worry about saving a kid's life?" she spat, instantly regretting it.

Hicks's smile was almost cruel. "You don't have an entire town relying on you, Special Agent Storm. Being politically correct is a luxury only those without power can afford."

"Cut it!"

Their heads turned to Travis, his muddy boots squelching as he crossed the distance, leaving a trail behind. "Screw this rain. Now's not the time."

Zoe nodded, unflinching despite the pressure in his voice. "The CSU needs to head to Tara's home."

Scott stepped in. "I called but they can't come in until tomorrow morning because of the storm. There are two patrol officers guarding the scene to ensure there is no contamination."

"The storm's going to wash away any tire tracks..." Zoe cursed.

Hicks scowled but didn't push further, instead turning to one of the officers. "Make sure the media gets the right story on this. No need for any unnecessary details."

Zoe ignored the mayor, but the thought of waiting until tomorrow morning seemed like an eternity. She grabbed a flashlight from the supply rack, her mind already mapping out the search. "I can't sit here. I'm heading out to her place. I'll coordinate with the units already there."

"You two go ahead. I'll speak to the father and see if I can get anything out of him," Aiden said.

Scott nodded, grabbing his own gear.

As they moved toward the door, Hicks's voice followed

them, dripping with desperation. "Find her. And make sure this doesn't turn into another disaster."

Zoe didn't look back as she pushed the door open and stepped out into the storm. The rain hammered down relentlessly as she and Scott jogged toward their cars. A realization crossed her mind—Tara meant 'star' in Sanskrit.

Their killer had succeeded in stealing a star. And they were unable to stop him.

NINETEEN

Zoe didn't like unknowns. But her whole life was cluttered with questions. The wipers made a squeaking sound against the windshield. Fat drops of water fell on the car like bullets. There was no lightning or thunder; just a downpour in this pitch-black darkness that was making her skin crawl. It reminded her of those stormy nights she spent in tents, sleeping next to that man when she was undercover. How she would stay up all night because she was so afraid *he* would wake up and touch her. How remote she felt from her regular life. He was of a medium build and no muscles. She was stronger and trained. But at nights he felt large, his presence looming. It was when he talked that she realized how dangerous he was, how he weaved magic with his words, and how often she had found herself on a slippery slope.

So she would just stare at the sky outside and wait for the black to turn golden.

"Still not used to the wilderness, huh?" Scott said from the passenger seat.

She knew he was making small talk to distract himself. "I was undercover, part of this man's... cult for almost two years," she recalled, her voice barely a whisper. "He was a sick man who had a fetish for impregnating women, and then have them and the kids basically work like slaves for his empire."

Scott's eyebrows dipped. "Did he...?"

"No, not with me. He tried at the beginning but I drugged his nighttime tea."

"What happened to him? Is he in jail?" he asked, hopeful.

She shuddered. "He's dead."

"*Dead?*"

The car went over a pothole, spraying arcs of water on either side.

"He allegedly committed suicide."

"Allegedly?"

"It's a long story." She had her suspicions. She knew the man; she had breathed the same air as him for too long to know he loved himself too much to off himself like that. But she also knew that some people get what they deserve.

"When I was a patrol officer years ago, we got a call for a domestic disturbance," Scott confessed in a shaky tone. "But I... was with a woman at the time." His cheeks flushed pink. "So I didn't respond immediately, thinking it was probably just a couple fighting. By the time I got there, he had beaten her up so bad that she went into a coma."

Zoe flinched, her grip on the wheel tightening. "Oh my God. Did she recover?"

"She did. But if I hadn't messed up, it wouldn't have happened."

"Why did you tell me that?"

"It's when I started drinking." He squirmed, clenching his fists in his lap.

They didn't talk after that.

. . .

The rain continued to hammer down as Zoe and Scott pulled up outside the Bennett home. The house was a modest, single-story building nestled in a quiet neighborhood, but the flashing lights of patrol cars had transformed it into a dreadful scene. The front door was open, and from the driveway, Zoe spotted one of the patrol officers, standing guard, his face pale with fear.

Zoe and Scott didn't waste any time, quickly making their way to the side of the house, careful to avoid the main entrance where officers were gathered. The rain had turned the ground into a muddy mess. Zoe's hoodie was already soaked through, but she barely noticed.

"We're not going inside," Scott said, his voice firm as he glanced at Tara's bedroom window. It was open just a crack, the curtains inside fluttering with the gusts of wind. "We don't want to risk contaminating the scene before CSU gets here."

Zoe nodded, already scanning the area around the window. "Agreed. But let's see what we can find out here. I'm assuming he didn't just take Tara and walk out the front door. Is there a back entrance? A backyard?"

"Yeah, but that door was locked from the inside. Her father said that the window to her bedroom wasn't closed all the way."

They moved cautiously around the side of the house, the ground squelching under their boots. Zoe's flashlight cut through the darkness, illuminating the small yard just beneath Tara's window. Despite the rain, she could make out several neatly arranged garden beds, filled with various plants and flowers. The sight struck her, even in the chaos—someone had clearly put a lot of effort into this garden.

Scott noticed it too. "Tara's dad must be into gardening," he muttered, his own flashlight sweeping over the plants.

She stood up, her gaze shifting back to the window. "Whoever took Tara must have opened the window from the outside. I'm surprised it wasn't locked."

Scott nodded, moving closer to inspect the window frame.

"Looks like they didn't break it. Might've used something to jimmy it open." He glanced down at the muddy ground beneath the window. "But with this rain, anything they might have left behind is probably long gone by now."

Zoe's flashlight swept over the ground, even though she doubted they would find anything. But then she spotted it—a faint shoe print, partially filled with water, just beneath the window. "Wait, hold on," she said, her heart racing.

Scott moved quickly to her side. "A shoe print," he said, crouching for a closer look. "It's faint, but it's something."

Zoe snapped a picture with her phone, the flash illuminating the print for a brief second. "We need to preserve this, even if it's just a long shot," she said, pulling a plastic bag from her pocket. She carefully covered the shoe print with the bag, weighing the edges down with some nearby stones. "Maybe CSU can find something in the morning. Particulate evidence, something."

Scott nodded, standing back up and scanning the area again. "They were here. But where the hell did they go?"

Zoe's mind worked, connecting the dots. "They knew what they were doing. They waited for the storm, knew it would cover their tracks. They were in and out in a flash."

Scott's jaw tightened, frustration evident on his face. "Damn it. This rain might have washed away most of what we could use."

"Maybe," Zoe said, standing up and looking back at the house. "But we've got this print, and the garden. Something feels off about all this. We'll get CSU out here first thing. Tomorrow morning canvass the neighborhood. Maybe someone saw something. A car, hopefully."

They turned back toward the front of the house, the rain still pouring down as they walked. Zoe glanced back once more at the dark, open window, her thoughts churning. Whoever had taken Tara was calculating, careful. But they had left something behind, and she was determined to figure out what it was.

* * *

The door creaked as Travis Hunter slipped inside his home, the faint light of dawn just beginning to creep through the curtains. His bones ached from the long night, and his head throbbed from the hours spent dealing with Mayor Hicks' rants and the mounting pressure of the investigation.

That's why he was happy where he was. He could never imagine running for mayor even though it had been suggested to him at one point. The day people's lives became pawns in personal ambitions was the day he would fail utterly and completely as a person.

He peeled off his wet coat and hung it by the door, his mind still racing with the latest events. The house was quiet, almost too quiet, as he made his way upstairs, dragging his feet.

When he got to his bedroom, Travis began to unbutton his shirt, each movement slow and deliberate, as if the fabric was made of lead. He could barely keep his eyes open and couldn't wait to go to sleep. Maybe this entire ordeal had just been a nightmare. He was pulling on a T-shirt when he heard it—the faint sound of the front door opening and closing, followed by soft, hurried footsteps.

He froze, his hand gripping the fabric of his shirt. Instinct took over, and he moved silently to the door, opening it just a crack. From the shadows of the hallway, he watched as Ryan slipped inside the house, drenched from head to toe. He was wearing a black hoodie, the hood pulled low over his face, but Travis could still see the fear in his face. Ryan's eyes darted nervously, his body rigid.

Fear crept up Travis' spine too. The uneasiness that had been gnawing at him for weeks had resurrected in full force.

This wasn't the first time Ryan had come home late with that same haunted look in his eyes.

His training whispered to him that this wasn't a boy who had never got over his mother's death; this was a boy who was hiding something. But what the hell was he up to?

His chest tightened, and he rubbed it absently, trying to ease the discomfort. He knew where it stemmed from. It was something he had buried deep down inside himself a long time ago that was now trying to get out. Travis pushed the door closed, his hands trembling as he tried to steady himself. "Get a grip, Hunter," he muttered under his breath. He needed to sleep, needed to clear his mind before he could think straight again.

But as he lay in bed, the silence of the house pressed in around him. He couldn't shake the image of Ryan's pale face, the fear in his eyes. He closed his eyes, hoping for sleep to take him. But when sleep didn't come and he opened them again, there was a girl standing at the foot of his bed.

She was young, no more than ten or eleven, her skin pale and waxy, her dark hair hanging limp and wet over her shoulders. Her eyes were hollow and jaundiced, staring directly at him with a look that sent icy tendrils of fear curling through his veins. She didn't move, didn't speak—just stood there, silently watching him.

A cold fist wrapped around Travis' heart. His body paralyzed with a terror he hadn't felt in years. He squeezed his eyes shut. This wasn't real. It couldn't be real. But when he opened them again, the girl was still there, closer now, her face inches from his, her cold breath ghosting over his skin.

Panic surged through him. He jerked away, turning over in bed—and there, lying beside him, was another young girl. This one was even younger, her blond hair tangled and matted, her eyes wide with an unsettling mix of innocence and despair. She was curled up next to him, as if she'd been lying there all night, her small hand resting on his chest.

"No," Travis whispered, his voice trembling as he pushed himself to the edge of the bed. "No, this isn't happening."

His mother had seen things, too. Visions that haunted her, drove her to the brink of madness. Was this it? Was he losing his mind, just like she did? Was this madness plaguing Ryan too?

TWENTY

Zoe's eyes thinned at the image on the screen. The new day had started on an encouraging note. She had finally gotten her hands on the CCTV footage from Seaside Sweets. The burglary had been tagged as a low-priority case following Lily's disappearance, but now this was the only solid piece of evidence that could lead them to their elusive killer.

"The CSU is combing Tara's room and that shoe print we found," Scott said, swinging the door to her little office wide open. "Jesus, it's cold in here."

Zoe didn't care. She had barely registered the chill seeping into her toes and fingers. Her eyes were glued to the footage. The timestamp displayed 11:28 p.m. "Got the robbery video. Check it out."

The grainy video showed behind the counter. The lights came on and a figure appeared in the frame. Zoe stilled in anticipation. The figure was wearing a brown hoodie, his size and shape distinctive of a man. But his hood was up, his hands in his pockets and his shoulders hunched.

He was avoiding the cameras.

With a gloved hand, he opened the compartment door to a

display case. He began sweeping all the desserts into a large box he'd picked up from the floor. As soon as he'd finished, he disappeared from the frame. Seconds later, the lights went off.

"Damn it." Zoe sat back with a huff. "He knew where the cameras were."

"Must have scoped the place as a customer at some point," Scott said.

She played back the video, zooming in on the hooded man. There had to be something here, she kept trying to convince herself. But the hoodie was a generic brown. No visible logo on it. "I'll send this to FBI."

"What will they be able to do?"

"They can enhance this frame by frame and detect something our eyes missed. That's our only shot."

Gloom settled on her shoulders like a heavy weight. Her mind spun in all directions, firing randomly, but she was getting nowhere. Aiden strolled into the office, carrying a tray of coffees.

"Did you guys find anything last night?" he asked, scowling at his tie, which was askew.

"A footprint. CSU is there. Anything from the dad?" Zoe asked.

"I didn't detect any signs of deception, but he's hotheaded. Very."

"He took four days to kill Lily." Scott's words tumbled as though outrunning his thoughts. "But Lily showed no signs of any kind of injury other than the strangulation. So what was he doing for four days with her? Deliberating?"

"It could be obsessive-compulsive pathology. The caretaker behavior is part of a compulsive cycle that the killer feels obliged to complete. Disrupting the sequence could cause significant psychological distress," Aiden explained. "We do know he's meticulous and most likely mirroring something important to him."

Zoe pulled up Lily's autopsy report again and read it line by line, hoping for a clue she might have missed. She'd gone over it countless times, but something kept nagging at her.

"Hold up," Zoe said, her tone shifting as she focused on a particular section. "The victim's stomach contents revealed traces of recently consumed food, including proteins and carbohydrates. The body showed no signs of malnutrition; in fact, it suggests that Lily was well fed in the days leading up to her death. The only damage was to the kidneys, which could be attributed to exposure to some kind of toxin while in captivity."

Scott stopped pacing, turning to her with a furrowed brow. "Well fed? So he was taking care of her?"

She nodded, flipping to the next section. "Yeah, and it says here, 'Hydration levels consistent with regular intake of fluids; no signs of dehydration typically seen in prolonged captivity.' He kept her well-nourished and hydrated."

Scott turned to Aiden. "You were right. He's being a caretaker. But why?"

Zoe chewed on the pad of her thumb—a habit Rachel hated. She could still feel Rachel flicking her hand away. "Are you sure we are clear on the finances of the Bakers? Tim and Mary?"

"We got those. There's nothing there."

"They don't owe anyone any money?"

He shook his head. "Why?"

"There's another possibility. Something more basic." Zoe floated the idea. "Hesitation."

Aiden pondered, then said, "Lily is the first victim."

The color drained from Scott's face. "Does that mean that he might not take four days with Tara?"

"It's a possibility." She nodded against that sharp blade of time pressed against her throat. It could nick her at any time. "Why these two victims? What do Lily and Tara have in common?"

"Lily was seven years old and Tara's eight years old. They are in different grades but same school."

"Maybe they knew each other then? What about Tara's father? What does he do?"

"He's an environmental scientist for a consulting firm. Has nothing in common with the Bakers," Aiden confirmed.

Zoe threw her head back, trying to connect the dots. There had to be a reason why these two girls were targeted. The killer had snuck into Tara's room to abduct her. It couldn't have been convenience. Was it random? Did he watch Tara from a distance one day and a switch flipped that he just *had* to have her?

"Could it be an obsession that he's following up on?" Scott voiced her train of thought. "He saw these girls and just had to have them."

"In my experience, obsession is linked to sexual acts. Are the cops still canvassing the neighbors?" Aiden asked.

"Yeah, they're there right now." He chewed his lip, trying to make sense of it all, when his eyes lit up. "Lily said there was a man she knew. What if Tara did too?"

Zoe straightened. "Kids talk to their friends, you know. We need to interview them. Maybe Tara talked about the same man to her friends."

TWENTY-ONE

Zoe and Scott walked down the hallway of Harborwood Elementary, the sound of their footsteps echoing off the polished floors. The school was quiet, the usual hum of children's laughter and chatter subdued as they made their way to the classroom. They exchanged a glance as they reached the door.

Inside, a group of young children sat in a semi-circle, their faces focused on a teacher reading aloud from a picture book. As Zoe and Scott entered, the teacher looked up, her expression softening. She stood, closing the book gently.

"I'm Ms. Davis," she said, extending a hand. "I heard about Tara. How can I help?"

"We're here to speak with Tara's friends," Scott said.

"Tara's friends?" She arched an eyebrow.

Zoe nodded, offering a polite smile. "Yes, we need to ask them a few questions. Just to see if they might have noticed anything unusual. Kids often share information with each other that they don't tell their parents."

"Who were closest to Tara?" Scott pressed, eager to move things on.

Ms. Davis nodded, her brow furrowing with concern. "Of course. Caleb and Mona were Tara's closest friends. They're a bit shy, though. I'll stay with you while you talk to them."

Zoe and Scott followed Ms. Davis to a corner of the room where two children, a boy and a girl, sat huddled together, their expressions anxious. Caleb was twisting his fingers nervously, while Mona clutched a stuffed animal to her chest. They looked up with wide eyes as the officers approached.

"You good with kids?" Scott muttered in Zoe's ear.

"I'm a delight," she responded, grinning widely. "Hi, Caleb. Hi, Mona." She crouched down to their level. "I'm Zoe, and this is Scott. We're here to talk to you about Tara, to see if you can help us. Is that okay?"

The children looked nervously at Ms. Davis, seeking reassurance.

"You're not in any trouble," Zoe added, her tone kind but direct. "We just want to know if you've seen anything that might help us understand what happened to Tara."

Mona glanced at Caleb, who gave her a small nod before looking back at Zoe. "Tara was our best friend," Mona whispered, her voice barely audible. "But we don't know what happened."

Zoe exchanged a quick look with Scott before continuing. "Did Tara ever talk to you about someone she knew? Maybe someone who wasn't from school?"

Caleb shook his head quickly. "No. She didn't know Lily, either. We never talked about her."

Scott leaned in slightly. "What about a man? Have you ever seen someone around who maybe didn't belong here?"

The children stiffened. Mona crushed the animal tighter against her chest. Caleb dropped his eyes.

Ms. Davis moved closer. "It's okay. You won't get into any trouble. Just be honest."

"It's okay," Zoe encouraged softly. "We just want to know if you've noticed anything that made you feel uncomfortable."

Mona fidgeted with the stuffed animal, biting her lip. Finally, after a long pause, she whispered, "Sometimes... I see a man in a gray car."

Zoe's heart skipped a beat. "A gray car? Where do you see him?"

Mona pointed toward the large window at the side of the classroom. "Out there, by the street. He's just... watching."

"Did Tara notice him too?" Zoe asked.

Mona nodded.

Scott's expression tightened, but he kept his voice steady. "When did you see him last, Mona?"

Mona's eyes grew wide with fear, her small hand trembling as she clutched her stuffed animal tighter. "Just... just before recess. Today."

The temperature in the room plummeted.

Ms. Davis blinked, panic taking over her aged features. "I... I... I had *no* idea about this, officers. I swear. I would have done something if I knew. Mona, why didn't you tell me?"

While Mona tried to explain, Zoe kept her eyes on Caleb. His cheeks were turning a scarlet red and he looked like he was going to throw up. The boy was hiding something. She opened her mouth, ready to probe more.

Scott's eyes followed Mona's gaze to the window, his heart pounding. "Zoe—"

Before he could finish, Mona's voice cut through the silence, trembling with fear. "There he is!"

Zoe turned sharply, her eyes locking on the window. Outside, partially obscured by the rain-speckled glass, was a gray car idling by the curb, its engine running. The silhouette of a man was visible behind the wheel, watching the school with a stillness that sent a chill down Zoe's spine.

Scott moved quickly, his hand already reaching for his phone. "I'm going to call it in."

But Zoe couldn't wait. He was just beyond her reach. All she had to was take the last plunge and grab him. What was he doing here anyway? Following the detectives? Working out who to take next?

Adrenaline flooded her. Her heart careened beat to beat. Next thing she knew, she was out of the school, running in his direction. She rounded the corner, eyes locked on the gray sedan as it started to pull away from the curb. Zoe didn't hesitate—she sprinted to her car, throwing open the door and practically diving inside.

The engine roared to life as she jammed the key into the ignition, her hands gripping the wheel with white-knuckled intensity. The man's car lurched forward, tires screeching as he took off down the street.

Zoe's breath came in short bursts as she slammed the car into gear and peeled out after him. The rain-slicked streets blurred past as she floored the gas, the car surging forward with a growl. The man was already way ahead, blasting through the stop signs, but Zoe was right behind him, every fiber of her being focused on catching him.

"Asshole," she muttered through gritted teeth, her anger throbbing in time with her pulse. She could see him checking his rearview mirror, his car swerving as he tried to put more distance between them.

The man made a sharp turn onto a side street, hoping to lose her, but Zoe knew these roads too well by now. First thing she had done was memorize the streets of this town. She took a hard left, cutting through a narrow alleyway, the car bouncing over the rough pavement. She emerged onto the next street ahead of him, catching a glimpse of the gray sedan as it barreled toward her.

"Come on," she hissed, her foot pressing the pedal to the

floor as she aimed for the next intersection. She took the turn sharply, tires squealing, and the car fishtailed, skidding to a stop right in front of him, blocking his path.

The man's car screeched to a halt, his tires sliding on the wet asphalt as he tried to avoid a head-on collision. Zoe jumped out of her car and yanked the driver's door open before he had a chance to react.

The middle-aged man looked up at her, his face pale. His receding hairline glistened with sweat, and he fumbled with the seatbelt, his hands shaking. "I'm sorry, I'm sorry!" he babbled, his voice high-pitched and panicked.

Zoe didn't wait for him to finish. She grabbed him by the collar and hauled him out of the car in one swift move, twisting him around and slamming him against the side of the vehicle. "You're under arrest," she snapped, as she cuffed his wrists.

The man didn't resist, his body trembling as he kept repeating, "I didn't mean to—please, I'm sorry."

Zoe tightened the cuffs, her breath still coming in short, angry bursts. "Save it," she said, her voice low and dangerous. "You have a lot of explaining to do."

TWENTY-TWO

"His name's Phil Malone," Scott read out from a file. He stood with Zoe and Aiden just outside the interrogation room, the mirrored glass separating them from the man on the other side. Phil Malone sat at the table, his fingers twitching nervously as they fiddled with his collar. Sweat beaded on his forehead, his eyes darting around the sterile room like a trapped animal.

Zoe crossed her arms, her gaze locked on Phil. "A bank manager, right? Doesn't exactly fit the profile we were expecting. What do you think, Aiden?"

"If I could detect psychopathy just by looking, I'd be charging a lot more for my services, Storm," Aiden replied with a trace of humor. "Does he have any priors?"

Scott flipped through the pages. "Nope. Other than a couple of DUIs a few years back, he's clean. No history of violence, no record of anything that would suggest he's a danger to kids."

Zoe frowned, her mind racing. "But he's been watching the kids. Does he have a family?"

"Divorced," Scott replied, his tone flat. "Wife left him about two years ago. She got full custody of their son. No visitation rights."

Zoe's eyes narrowed as she watched Phil through the glass. The man was clearly scared, his hands trembling as he fidgeted with the collar of his shirt. "So, what's he doing hanging around an elementary school?"

Scott shrugged, a slight tension in his shoulders. "That's what we're about to find out."

"He looks too nervous, so this should be easy. Unless this is an act in which case I'll jump in. I can hang back here and observe," Aiden said.

Zoe and Scott exchanged a look, before entering the interrogation room. It was stark and utilitarian, designed to strip away any sense of comfort. The walls were painted a dull, institutional gray, and the fluorescent lights above cast a harsh, almost clinical glow over everything. A single metal table sat in the center of the room, its surface cold and uninviting, with two rigid chairs on either side.

Phil looked up sharply as the door opened, his eyes wide with fear. He swallowed hard, his Adam's apple bobbing nervously as they took their seats across from him.

"I'm really sorry," Phil blurted out, his voice shaky. "I didn't mean to cause any trouble. I—I'll stop going to the school, I swear."

Zoe glared at the sweaty man, twitching uncontrollably across from her. His right hand had a noticeable tremor as he pulled out a handkerchief from his pocket and began dabbing his forehead with it. Instead of stuffing it back in his pocket, he kept dropping it on the floor.

He was too sloppy. And something told Zoe that the tremor in his hand didn't stem from anxiety.

She leaned forward, her gaze steady, but her tone softened slightly. "Phil, we need to know why you've been hanging around the school. Who are you watching? And why?"

Phil hesitated, his hands wringing together on the table. He opened his mouth, closed it again. "My son... Caleb. I'm just... I'm just trying to see my kid."

Scott and Zoe exchanged a glance, the pieces beginning to fall into place. Zoe remembered how quiet Caleb had been when Mona mentioned the man in the gray car. It was as if he had been hiding something, something that now seemed all too clear.

Her shoulders slumped in defeat. They had just walked into a custody situation.

"Your son goes to Harborwood Elementary?" Zoe asked.

Phil nodded, a tear slipping down his cheek. "My ex... she doesn't let me see him. She got full custody after the divorce, and she cut me off. No visitation, nothing. I just... I just want to see my boy, make sure he's okay."

Scott leaned back in his chair, the tension releasing from him like a hiss. "So you've been driving by the school, just to catch a glimpse of him?"

Phil nodded again, his hands shaking as he wiped his face. "I know it's wrong, I know. But it's the only way I can see him. I just park there for a few minutes, watch him during recess. I don't go near him. I don't talk to him. I just... I just want to know he's safe."

Zoe's mind flashed back to the way Caleb had sat quietly while Mona spoke, the way he hadn't said a word about the man in the car. "Caleb knows, doesn't he? He knows you're there."

Phil's face crumpled, and he nodded, tears flowing freely now. "He saw me once, a few months back. I waved, and he... he smiled. But he never said anything. I don't want to scare him. I just want to be close to him. Please, I'm begging you, don't take that away from me."

Was this the man Lily saw? "Do you know Lily?"

He frowned, confusion marring his face before recognition

struck. "Lily *Baker*, you mean? The dead girl in the woods? What does that have to do with me?"

Zoe noticed the tremor in his hand. "Is that just a nervous tick?"

He hid his hand under the table and his lips flattened into a thin line. "Parkinson's. My father had it too. Symptoms started around now."

There were no hesitation marks on Lily's skin. A tremble like that wouldn't have led to those clean striations. Disappointment filled her to the brim. "You can leave for now. But stay away from that school, Mr. Malone. It makes children uncomfortable, you lurking around."

"You don't want to end up on a registry." Scott's smile was brittle.

Phil swallowed hard and nodded.

They left the room and Zoe almost felt bad for chasing him down and throwing him into her car. "Maybe I should buy him a milkshake."

Scott's lips twitched into a smile. "It was a good shot. But Lily might have been referring to another man."

* * *

The rain came down in sheets, creating a murky backdrop for the gathering of reporters huddled under their umbrellas. Regina stood before them, her raincoat pulled tight around her, droplets running off the brim of her hat as she faced the small group of media representatives. The scene was bathed in hues of gray and black. Regina fought the wave of moroseness that was threatening to pull her under. Despite Harborwood being in the Pacific Northwest and being more used to clouds than sun, the town was still a place of comfort. A town forged in old bonds and loyalties.

But now that briny ocean breeze had gotten too chilly, the

lush leafiness had become a thick green maze and that mist was turning into smog.

She took a deep breath and her voice carried over the patter of rain. "This morning, I stand before you with a heavy heart. Tara Bennett, one of our own, is missing. And just days ago, we found Lily Baker, a young girl who had her entire life ahead of her, dead. Harborwood was once a safe town, but today, it feels like anything but. Our children, our most vulnerable, are not safe."

The reporters murmured among themselves, pens scratching across notepads, cameras flashing intermittently. Regina continued, her tone sharpening. "And while our children are at risk, Mayor Hicks is more concerned with his political agenda than with the safety of our community. I have dedicated myself to making real changes. Just last year, I oversaw the construction of a new school for children with special needs—a place where every child can feel valued and safe."

The rain intensified, but Regina's voice remained steady. Then, a reporter, a young woman with sharp eyes, stepped forward, her voice cutting through the sound of the storm. "Regina, there are rumors circulating that the ground the school is built on isn't stable. Something about it being prone to erosion and unsuitable for heavy construction. Can you comment on that?"

Regina's heart skipped a beat, her confidence wavering for just a moment. No one had asked her that question before. She rearranged the papers in her front of her fruitlessly. She forced a smile, though it didn't quite reach her eyes. "Those are just rumors, completely unfounded. The school was built with the utmost care and consideration for the safety of the children."

The reporter didn't seem entirely convinced, but Regina quickly shifted the focus back to the issue at hand. "Right now, our priority is to find Tara and ensure the safety of all our children. That's what we should be focusing on. As mayor, the first item on my agenda would be to increase police funding in this town. We have brave officers on our force, but they are held back by limited resources. By expanding our police force and ensuring we can afford access to the latest technology and skilled consultants, we will make our town safe *again*."

As the cameras clicked and the questions continued, Regina wrapped up her statement and began to walk away from the group, her mind still reeling from the unexpected question. Away from the prying eyes and flashing lights, she grabbed Connor's elbow, pulling him aside with a firm grip.

"What the hell was that about?" she hissed. "The question about the ground—where did that come from?"

Connor shrugged and was already thumbing his phone. "Hicks must have planted that question. It's just opposition research—trying to make you look bad."

Regina's eyes narrowed, anger simmering beneath the surface. Connor was orchestrating her entire life. *She* was the candidate. If she won the election, *she* would be the mayor. Then why did it feel like she was living someone else's life?

"I followed you the other night, Connor. I know where you went."

Connor's expression froze, his eyes widening slightly. He looked around to make sure no one was listening, then leaned in closer, his voice barely above a whisper. "It's to save our asses, Regina. Everything I'm doing is to make sure we stay on top of this. Trust me, it's all part of the plan."

Her grip on his arm tightened. "What do you mean? Is something going on that I'm not aware of?"

He released an exasperated breath. "We're running low on cash."

"*What?*"

"Yeah." Despite his puffed chest and hands on his waist, he

kept shifting on his heels. "We've been aggressive in our approach which has been good for our numbers—"

She almost lunged at him, her blood frothing. "Where did the money go, Connor?"

"Advertisements are expensive." He held his ground. "But it's a necessity. That's why I went over there. We need to cut our losses."

"How bad is it?"

His expression was as hard as stone. "If we don't trim the fat or find extra resources, we got a month."

Regina's stomach folded. The election was in six weeks. What was she going to do?

TWENTY-THREE

"Do you get tired of it?" Aiden asked.

"Tired of what?"

"Chasing closure for other people?"

She swallowed. "Yes."

"Then why do you do it? Why are you here?"

Zoe sighed. She was tired of him picking at her brain. "Am I that interesting?"

"Sorry?"

"Don't you have psychopaths and people with split personality disorder who would be more fun to talk to?" She groaned, throwing her head back. Aiden bit his lip, fighting back a smile. "Oh, so now you think I'm funny?"

"Amusing is more accurate. But to answer your question, yes, you're a one-woman show."

"I'm here to entertain you?"

His eyes sparkled. "Not going to lie, Storm, but maybe a little bit."

Her stomach growled. "In that case, I need some calories to keep the Zoe Storm show going. Pizza?"

"With pineapple?"

"That's blasphemy."

* * *

Zoe lay in bed wide awake, staring at the cracks in the ceiling. She was wearing earbuds and listening to Puccini's "Nessun Dorma" from the opera *Turandot*. A rich voice tore through the gentle swell of the orchestra. As the piece progressed, the intensity grew, the singer's voice rising with a powerful surge of emotion.

The rising crescendo loosened the strings that had her insides tied into a knot. She imagined the cracks in the ceiling mending on their own. But impatience ran through her. An itch, a tickle, a pebble in the shoe. She waited for the music to calm her, to ebb away the currents that pulled her under. But after another minute, the song was nothing but noise in her ears. She removed her earbuds with a huff and her ears ached in the sudden silence.

She sat up and looked around the empty motel room. It was so impersonal. Nothing but a collection of basic necessities used by a gazillion drifters before her. She would also move on, go to another place and crash for a few months, and no one would know she had been here. She was just passing by and she always would be unless she strengthened her roots to her past. But time was withering those away. All she had left of Rachel and their time together were memories that would fade with time.

And then what was she without them? Gina had a family. The only thing left of Zoe would be archived cases in the FBI.

She tried sleeping but the uneasiness was like fizz pumping through her veins. With an irritable groan, she got up, wrapped her fluffy robe around her and padded her way to Aiden's room. Something told her that he wasn't sleeping either.

When she knocked on the door, he opened it in a second.

"Storm." His eyes swept over her robe and bunny-shaped shoes. "Interesting choice."

She scowled and pushed past him. "I knew you slept in a suit."

"Why don't you come in?" he said sarcastically, shutting the door.

Zoe's eyes slid over his room—an organized stack of files and psychology books sitting on the table, the bed made with such precision that she knew he hadn't gotten in yet. "Can't sleep?"

"I don't sleep." Aiden shook his head, hands in his pockets.

"What?"

"I have insomnia," he admitted bashfully.

"Then why did you buy a new mattress?"

"So that I can lie on it without breaking my back."

Zoe nibbled on her thumb, noting how even Aiden didn't have any mementos of his life—no pictures or signs of anything beyond the daily grind of combing through evidence and people's minds.

"What's bothering you?" he asked.

"I don't know what man Lily was referring to. It could just be Phil?"

"Unlikely." He sank into a chair. "Didn't that guy from the fishery, Andy, who saw Lily, say that she wanted to go say hi to someone?"

"Yeah..."

"And it was none of her friends, but it was someone she recognized."

"But Tara was abducted from her home at night. The killer had risked an abduction in broad daylight."

When her phone rang, Simon's name flashed on it.

"It's 11 p.m.," Zoe pointed out instead of the customary hello. "Why are you calling me this late?"

"Because I'm sitting here and reviewing your IT request to pick apart a perfectly good CCTV footage," he replied, his voice craggy with sleep. She could hear the hum of the running dishwasher.

"We got a second missing girl, Simon. One was found dead. With creepy ropes and a message in the woods."

The minute she said his name, Aiden swiftly turned on his chair, giving her his back and engrossing himself in a book.

"Creepy ropes? How many were there?"

She knew she didn't have to hide anything from him. "Three. There's nothing in any database about a similar MO. Aiden believes it's three victims, and I agree."

He whistled. Dishes clanged. "Z, my hands are tied. How are you and Wesley working together?"

When he said Z, a current ran through her. She didn't feel any want or desire. It was like an old feeling trying to resurrect. "Great. He says hi. What's the problem? Budget?"

"We're stretched thin. IT is overloaded. Oh, Aiden is with you? It's late..."

Zoe sensed that sharp tilt to his tone, but she refused to acknowledge it. He was married. Why would he care?

"Children, Simon. These are kids!" Her voice climbed higher. Ever since she'd held Gina's twins in her arms, she knew she had become soft. She finally understood something that was both illogical and pure truth—how the value of a person was inversely in proportion to their size. From the corner of her eye, she saw Aiden focusing too hard on the same page, his grip tight on the spine.

"Harborwood isn't the only place with a child killer."

Zoe slumped into a chair and rubbed her eyes. "I know. I know. You're right."

She had worked all kinds of disturbing cases. Whenever she found herself in the midst of a disturbing case, staring into the eyes of someone whose world had been blown to smithereens by someone wielding a hammer, she painfully remembered that she had somehow dealt with worse.

Somehow there was always something worse out there. But evil was a funny thing. It didn't have a gradient; it just had different shapes.

"Listen. I'll try my best," Simon said, his voice softening. "I can't make any promises, but you'll have to be patient."

"Okay." At least that was something. Maybe she could learn how to work ultra-savvy software and analyze that video herself.

Nancy's voice could be heard in the background. "Who are you talking to?"

"Oh, it's just work. Dale," Simon said.

"Okay, I'm going to bed!"

A hot flush crept over Zoe's face, making it throb.

"Sorry about that," Simon said. "Where were we?"

"You don't have to lie to your wife that you're talking to me," she said in a hard voice. "We were just talking about *work*."

"Ah... come on, Z..."

"Don't Z me!"

He sighed. "She's sensitive about you. She gets insecure. I just didn't want to get into another fight with her over you after a long day."

Confusion muddled her brain. "Over me? Seriously, Simon? Why does your wife think I'm the other woman?"

He fell silent. A loud silence that pierced Zoe's eardrums. "You're not. But we used to be together."

"That was years ago, before you even met her..." she whispered.

"And she gets awkward about it. I'll let you go." He cleared his throat. Before Zoe could reply, he hung up.

She kept the phone pressed to her ear, rehashing the conversation. Maybe she was too hard on him. She knew somewhere that Simon still held a torch for her. Who was she to have an opinion on what he was telling his wife? Why was she getting involved? She had bigger things to worry about.

Suddenly, she remembered she wasn't alone. Aiden was

now facing her, his expression stony. Was he judging her? It was an inappropriate conversation to have with a boss. She thought she was going to explode. Her nerves were jangled under her skin, threatening to puncture their way out.

"Sorry about that." She lowered her gaze.

Aiden shrugged, as unreadable as ever. And she felt it in her bones—the judgment. Wasn't he a shrink? Wasn't he supposed to *talk* and not judge? "I should go."

Aiden made no attempt to stop her and she felt like an even bigger idiot. For a second, she'd thought they were maybe even friends.

When she got to her room, she twisted her hair in a bun and opened the preliminary reports submitted by the patrol officers and the CSU. None of the neighbors saw anything. The abduction had happened around midnight—too late for any neighbors to be out and about. And due to the storm, no one heard anything either.

The CSU had tagged the shoe print as priority. She studied the report, mulling it over. The shoe size was 10.5, which was standard for an adult male in the US. Based on the pattern, it was Nike. Another generic brand. Particulate evidence of tiny particles of limestone dust and some traces of rust. Could this be an industrial site of some sort?

Lily had an allergic reaction to devil's club—a plant not found in the woods where her body was discovered. But perhaps devil's club was present at the site she'd been taken to before she was killed.

TWENTY-FOUR

The next morning Zoe pushed open the door to the small café, the warm scent of coffee and freshly baked pastries washing over her as she stepped inside. The place was cozy, with a few patrons scattered around the tables, quietly sipping their drinks or typing away on laptops. Even the cafés were glum. She missed the big city buzz that trickled into the smallest and most unassuming nooks and crannies. In Harborwood, it was the ocean breeze that penetrated everything. Out the window, she saw a ship half cloaked in the fog in the distance. She couldn't tell if it was moving closer or further away.

The line at the counter was short. It was a small town. No big queues and no restaurants open after 9 p.m. Her mind was still buzzing with the details she had absorbed the night before. The locals would know the woods well. They hadn't heard anything from the neighboring towns. No sightings.

When it was her turn, Zoe ordered a strawberry milkshake, one of her favorites. As the barista prepared her drink, she glanced around the café. That's when she saw him.

Keith was sitting at a corner table, half hidden behind a large newspaper. His shoulders tensed the moment their eyes met, and he tried to sink lower in his seat, the newspaper rising like a flimsy shield between them. Zoe couldn't help the small, amused smile that tugged at her lips.

It was his lucky day that she didn't have time to harass him, but she wasn't going to let him off that easily.

When her milkshake was ready, Zoe picked it up and turned back to the counter. "One more, please," she said to the barista, looking at Keith over her shoulder. He peeked over the edge of the paper, clearly exasperated. The second milkshake was quickly made, and Zoe took both drinks over to Keith's table.

Keith stiffened, the newspaper crinkling as he tried to pretend he hadn't noticed her. But Zoe wasn't fooled. She walked up to his table and set the second milkshake down in front of him without a word.

Keith slowly lowered the newspaper, his eyes narrowing as he looked up at her. He said nothing and just watched as she turned to leave, his gaze burning into her back as she made her way to the door.

It was Rachel who had loved milkshakes. Zoe hoped that Keith remembered that about her and would unravel whatever secret he was holding.

* * *

To Zoe's irritation, she and Aiden carpooled to the station together. She had managed to squeeze a moment of privacy to get coffee, but the car ride had been agonizingly quiet. So quiet that at one point she had to hum to pretend she didn't notice Aiden stealing glances at her. The station reminded her of a beehive. Unlike her first impression, where everyone moved around lost and asynchronized, there was an efficiency and urgency plugged into their movements.

They weren't dealing with the first missing girl in Harborwood anymore—it was a string of kidnappings. She headed straight for the old coffee machine when she realized to her dismay that it was out of order. She had been hoping more sugar would help her think.

"There you are!" She hopped to Scott as he rounded a corner. "Do you know any industrial site that would have devil's club growing nearby?"

He blew out a breath, the wheels churning behind his shifty eyes. "Let's pull up a map." He went to his desk and rummaged through the stacks of rolled paper. Scott's desk was devoid of any personal memorabilia. No pictures, no trophies, no handmade craft. Even her desk back at the FBI field office had drawings her nephews had done for her. He unrolled one of the maps of the area.

"Isn't this information computerized? Some software that could help us narrow it down?" Zoe asked.

He looked at her flatly. "We don't even have enough cell towers in the National Park, Zoe."

"Yeah." She frowned at the map of Harborwood. A slice of land, mostly crowded with green spaces, and ocean on the other side. "Okay, so devil's club is common enough in Harborwood. According to the rangers, these are the best known spots." He uncapped a marker and drew disjointed circles in three areas.

"Are these the only ones?"

"Well, no. If someone is planting them randomly in their backyard or stray ones pop in the woods then there's no way of knowing."

Zoe scratched her head. This is why she didn't like the woods. A city, she could map. She could know what happened in every building, on every floor. But the woods were elusive, guarding secrets, and unfortunately, *too* vast in Washington.

"Okay, according to the analysis of the shoe print by the CSU, there were significant deposits of limestone and rust. So we are looking at an industrial site? An old one, I assume, based on the rust?"

"That's a good start." He flipped through some old records. "We got two potential places. Neither of them are close to where Lily was found."

* * *

Zoe trudged through the thick underbrush, her boots sinking into the damp, moss-covered ground with each step. The dense canopy overhead blotted out most of the light, casting long and hulking shadows like the day was speckled with nights. She walked guardedly behind Scott, who seemed to be more comfortable with the dizzying woods. The air was heavy with the scent of wet earth and decaying leaves, and the only sound was the rustling of the trees and the occasional snap of a twig underfoot.

"This place used to be a manufacturing hub," Scott said, his voice low as he ducked under a low-hanging branch. "Back in the fifties, it was a factory that produced parts for ships—engine components, propellers, that sort of thing. But when the industry dried up, so did the factory. It's been abandoned for decades, just left to rot out here."

Zoe nodded, her eyes scanning the trees ahead for any sign of movement. "You'd think someone would've torn it down by now. Or at least fenced it off."

Scott shrugged. His gaze fixed on the faint outline of a building just visible through the trees. "Too expensive, I guess. It's in the middle of nowhere, so no one bothered. Now it's just a ghost of what it used to be—half-collapsed, rusting away."

"I hope second time's the charm."

The old industrial site finally came into view. The factory loomed ahead, a hulking mass of crumbling concrete and rusted metal, overgrown with vines and surrounded by dense forest.

The windows were shattered, and the roof had partially caved in, leaving gaping holes that allowed the rain and elements to eat away at the remaining structure.

They moved cautiously—Zoe's eyes sweeping the area for any signs of recent activity. The ground was littered with debris —broken bricks, twisted metal, and remnants of old machinery. They circled the building, their flashlights cutting through the gloom as they searched for any clue that might lead them to Tara.

"This place is a death trap," Scott muttered, kicking aside a piece of rotted wood.

Zoe nodded, her senses on high alert. "It's isolated, hidden... the perfect place if you don't want to be found. I don't see anyone."

Just as she finished speaking, a faint noise reached her ears —a rustling in the bushes, too deliberate to be the wind. She whipped her head around, her flashlight beam catching the movement. A figure darted out from behind a rusted metal pipe and bolted into the woods.

"There!" Zoe shouted, already breaking into a sprint.

Scott was right behind her, their feet pounding against the uneven ground.

The man was fast, but Zoe was faster. She pushed herself harder, adrenaline surging through her veins as she closed the gap between them. The figure was ragged, his clothes dirty and torn, his hair matted.

"Stop!" Zoe called out, but the man only ran faster, his breath coming in ragged gasps.

She weaved through the trees, branches tearing at her face, the ground slick and treacherous underfoot. Something caught her foot and she went crashing face down. Her nose crushed against the mud. But Scott shot past her. With one final burst of speed, he lunged forward, grabbing the man by the arm and yanking him to the ground.

They fell with a grunt, the man's body twisting as he tried to scramble away, but Scott pinned him down. "Easy there."

Zoe got up and realized she'd twisted her ankle—luckily she hadn't sprained it.

"You okay?" Scott asked over his shoulder, his arm digging into the neck of the motionless man.

"Yeah..." She dusted off the mud on her jeans.

Scott turned him over. The man's eyes were wild, darting between Zoe and Scott as he tried to catch his breath. "I wasn't doing nothing!" he stammered, his voice shaky. "I just... I just crash there sometimes, okay? I don't want no trouble!"

"What's your name?" Zoe asked, slightly winded, kneeling beside him.

"Jimmy."

Jimmy had blotchy skin and corroded, missing teeth. His head was splattered with bald spots and his arms were peppered with needle marks. A distinct foul smell emanated from him—meth and lack of shower combined.

"You crash there?" Zoe repeated, unconvinced.

"Yeah, I just spend the nights."

"You're lying. There was no sleeping bag or blanket or pillow or clothes or anything that would indicate that you spend the night here."

He licked his lips, fear palpable on his face. "I don't own anything!"

"So if I check you right now, I won't find any drugs on you?" Scott raised his eyebrow.

Zoe studied his face. He looked desperate, scared—like a man who had been living on the edge for too long. "Jimmy, why don't you answer our questions and maybe Detective Cohen over here won't go through your pockets?"

Scott exchanged a glance with Zoe, his expression serious, but she just shrugged.

Jimmy hesitated, his eyes flickering with uncertainty. "I was here to make a drop."

"What drop?"

"GHB."

Scott frowned. "Gamma hydroxy-butyrate."

Zoe recognized the drug. It could simulate unconsciousness, confusion or even seizures. "For whom?"

Jimmy hesitated again but Scott turned him around and pressed into his neck, he nodded desperately. "All right! All right! It's just this kid, okay? I've been selling to her for over a year now. I meet her here."

"We need a name, buddy," Scott reminded him.

"Bella. Bella Baker."

Dread washed over Zoe. It was Lily's sister.

TWENTY-FIVE

"How important is family to you?"

Zoe growled. "How is this relevant to my psych evaluation?"

"Everything that makes you you is important," Aiden said with a shrug.

"It means everything to me."

"It's important to have that anchor in a job like this. Something to go back to after dealing with so much..."

"Horror." She spelled it out for him.

"Exactly."

"Do you have an anchor too? You must have dealt with worse people than me."

He chuckled and gestured around his office. "My anchor is this. These books. These theories."

"Feels flimsy. No offense."

"None taken." The corners of his eyes softened.

"Sometimes, I'm afraid," Zoe confessed in a small voice, playing with the sleeve of her T-shirt. To her dismay, she was getting too used to Aiden's handsome face and soothing voice, and the scent of coconut that always lingered in his office.

"Afraid of what?"

"Of changing too much. What if I lose myself in these horrors I see every day?"

* * *

Dressed in an oversized plaid shirt and her dark hair cascading down the side of her face, Bella's body was caved inward and away from Zoe and Aiden. She made every effort to make it clear that she had no desire to be in the interrogation room. Her face was disinterested but her eyes screamed rebellion.

Zoe knew girls like Bella. Girls like Bella hardened because they knew betrayal from an adult close to them. Their problems started at home, where they were the victim of a negligence or an evil. But Zoe also knew that the way to deal with these kinds of girls was not to be gentle.

Bella was a wounded animal. She only understood harshness.

"We found your dealer. Jimmy," Aiden said.

There was the slightest flicker of surprise in her eyes, but she quickly rolled them to hide it. "I don't know what you're talking about."

"He's willing to testify and I'm more than willing to get a court order to check your school locker and your room," Zoe warned.

Bella frowned. "Can you do that?"

"GHB is a controlled substance. You are seventeen but you might be charged as an adult and face up to five years in prison."

They had Bella's attention now. Her lower lip jutted out, like she was trying not to cry. "I want a lawyer."

"That's your right." Zoe made to stand up. "I was hoping this would be a voluntary interview but I'll also call your parents—"

"No!" She jerked forward in her seat. "Don't call them. Please."

"Then talk to us," Aiden said, as Zoe sat back down. "Why are you using GHB?"

"Because Lily is dead." Bella looked at them in horror. "What do you think happened? My parents blame me. I should have kept an eye on her. And they're right..." A fat tear ran down her cheek. "Because of me, someone strangled her."

"Jimmy said you've been buying from him for over a year, Bella," Zoe said.

Her nostrils flared and she wiped her nose with her sleeve. "Let's just say my issue with my parents started way before they decided I was a monster for letting Lily get away."

"What kind of issue?" Aiden pressed.

Bella swallowed hard, her brows pulling together. "It's... whatever. Your run-of-the-mill shit. A mother who doesn't leave you alone and a father who works too much to care about anything else."

Zoe sensed she didn't want to talk about it. But there was a sadness to her. "Did she pay more attention to Lily than to you?"

She scoffed, sarcastic. "Of course she does. I'm too old now. But Lily is... was... younger and more malleable, I guess."

"That's an interesting choice of word." Aiden pushed his glasses up his nose, a deep groove forming between his eyebrows. "Were you jealous of Lily?"

"No!" she said, aghast. "Of course not! Why would I be?"

"Sometimes relationships are complicated. You can hate the attention you're getting but at the same time you miss it when it's directed at someone else. The cycle of toxicity," Aiden explained gently.

It was a feeling toward Rachel that Zoe had furiously avoided. All her memories of her were tainted by the secrets her mother kept. It was so easy for her mind to tilt just a little and drop into resentment and anger. But she had locked that part of her away and only nourished it from time to time. She glanced at the little cut on her hand from destroying that car—a staunch reminder.

"I loved Lily. I didn't want to hurt her. I never did." She lolled her head, playing with a strand of her hair. "I just use because it's easier that way."

"You were close to Lily," Zoe said. "Did she ever mention a man watching her or a man she was friends with?"

"I told you I don't know." She shrugged exasperated. "If I suspected some pervert was hanging around Lily then I would have said something!"

"You do know that Tara Bennett is missing?"

Bella's face paled. "Are you insinuating I have something to do with this? I don't even know her."

A sharp knock on the door and Travis popped his head in, gesturing them to come out.

Zoe and Aiden followed Travis outside into the narrow hallway with peeling brown wallpaper and flickering yellow light above. Travis avoided their eyes as he rocked back and forth on his heels. Before he said a word, Zoe knew what he was going to say. She could feel the utterly revolting words that were going to come out of his mouth seeping into her skin.

"It's... Tara," he croaked in a small voice. "Rangers found her body in the woods."

* * *

The clearing was small. Tall trees stood around it and Zoe swore they were leaning closer, like they wanted to cradle it lovingly. The ferns clawed at her legs as she brushed past to get a closer look. As she approached the scene with heavy steps, she was filled with a cold sensation. The rangers had gathered around the scene, their faces drawn.

When they parted to let Zoe through, her stomach dropped and her blood ran cold.

Tara's body lay crumpled against a tree, half concealed by the thick underbrush, her clothes streaked with mud and the color of her skin pallid. Sunlight filtered through the canopy, casting dappled shadows on her, like she was in rippling waters. For a moment, Zoe thought she saw her move. But the little girl set against the massive, century-old tree looked like a doll. She couldn't tear her eyes away.

This time only two ropes with nooses hung from the branches. One was empty and one had a picture of Tara.

The CSU was already there collecting samples and gathering evidence. The coroner was bending down next to Tara, examining her. But Zoe noticed a sheen of sweat coating his forehead despite the chill hanging in the air.

Because Zoe noticed everything. Especially how there was one empty noose that was left hanging. One more noose for one more victim.

With a gloved hand, she carefully peeled away the photo of Tara from the second rope, and read the scribbled message on the back:

The outcome wasn't what I hoped for, but perhaps it's for the best. Everything concludes when darkness falls.

TWENTY-SIX

Tara Bennett had an overbite. She had two dimples digging into her skin. Her hair was dark and curly. She wore thick glasses, which she hated. She was only eight years old. She had been looking forward to the new *Paw Patrol* movie to come out.

Zoe breathed through the weight pressing on her chest. She stared at the photo of Tara, wondering what she would have looked like had she been allowed to grow old. In the distance, she saw an elderly couple walking along the beach—their backs hunched and gait agonizingly slow. They probably hated being old, tired of living in a body that was a shell of what it used to be. But Zoe knew that growing old was a blessing. She had seen too many bodies deformed in unimaginable ways and lives taken for the most ridiculous reasons.

She set the picture aside and stared into the dark, treacherous waters of the Pacific Ocean. It was like a big pool of ink. The water looked thick and velvety from here. The sky was blanketed by clouds. A breeze chilled her scalp and she took deep breaths to clear her mind.

A group of kids were playing at the beach. Three boys. Two

of them were older and bigger than the third one. She watched them idly, dark thoughts crossing her mind—how were they destined to die?

And then she noticed the two big boys shove the younger one, who stumbled backward, crying. The older ones proceeded to harass him, snatch his backpack that he was desperately trying to hold on to, ruffling his hair and roughing him up.

Anger spiked in Zoe. She hopped off the rocks she had perched herself on and barreled toward them, her blood pounding hard in her veins. "Hey!"

The three of them looked at her. But all she saw was red. Something that had to be fixed, something that was *wrong*.

"Get away from him!" she screeched, standing like a wall between him and the two boys.

The older boys staggered back but not before one of them retorted, "Why don't you mind your own business, bitch?"

She fisted her hands and revealed her badge. "Say that again and I'll teach you a lesson."

The older boy's eyes widened. Behind Zoe, the little one started crying. He got up and rushed to the other older one, hugging him. He was probably his kid brother. The three of them looked at Zoe with frantic, panicked eyes. That's when Zoe realized how young they were. The older ones were not even sixteen.

Has she just threatened children?

She opened her mouth to apologize, but the boys suddenly hightailed it from there, disappearing into the night.

Zoe plopped down, her knees digging into the sand. This wasn't her, at least not like this. She was usually careful, studying her target and not acting impulsively. But now she was losing it.

* * *

"Hello, Mr. Hunter. It's good to see you back." Melissa, a bony woman who wore only white dresses, smiled at him.

Travis didn't return the smile. He crossed his arms and pouted. He didn't want to come back here again to his old therapist. The office with its beige colors, posters containing quotes about mental health, and a collection of succulents and snake plants to add a splash of serenity and color irked him. It was ridiculous, he thought. It made him feel weak, like he was on display.

"You know," Melissa said, capping a pen in her hands, "it's not a weakness to be here, Travis. I have many patients who are doctors, nurses, firefighters, cops... your job comes with baggage that you shouldn't have to process alone."

"Back in the day, people got over world wars without therapy," he grumbled. "And yet here I am."

"People also got by without modern medicine and yet we use them. Now tell me, why are you here?"

"I'm sure you're reading about what's happening in this town." He pulled at a thread on the orange couch.

"Yes." She pressed her lips in a thin line. "I can't imagine how traumatizing it must be for you. It must be reminding you of your late sisters. Are you hallucinating again?"

Travis looked up, his breath catching in his throat. They were standing behind Melissa like wraiths with empty eyes. When he blinked, they disappeared. "No. That time is behind me."

"Are you still taking your medication?"

"I haven't taken it in years. Don't need it. I'm just on medication for my high blood pressure."

"This case might open wounds that have healed. You might relapse."

If Melissa knew that Travis was seeing his dead sisters standing behind her, she would prescribe him medication or worse, declare him unfit for duty. He couldn't afford to sit at home. And nothing felt more imperative than untangling the mystery of his son. Despite the chaos that surrounded him at work, all the world's problems dwarfed in front of his child. That was the curse of being a parent.

"That's not the only reason I'm here."

"Then what is it?"

"My son, Ryan." His voice trembled. "I worry about him."

"I remember you told me you always felt there was a distance between you two. Has something changed?"

He nodded. "He's involved in something. He stays out all night and when he's home he locks himself away in his bedroom. He doesn't talk to me. I want to respect his privacy so I've been holding back on going through his stuff. But I called his school yesterday and they said he's been ditching classes."

Melissa nodded, sympathetically. "He's seventeen years old, Travis. Teenage years can be very turbulent. Especially for someone who lost his mother at a young age. Have patience."

"I don't have patience, Doc." His voice was laced with desperation. "If I ignore him... what if he... what if he's on some wrong path?"

Melissa stared at him, puzzled. "Do you suspect something concrete?"

What if his darkness had spilled over into his child?

"No," he lied.

"It's possible that you're deflecting."

"Deflecting?"

"That the deaths of Lily and Tara are weighing so heavily on you that subconsciously your mind finds it easy to focus on Ryan."

Travis turned her words around carefully. The pressure in his chest returned with full force. With trembling hands, he picked up a glass of water and guzzled it.

Melissa watched him warily. "Are you okay?"

"I just can't talk about it. Not today."

"Okay... not today."

* * *

Scott knew he shouldn't drink. He had worked too hard to give it up. But why were bad things so easy to give in to? Was he using the deaths of Lily and Tara as an excuse? Maybe if *he* was better, they would still be alive. The cab glided haphazardly through the winding, dirt roads of Harborwood.

There was an itch stuck in his throat. It scratched him every time he took a breath. Only one thing could make it better—that rich, smoky liquid with notes of oak and his damnation. He loosened his tie and clenched and unclenched his fists, suddenly clammy.

"You all right?" the cab driver asked, watching him squirm in the rearview mirror.

"Yeah," he replied curtly, his hands finding a flask in the inside pocket of his coat. He weighed the empty leathery flask in the palm of his hand. It was his father's flask—the only thing Scott had inherited from him other than a weakness for alcohol. He had kept it all this time.

He flicked it open and took a whiff. The smell alone was usually enough to help his nerves. But tonight his stomach was full of those nerves.

The smell wasn't enough. He needed to lose himself.

When the cab reached his destination, he tossed some bills at the driver, telling him to keep the change, and climbed out of the car. He waited for his numbing thoughts to revive with force and tell him to go back home.

But he couldn't. Not tonight. Because nothing mattered. Because if there was one thing that could stop him from drinking again, it was *her*.

He swayed slightly, the memory of Tara coursing through his veins, the biting emptiness amplifying inside him.

He paused at her door, his hand hovering over the worn wood, hesitating. But the memory of Lily's and Tara's pale faces, and the loneliness that seemed to stretch endlessly before him drove him forward. Before he could change his mind, Scott knocked on the door, the sound sharp and urgent in the stillness.

A moment later he heard the soft shuffling of footsteps on the other side. The door creaked open, and Carly stood there, her expression shifting from surprise to concern as she took in the sight of him—disheveled, eyes glassy, the scent of whiskey hanging heavy in the air.

"Scott?" she said softly, clearly concerned. "What are you doing here?"

He didn't answer right away, his gaze fixed on her. He couldn't find the words, couldn't articulate the mess inside him. All he knew was that he needed her—needed something to make the pain stop, even if just for a moment.

Before he knew what he was doing, he stepped forward, closing the space between them. His hands reached out, cupping her face as he leaned in, his lips brushing against hers. The kiss was desperate, almost frantic.

Carly tensed, her hands coming up to his chest to push him away, her breath hitching in surprise. "Scott, wait—" she began, her voice muffled against his lips.

But he didn't stop, couldn't stop. He should. What the hell was he doing? His restraint had been stripped away, leaving only the raw need and the pain he'd been drowning in for far too long. He deepened the kiss, his fingers threading through her hair as he pressed her against the doorframe.

Carly sighed. Her body molded into his and she returned the kiss. He pushed her to the bedroom that he used to frequent too often and began unbuttoning her blouse.

"What happened?" Carly, letting him undress her.

He didn't want to talk. He just wanted to forget. "She's dead. They're all dead."

TWENTY-SEVEN

Regina poured herself a drink. It was never too early to drink. Not when you were running a campaign. She took a deep sip, letting the burn slide down her throat, steadying the tremor in her hands.

She leaned against the kitchen counter, staring out the window at the overcast sky. The world outside seemed bleak. The waves crashed against the rocky shore, sending up sprays of mist. The sound of her phone buzzing on the counter snapped her out of her thoughts. Regina ignored it, taking another long drink instead.

She was aware of the risks when she announced her candidacy. There was *one* glaring, black spot on her otherwise clean life, and it was that bloody school for kids with special needs. Opening her life up for Hicks to slice and dice, there was a chance that what she did would be unearthed. Connor had been the one to plant the seed in her mind. He'd always been so good at making her see the bigger picture, at pushing her toward decisions that were... less than ethical but necessary, as he would say. It only felt like yesterday when she made the worst decision of her life that helped her public image the most.

"Regina," he had said, leaning back in his chair with that infuriatingly calm demeanor of his. "This school could be your legacy. Think about it—building a place where blind children can learn, can thrive. It's a PR dream. The votes will come pouring in."

"But the soil," she had argued, her voice tight. "The reports say it's unstable. There's a reason that land's been vacant for so long."

Connor had dismissed her concern, his smile sly. "So we get a different report. One that says what we need it to say. You're not going to let a little dirt stand in the way of something this big, are you?"

"*Connor.*" She leaned forward across the table. "This is a *school*. For *children*. The report clearly states that it's inadvisable to build something big on it."

"And all I'm saying is that scientists and geologists are wrong *all* the time!" He raised his hands. "We'll get another opinion—"

"This was our second opinion. I think we know our answer."

"Are you seriously going to let this stop you? You and your entire team—including myself—have slogged their asses off for *months*. Imagine the number of jobs this would create. Architects, contractors, teachers, accessibility consultants. We've involved lawyers, secured sponsorships—"

"I know all that!" she snapped, jumping up. "I know a lot of work has already been done."

"No, you don't. You just sign the paperwork, Regina," he said with an intensity she didn't recognize. Connor was usually flippant and dismissive. Not that he didn't care or didn't work day and night, but he wasn't one to display his passion. "It wasn't you who was working late hours, not going home, skipping their kids' birthdays to make this project work. We poured our blood and sweat into this—"

"I understand." She massaged her eyelids. "But there are some things we just cannot compromise. Safety is one of them."

"Nothing will happen, Regina. The reports say that the risk is medium to low. Not even medium. But this opportunity will *never* come again. It's too late for us to back out and not piss off a bunch of people who would not want to work with us ever again. Not to mention, it will take us years to start from scratch and get all the approvals." He was almost begging her now. A rare sight. "Regina, my future is also on the line. If I thought this was going to blow up in our face, then I would have backed out. But I'm in this. Because I *know* nothing will happen."

Regina was so close to fulfilling her dream. She could taste that victory. Finally, there was a project that was nearing completion after years of dealing with corporate and government red tape. And maybe Connor was right—why would he take such a big risk if he didn't have any confidence in it? The report said medium to low not high.

She'd known it was wrong, felt it deep in her gut. But Connor had a way of making the wrong things seem right. So she'd done it. She'd paid off that man. The money had been enough to sway him, and just like that, the report had been changed. The soil was suddenly perfect for construction, and the school had gone up without a hitch, fulfilling her lifelong dream and cementing her position as a leader in the community.

A gamble for the greater good.

Regina downed the rest of her drink, the glass clinking against the counter as she set it down harder than she intended. The guilt had been easy enough to ignore at first, drowned out by the applause at the ribbon-cutting, the praise from the community, the boost in the polls. But now, with reporters digging around, with that question hanging in the air... it was all starting to unravel.

She couldn't shake the feeling that the ground beneath her was about to give way, taking everything she had built with it.

The door creaked open behind her, but she didn't need to turn around to know who it was. With a sigh, she pushed the empty glass aside. "If this goes south, Connor, I'm not going down alone."

When Connor didn't reply, Regina turned around to find him standing still, his eyes cold. "Something has happened, Regina."

TWENTY-EIGHT

The car went over a bump, jolting Zoe out of her state of numbness. The streaming blur of green was easy to get lost in. She pulled at her seatbelt, which suddenly felt too tight on her chest. A feeling of impotence had gripped her.

Aiden turned on the AC and directed it at her.

"Thanks." She scrutinized his face and how seemingly unaffected he was. Always in deep thought, cutting and dissecting interactions, but at the same time so far removed from it. No wonder she would sometimes forget he was there; he seemed to seamlessly blend into his surroundings. "I feel like shit, Aiden."

"So do I, Storm," he admitted in a small voice.

They shared a moment of understanding. "Do you have any theories?"

"A couple."

"Like what?"

He took a sharp turn and the rising sun flicker-flashed through the trees overhead. "Something about his last message was off. It was too simple."

"Simple? What makes you say that?"

"It wasn't as lyrical as the first one. It was written more directly, lacking subtlety. The tone shifted from..." His face scrunched as he searched for the right words. "He sounds resigned now. Like he's already given up."

"Tara wasn't held captive as long as Lily was. Do you think there's been a shift in his psyche?"

He nodded, touching his glasses. "Something has changed. Perhaps the fact that he got away with two murders has led to a satiation effect, reducing the compulsive reinforcement he previously experienced. Although he didn't perceive it as a game, the psychodynamic engagement with us—the cat-and-mouse interplay—has lost its intrinsic appeal."

"This case isn't just changing us, it's changing him too."

They were one of the first to arrive at the station. Uniforms in night shift were packing up, ready to head home. They nodded at her, some smiled and made small talk.

They asked questions that she didn't have the answers to. But she was determined to find out. Three ropes, three nooses. Two victims so far. A current rippled through her veins as she made her way to her little makeshift room, carrying a large whiteboard she had purchased at a local store.

And then they got to work. She jotted down names, forensic details, and lists of suspects and possibilities. Aiden started a linguistic analysis of the two messages—something about checking stylistic features and sentence structure.

The CSU had fast-tracked analysis of the note left at the scene. As expected—no fingerprints or DNA. Her phone vibrated. When she saw who it was, her stomach dropped.

> *Simon: IT is overloaded but I'm trying. I don't like how we ended our conversation. Can we talk?*

Zoe didn't want to talk to him about anything other than work. It irritated her that he was digging up old feelings and triggering memories long forgotten.

"Sorry." Scott shuffled into the room carrying a tray of coffee and a bag of Sour Patch Kids. "I slept in."

Zoe studied him with skepticism. He had slept in. His hair was ruffled, the suit he was wearing yesterday was now crinkled, shirt buttoned improperly, and there was a fading red spot under his collar. She hadn't realized that he was seeing someone. She met Aiden's eyes but they said nothing.

"That's a nice perfume. I have it too," she said casually, looking at the whiteboard.

Scott growled. "This is embarrassing."

She ripped open the bag and grabbed a fistful of the candy. "Okay, so I called the coroner this morning. He'll send his report this afternoon. Let's look at our suspects."

He exhaled and leaned against the table, next to her. "Okay, so we got Bella Baker. Could she fit the profile?"

"She's a messed-up teenager on drugs with some deep-rooted parental issues," Aiden said, sighing. "But she's not a killer."

"That would explain why Lily was cared for and well fed before she was killed." Scott raised an eyebrow. "What if she has some split personality or psychosis type of issue?"

"There would have been signs both during the interrogation and from her medical history, and I checked..." Aiden said. "Plus, the shoe print you found outside Tara's bedroom? Bella's feet are much smaller."

Zoe rubbed her temples. The connections were noodling with no starting point to entangle them. "We should look into Bella's associates. Maybe she has a boyfriend."

"I'll ask uniform to follow up on that. What else do we got?" Scott asked.

"The problem is the connection between Lily and Tara."

Frustration clawed at her. "Lily is seven years old and Tara eight. They don't have any mutual friends; their paths didn't cross at school according to teachers and friends. Their families don't know each other."

"It is premeditated, but is our killer selecting girls randomly?"

She glanced at the two pictures pinned to the top of the whiteboard. They looked so different from each other—their skin and hair were different. "Usually, there's a type. Something more than just prepubescent ages appealing to the killer. Something simple like hair color. Or even glasses."

"Glasses?"

"The first case Aiden and I worked on was a killer who targeted people with bad eyesight." She cracked her knuckles. "Remember that one?"

"He was popping eyeballs with ice picks," Aiden said, his voice devoid of emotion. "There is something linking the two."

"Did your tech guy get back to you with the video tape?" Scott asked.

"Not yet. I think I'm going to have to take a crack at it myself. Access the software and learn how to use it." A thought was simmering inside Zoe's mind. "Are the woods being searched?"

"As we speak."

She marked the two spots where Lily's and Tara's bodies were found. The locations were far from each other, at least a fifteen-minute drive. And the woods were dense and removed from any trails. Whoever the killer was, they carried their bodies deep into the woods. Probably for privacy while they set up the stage.

"You'd almost think that this killer has some kind of experience," Zoe said. "The murders are too cleanly orchestrated."

"Every Tom, Dick, and Harry watching cop shows and

accessing the Internet knows everything they need to know about this," Aiden pointed out.

A sharp knock on the door interrupted them. Terri, an officer, walked in and handed a report to Scott, muttering something in his ear before leaving.

Scott flicked through the pages, a frown marring his face.

"What is it?" Zoe asked.

"When Tara went missing, I asked to pull Logan Bennett's financials like with the Bakers. You know, to check if he owed anyone any money."

"Does he?" she asked hopefully.

"The opposite. He's flush with cash. For the last three years, every month five grand is deposited into his bank account. But it's not his salary." He showed them the report.

It was a wire transfer from a company called Global Holdings Inc. "That's a good chunk of money. Does he have a side hustle?"

"Nope. No sources of passive income. I looked up the company online but I can't find anything on it."

"It's a generic name. Who are they and why are they paying him?" Zoe said.

TWENTY-NINE

Zoe was back doing what she hated the most.

Meeting families of loved ones lost to violence.

The house was a modest, single-story structure, the kind that had seen better days. The lawn was overgrown, the weeds choking what little grass remained. The windows, though clean, were covered with heavy curtains, blocking out any glimpse inside. It was a house that seemed to want to be left alone, much like its owner.

As they approached the front door, Zoe noticed the faint smell of stale cigarettes and something else—metallic and sharp, like fear. She exchanged a quick glance with Aiden before knocking. The door creaked open almost immediately, and Logan stood staring at them.

Logan was in his late forties, his hair thinning and streaked with gray, and his eyes bloodshot, with dark circles beneath them. His hands trembled slightly, one of them clutching a cigarette, the other a beer bottle.

"Mr. Bennett," Zoe began softly, "we're very sorry for your loss. But we need to talk."

Logan nodded, his expression blank, as if he hadn't really heard her. He stepped aside to let them in. The inside of the house was dimly lit, the air thick with the smell of cigarettes and negligence. The living room was cluttered with old furniture, magazines stacked haphazardly on a coffee table, and empty beer bottles scattered across the floor.

Tara's picture hung on the wall. She had dressed as Dorothy for Halloween. It was the only bright spot in the house.

"Sit down if you want," Logan muttered, collapsing into an old armchair that groaned under his weight. Zoe and Aiden took a seat on the worn-out sofa across from him.

"We appreciate you talking with us, Logan," Aiden said, his tone measured. "We understand this must be an incredibly difficult time."

Logan took a long drag from his cigarette, exhaling slowly as he stared at the floor. "Yeah, well... what do you want?"

Zoe braced herself. "Logan, we're trying to understand more about what might have happened. We need to ask you about some payments that have been going into your account every month from a company called Global Holdings Inc. Can you tell us about this company?"

Logan's eyes snapped up, narrowing as he looked between them. His grip on the beer bottle tightened. "What's that got to do with Tara? You think money's got anything to do with my little girl?"

"We're just trying to get the full picture," Aiden said calmly. "We're not accusing you of anything. We just need to know if these payments are connected in any way to what happened."

Logan's face flushed with anger. He slammed the beer bottle down on the armrest, causing Zoe to flinch. "You come here, into my home, and start throwing around accusations? My daughter's dead, and all you care about is some goddamn money?"

"Logan, we're not accusing you," Zoe said, keeping her voice steady. "We're just trying to find out the truth."

"The truth?" Logan spat. "The truth is that you have no goddamn idea what's going on. You couldn't save Lily, you couldn't save Tara, and you sure as hell won't be able to save the next girl. You have no idea who's behind all this. Just chasing your own tails."

A cold nub settled in the pit of Zoe's stomach. How was a killer able to leave clean crime scenes in a place like Harborwood which never witnessed violent crimes like this?

"Mr. Bennett, we need to follow up on anything that looks suspicious—"

"*Suspicious?*" he barked, his eyes blazing. He stood up abruptly and paced the room, his agitation growing with each step. Zoe could see the strain in his movements, the barely contained rage simmering just beneath the surface. "So you want to pin this whole thing on me? Is that how you save your incompetent asses?"

"We're not pinning anything on you, Logan," Aiden said, rising slowly from the sofa. "But we need to know where the money's coming from, because it could be important."

Zoe stood up, feeling the tension in the room rising. "If you know something, anything, that could help us find out who hurt Tara, you need to tell us."

Logan turned to face them. "It's a side hustle I have. Freelance accounting work I do for a small company. It has nothing to do with what happened to Tara. You want to help?" He pointed to the door. "Then get the hell out and find out who killed my daughter instead of wasting your time harassing someone who just lost every damn thing!"

Blood rushed to Zoe's face. This was a bad time, but they also needed answers.

"We're sorry for your loss, Logan," Aiden said quietly. "If

you remember anything, or if you change your mind, you know where to find us."

Logan slammed the door shut behind them with a force that made Zoe almost lose her footing. Outside, the clouds swollen with moisture had finally burst, leading to a drizzle that fell on them like little icicles. Zoe winced at the cold drops dripping down her neck.

"There's an extra umbrella in the car," Aiden said as they jogged down the jagged path.

"It wasn't the best time to talk to the guy. He's a single dad. I can't even imagine what he's going through," Zoe said.

"Yeah..." he said, seemingly unaffected by the drizzle leaving spots all over his suit. "He's lying."

"Yeah?"

"He showed classic signs of deception. He's hiding something. Check with the bank and see if they're willing to cooperate and share KYC records. If not, then we'll have to get a court order." He opened the back door of the car, retrieved the umbrella and handed it to Zoe.

"Thanks." She bit her lip.

"Why don't you head to the station? I have an errand to run."

"Errand?"

He tried to maintain his composure. "Between you and me, this case has been hard on Chief Hunter. He's already been under a lot of pressure from Mayor Hicks and I think his teenage son has been playing up. I want to offer an ear."

"Yeah. Of course. You take the car. I'll call a cab."

Zoe watched his car race away and cast her eyes on the lush, wet greenery surrounding her, the tip of a snow-capped mountain visible in the sky. Her chest tightened, thinking about the scars this case would leave on Harborwood.

When darkness falls...

Zoe went over and over the words, almost willing the letters to rearrange themselves to reveal a clue or the killer's identity. There was an end to this. Three ropes, three nooses, and three victims. Why three? Why *them*?

She clasped her fingers in front of her, stretching out each clue and potential lead in her mind.

The court order to obtain the list of children enrolled in the school system had come through. She was looking for girls under the age of twelve, assuming that the killer would continue his pattern of targeting prepubescent girls.

There were 475 girls under the age of twelve in Harborwood. Apart from the names Helena and Maia having something to do with light, Zoe had no idea how many other names meant *light* or anything to do with light. She let out a growl and sat back on her chair. An ache began hammering at the side of her head, like a woodpecker.

Terri, a patrol officer, poked her head in. "There's someone to see you, Agent Storm."

Zoe followed her outside to find a tall, strapping woman with short hair and a power suit standing with her arms crossed. She recognized her from the billboards around the town.

"Regina Warner."

"Agent Storm." Regina gave her camera-ready smile, her pearly white teeth gleaming. "It's good to finally meet you. Chief Hunter has told me good things about you."

"Thanks." She shook her hand.

Regina's eyes did a full sweep of her. And Zoe couldn't tell if she was being judged or sniffed. It was a thin line. "I know you have been updating Mayor Hicks on your progress. But I wanted to personally ask how everything's going."

"Two girls are dead, Ms. Warner. It's not looking good."

"Of course." Her eyebrows dipped. "I have suggested to

Mayor Hicks that he should impose a curfew and dispatch more police to the schools."

"I can't say that's not unreasonable considering what's going on."

"Well, that's if he agrees to it." She rolled her eyes. "Do you have any solid leads?"

"We can't discuss that with anyone."

"Fair enough. What kind of sick bastard does this to children and leaves cryptic messages and empty nooses?" She shuddered. "Makes me sick to my stomach. I hope you catch him. And if there's anything I can do to help then please let me know."

"I will. Thanks."

Regina turned around and walked away, her heels clanging on the floor and echoing in the empty hallway.

Something Regina had said snagged in her brain. How did she know about the messages and the ropes? As far as Zoe was aware, that information hadn't been made public.

When she turned, she almost walked into a wall. It was Scott. "Was that Regina Warner?" he asked, looking over her head.

"How does she know details about the crime scene? Like the nooses and all?" She asked, hitching her thumb in Regina's direction.

He shrugged. "It's a small town, Zoe. Uniform, rangers, they're probably discussing this case with their friends and family."

Her chest deflated. Harborwood had a lot to learn. "Instruct everyone not to share *any* details with outsiders."

"Why?"

"Because it encourages copycats."

Realization crossed his face. "Right. I suppose. None of us thought that way." His phone trilled, and when he answered Zoe watched the expression on his face change. A fierceness flashed in his eyes and his jaw hung open. "Okay… yeah. I'll call you back with the team. Sure. Thanks."

"What happened?"

"The killer messed up," he said with a satisfied grin. "He left DNA on the rope at Lily's crime scene."

THIRTY

Zoe stood at the window of Travis Hunter's office, her gaze fixed on the bleak, overcast sky. The clouds hung heavy. She sensed there was a storm whipping on the ocean from the early telltale signs of the leaves fluttering in fast winds.

Travis sat at his cluttered desk, his fingers tapping rhythmically on a stack of old case files. His face was bloated and there were dark circles under his eyes. Mindlessly, he began rubbing his wrist, staring off deep into empty space. Zoe hadn't spent that much time with the chief. But compared to the first day she met him, he had lost a significant amount of weight. The ring he always wore on his wedding finger had come loose. But she also noticed the small signs that he was losing it. Aiden was right. They exchanged a loaded glance.

Scott paced the room, holding his phone. As soon as it buzzed, he tapped the speakerphone button, the crackle of static giving way to a clear, crisp voice.

"Dr. Camden, it's Scott," he said, leaning closer to the phone. "I've got Chief Hunter, and Agent Zoe Storm and Dr. Aiden Wesley from the FBI here with me. You're on speaker."

"Good to hear from you, Scott," Dr. Camden said. "I've got

the preliminary results on the ropes from Lily's crime scene. The analysis took a bit longer than usual; there were some complexities other than the backlog."

Zoe turned away from the window, her attention sharpening. Complexities wasn't what she wanted to hear.

"What kind of complexities?" Travis asked.

"We ran multiple tests on the ropes," Dr. Camden explained. "Most of it was inconclusive—too much degradation, environmental contamination, no fingerprints, you know the drill. But one of the ropes, the one with her picture clipped to it, had a small amount of DNA that didn't belong to Lily."

Zoe's pulse quickened. This could be something. "How small are we talking?" she asked, stepping closer to the desk.

"Small enough that we could only get a partial profile," Dr. Camden replied. "We used a technique called Low-Copy Number analysis, which amplifies the DNA, but it's risky—sometimes you get artifacts or contamination. This time, though, we were able to confirm one thing."

Zoe felt a flicker of hope. "And what's that?"

"It's male DNA," Dr. Camden said, "and more specifically, the individual has a mutation in the HFE gene—hereditary hemochromatosis."

Zoe looked at Aiden, trying to gauge his reaction, but he just shrugged. "Hereditary hemochromatosis?" she repeated, the term ringing a bell. "That's the condition where the body absorbs too much iron, right?"

"Exactly," Dr. Camden said. "It's relatively common in people of Northern European descent. The mutation we found is on the C282Y allele, which is one of the more typical ones associated with the condition. People with this mutation can accumulate toxic levels of iron over time if left untreated."

Travis played with his wedding ring. It slipped from his grasp and rolled toward Zoe who picked it up and handed it back to him.

"Any hits on CODIS?" Travis asked.

"We ran it through CODIS, but with only a partial profile it's like searching with a hand tied behind your back. No hits came up," Scott said.

Zoe felt the flicker of hope dimming. "Are there any symptoms of this which might help us narrow it down?"

"Symptoms are non-specific like fatigue and joint pain. And for most patients, it will show up later in life when enough iron levels have accumulated."

Scott hung his head low and rubbed his palms. "Is there any other information you can get from this sample?"

"Unfortunately, no," Dr. Camden admitted. "The condition affects a significant proportion of the population, especially in regions with a high percentage of people of Northern European ancestry. We can definitively say we are looking at a white male. But with the amount of DNA we have, we couldn't create a full profile—just enough to identify the condition."

"Can you rerun the sample and do more tests?" Aiden asked hopefully.

"We can't do that without risking degradation. If we do then we risk losing the sample altogether. If you make an arrest and this case goes to trial, the defense will be unable to run any tests to verify our findings."

"That could compromise the whole case," Zoe agreed. "ND grounds for a mistrial."

Scott sighed in frustration. "So we're stuck with this? A genetic breadcrumb that leads nowhere."

"For now, yes," Dr. Camden conceded. "But it's not a dead end—just a detour. The DNA we do have could help eliminate suspects or corroborate other evidence if you find it. Think of it as one piece of the puzzle, not the whole picture."

Zoe's mind churned. They needed more than pieces. But this was a way forward. They were one step closer to identifying the killer.

"What are our options here?" Travis asked.

"You could go down the route of looking into local medical records, though privacy laws make that nearly impossible," Dr. Camden said. "People with hereditary hemochromatosis often need treatment, like phlebotomy to reduce iron levels. If there's a specialist in town, they might have records, but getting access to that data... you'd need a court order, and even then, it's a long shot."

Zoe felt a wave of frustration. They were so close, yet so far. "Thanks, Dr. Camden. Let us know if anything changes."

"I will. And good luck."

"It's something, but it's not enough," Zoe said, breaking the silence choking the room. "We're still grasping at straws."

Scott's eyes lit up. "We can run a volunteer program, Travis. It's a small town. We can invite people to come and get tested for this condition."

Travis flattened his mouth, unconvinced. "Why would the killer come out and volunteer if he knows he has this condition?"

"Maybe he doesn't know?" Zoe offered. "Dr. Camden said that the symptoms don't appear until much later. He might not even be in treatment for it."

Travis pondered this, his eyes doing a calculation. "There will be a significant proportion of people who will not show up, Agent Storm. Not because they don't care or are guilty but who wants to give out their DNA to anyone, especially the police, effectively the government?"

"It's also a privacy issue," Aiden said.

"The one thing Americans care about most after freedom." Travis's eyes bore into Zoe. "You'll have to find another way to do this, Agent Storm and Dr. Wesley."

. . .

The rain fell in heavy sheets, turning the parking lot into a glistening expanse of wet asphalt. The streetlights cast a dim, yellow glow, reflecting off the puddles that had formed throughout the day. Travis Hunter stepped out of the station, the cold air hitting him like a slap. He pulled up the collar of his coat and opened his umbrella, the rain drumming steadily against the fabric.

As he made his way toward the parking lot, he spotted Scott standing by his car under an umbrella as he fumbled with his keys.

"Scott," Travis called out, raising his voice over the downpour. Scott looked up, surprised, then quickly turned back to his car, his movements stiff.

Travis approached, the sound of his footsteps muted by the rain-slicked pavement. "You got a minute?"

Scott glanced at him, his expression wary. He nodded, though it was clear he wasn't in the mood for a chat. "Sure, what's up?"

They stood there, huddled under their umbrellas, the rain creating a near-constant hiss around them. Travis hesitated for a moment, choosing his words carefully.

"A friend of mine was at the bar the other night," Travis began, keeping his tone neutral. "He said he saw you there."

Scott stiffened slightly, but didn't look at Travis. "So what?" he muttered, his voice barely audible over the rain. "I can go to a bar if I want."

"He said you were drinking."

Scott's head snapped up, his eyes narrowing. "What's it to you, Travis? It's none of your goddamn business."

His patience was wearing thin. "It is my goddamn business," he snapped. "It's my business to make sure the people under me are okay."

Scott scoffed, turning back to his car. "I'm fine. I ordered a drink. It's no big deal."

Travis wasn't going to let him off the hook that easily. He took a step closer, his umbrella nearly touching Scott's. "You were doing really well. You've been sober for over two years now."

Scott's face tightened, and for a moment, he didn't respond. When he finally spoke, his voice was low, almost resigned. "I do this sometimes, okay? When I'm stressed, I order a drink and sniff it and hold it. The ritual calms me down. But I didn't *drink.*"

Travis studied Scott's face, the hard lines of stress and something else—something darker—etched into his features. "Are you hiding something, Scott?"

Scott's body tensed, his jaw clenching. "No," he said, immediately defensive. But the denial lacked conviction. Travis' eyes bore into him as he waited. Finally, Scott exhaled sharply, his shoulders sagging in defeat. "I went to see Carly."

Travis blinked, momentarily taken aback. "Carly? Why the hell would you do that? You know that woman is toxic. God knows what she's doing raising a child."

Scott's eyes flashed with anger, and before he could stop himself, the words were out. "If Carly's so bad, then maybe you shouldn't have slept with her when I was dating her."

The words hung in the air between them, sharp and cutting. Travis felt like he'd been punched in the gut. He stared at Scott, stunned into silence.

Scott didn't wait for Travis to respond. Instead, he yanked open the car door and got in, slamming it shut behind him. The engine roared to life and Scott sped out of the parking lot, the tires splashing through puddles as he disappeared into the night, leaving Travis to marinate in shame at having betrayed his friend.

THIRTY-ONE

"Just trust your instincts, Agent Storm." A dimple appeared on Aiden's cheek. "Your instincts will never fail you."

Zoe hadn't noticed his dimples before. She liked it. "Haven't your instincts ever failed you before?"

"No."

"Aren't you self-assured?" she teased lightly.

He cracked another smile. "If your instincts failed you, then it's because you were too scared to actually listen to them."

Zoe pondered his words. She knew deep in her bones she wouldn't keep her promise to Rachel to not look into her death—she just didn't have the stomach. "I suppose you're right. But your instinct definitely failed you when you decided to decorate your office with that.*"*

He turned his head to follow her gaze at the Pollock painting on the wall behind him. "That's a classic! What are you talking about?"

"Why didn't you pick something easy on the eyes? Like a Monet or a Van Gogh?"

> He made a show of taking notes. "Patient has a shockingly poor taste in art. Unfit for duty."
>
> Zoe laughed.

* * *

There was something charged about that morning. An electric hum that clung to Zoe's skin like static as she walked along the docks to the station. The water in the harbor lay almost perfectly still, a mirror reflecting the muted colors of the sky, broken only by the occasional ripple as a lone seagull dipped low to skim the surface. The boats, varying in size and age, bobbed gently in their moorings, their hulls creaking softly like an old man's bones.

Her phone rang. "What's up?"

"I finished my linguistic analysis of the messages," Aiden said, sounding unusually hesitant. "And I found something intriguing."

"Like what?" Her heart skittered.

"Both messages refer to conclusions or endings and contain metaphors. I did three types of analysis—lexical, syntactic, and stylistic. The first message had frequent use of first-person singular pronouns, unlike the second message that had third-person and impersonal language like *the outcome, everything concludes*. The first message also contains more poetic terms like *climbing a hill, plucking a flower, stealing a star—*"

She stopped in her tracks, watching the seagulls pick away at the carcass of a dead bird. "The second one had generic phrases like *perhaps it's for the best.*"

"Exactly. In terms of sentence structure, while both use contractions, the first one was a mix of short and complex sentences with multiple clauses but the second had two sentences of moderate length and simpler structure. Also, the tone has shifted from urgent, personal, and emotive to reflective, impersonal, and resigned."

Zoe raked over the words that were embedded in her head. "Yeah, the second was more formal too. First one was poetic, less generic expressions."

"Now you're getting it." A pause. "According to the program, there is a fifty percent chance that the two messages were authored by two different people."

"What?" Her voice splintered. "*Two?* Isn't it possible that the killer's psyche is evolving with the killings?"

"It's a possibility and to be fair, the two messages were very short but... the crime scenes are too clean, Storm. Especially for a town that has no history of violent crimes and incidents. Chief Hunter and I have looked into every newcomer in town and they all checked out. We can't rule this out."

"So there might be two killers."

"It's easier for two to orchestrate something like this." A phone rang in the background. "I'll give my findings to Scott. You coming?"

"Yeah, I'll be there soon. See you."

Zoe was getting used to the smell of salt and seaweed. Her mind was still in turmoil over Aiden's suggestion. Her foot caught in the old ropes coiled on the ground and she almost stumbled forward. A hand appeared around her elbow, steadying her.

"Easy there." It was Keith.

"Hey." Zoe blinked, not quite sure how he'd found her.

He withdrew his hand, stuffing it in his pocket, and looked over at the ocean with narrowed eyes. "How's the case going?"

"I'm sure you've been watching the news." She slurped on her milkshake.

His gaze remained on the plastic cup longer than it needed to. "It was your mother's favorite. I, myself, was more of a chocolate milkshake guy."

She tried not to beam. But she only knew bits and pieces about her mother. "What else did she like?"

"The ocean." A rueful smile tugged at his lips. "She always used to dream about living out here. She spent some time in Lakemore as a teenager and wanted to go back. She wanted to do a lot of things."

But she was killed. Someone forced her to take pills and then drowned her in the bathtub. And her dutiful daughter Zoe cleaned up the crime scene before calling the police. The knot in her chest tightened. The knowledge of what she had done choked her. It was necessary, she *had* to. She knew that. It's what Rachel had wanted. She had done the right thing. But if it was the right thing to do, then why did she hide it?

"Gina has two kids. Twins," Zoe said. "I wish she got to see that."

"Grandkids, huh?" He chuckled. "Time goes by fast."

"Why didn't you ever contact her?" She regretted it the moment she asked the question. A shadow engulfed his face.

He pretended to check his watch. "Running late for an appointment."

She didn't stop him as he hightailed from there. She had made progress. He had approached her of his own accord. She could wear him down. But he was like a wounded animal. The only way he would come to her was if she stayed away, even though as time ticked by and her patience ran thin, it was the hardest thing to do.

Zoe was right about there being something different in the air. Her pulse quickened as she got out of the car. The parking lot was packed with people, signs waving, and voices raised in angry shouts. The morning had brought more than just tension; it had brought a storm. As she drew closer, she could make out the signs: "Justice for Our Girls!" and "Do Your Job!"—the words hit her like punches to the gut.

The crowd was larger than she'd anticipated, and louder too. Patrol officers stood at the entrance, blocking the tide of angry townspeople. The reporters were in the thick of it, cameras rolling, firing off questions that only fueled the fire.

Zoe's heart sank as she spotted Logan, Tara's dad, near the front. His face was twisted with anger, and he was shouting at the officers, demanding answers they couldn't give.

"How do you sleep at night?"

"How many more girls have to die in the woods?"

"Why haven't there been any arrests yet?"

Reporters with cameras slung over their shoulders moved through the throng of people. All the fear, grief, and anxiety had all boiled into anger. When emotions didn't know where to go, they all headed to fury. The rage that boils blood. The frustration that feels like needles running through veins. When reality bends and everything looks wrong and unfair.

It's in that heat that the animal takes over, when logic and calmness flee. And all animals need a prey.

There was no way around it—Zoe would have to push through the angry mob. She squared her shoulders and started to work her way through the mass of bodies, trying to keep her head down. But she didn't get far.

"Hey! It's her! FBI!" Logan's gaze locked onto hers, recognition flaring in his eyes. "You!" he shouted, pointing a finger at her. "You're the one who's supposed to be protecting us! Why aren't you doing your job?"

"It's the FBI. They're all corrupt!" someone yelled.

The crowd surged, closing in around her. Hands reached out, grabbing at her arms, her coat, anything they could hold on to. Zoe's heart pounded as she tried to keep her footing, but she was surrounded by a wall of hostility that was closing in.

"My daughter is dead!" Logan yelled, his voice rising above the chaos. "What the hell are you doing about it?"

Zoe tried to speak but her voice was drowned out by the roar of the crowd. "Please let me through! We are doing everything we can!"

Panic clawed at her throat as she struggled to break free from the hands pulling at her.

Suddenly, a familiar figure pushed through the crowd—Scott. He moved with a determined urgency, his face set in a hard line as he reached her side. "Back off!" he shouted, as he pushed people away from Zoe. "Get back!"

For a moment, Zoe thought that everything was going to be fine and she would be pulled into the safety of the station. The next second, someone lunged.

A flash of metal slicing through the air. Zoe's eyes widened in horror as the knife cut across Scott's face.

THIRTY-TWO

Scott cried out, sinking to the ground, his hands and face covered in blood. It was everywhere. Zoe's screech rose above the noise of the crowd. And then chaos erupted. Someone screamed that there was a knife. Another one thought it was a gun.

People pushed and shoved, some trying to get away, others closing in. It was a stampede. The officers at the entrance charged in, batons raised, trying to force the crowd back. Zoe dropped to her knees beside Scott, his hand pressed to his bleeding face. "Scott, the ambulance is on its way." She was already on her phone. "You hang in there, okay?"

Zoe inhaled the scent of antiseptic and bleach. Unlike most people, she loved hospitals. She never saw it as a place of sickness and death; she saw it as a place where lives were saved. She had witnessed too many deaths that could have been avoided. Sitting on one of the steel chairs outside the ward, she stared at the blue curtain, behind which Scott was being treated.

A: You okay, Storm?

Z: Yeah, just waiting for the doctor to give me an update on Scott.

The blue curtain ripped open and one of the nurses popped her head out. "You can come in now, Agent Storm."

Scott lay on the bed. A deep gash ran from his cheekbone down toward his jaw, the stitches neat but angry-looking. The skin around it red and swollen. The collar of his shirt was stained with dried blood.

"Wow. I'm going to call you Scott Scarface," Zoe teased. Scott grimaced and crossed his arms. "Thanks. For saving my ass there. I would buy you a drink but..." She laughed while he glared at her. "Sorry. I make jokes when I'm uncomfortable."

"Clearly."

"That was wild. What happened at the station." She perched on a stool next to him. "I'm guessing that doesn't really happen here?"

"Never. We weren't ready. Terri told me she got an invite on Facebook to join some event happening at the police station but she didn't think much of it until people started showing up with pitchforks."

"A Facebook event?" Zoe had an idea. "I suppose it's a small community..."

"What are you thinking?"

"Sometimes killers who are cuckoo, like this one, leave traces on social media. Like odd posts or pictures."

His lips puckered in thought. "You think this killer might be posting weird poems or some shit?"

"It's possible."

"I'll ask Terri to look into it."

The curtains ripped open again and a lanky man with a long neck and clumps of white hair and wrinkled skin approached the bed, holding a clipboard. "Detective Cohen? I'm Dr. Vic Parsons. I saw the news. Welcome."

"Can I leave?" he grumbled.

Dr. Parsons coughed. A smoker's cough, Zoe noted. His eyes glazed over Scott's stitches. "You can after you get your tetanus shot. As per your records, you haven't had one in over twenty years. Do you have any other symptoms?"

"Nope."

"Don't like hospitals very much, do you?" the doctor said with a snicker.

"Nope."

"I like hospitals," Zoe said, and shook his hand. "Thank you for what you do. I'm Zoe Storm from the FBI."

Dr. Parsons beamed at her. "It's refreshing to meet someone who likes my place of work. My grandkids think I work at a cemetery." He turned to Scott. "Your stitches will begin to dissolve in the next few days and be fully dissolved in weeks or months, worst-case scenario. The nurse told me that the cut wasn't deep enough for us to worry about any bone damage so I'll spare you X-rays and CT scans. But if you experience any unusual symptoms at all, you come right back, understood?"

"I will." Scott started to get up and winced.

"You'll be in pain. Just take extra strength Tylenol." He looked at Zoe and winked. "Take care of this one."

"Yes, sir." She did a little salute. Dr. Parsons chuckled on his way out.

"How are you so chirpy after everything?" Scott accused her sharply. "Two girls are dead. One can go missing anytime. And people want to kill *us*."

A jolt ran through her at his biting words, an angry reminder of how everything had been going wrong since she arrived in this town. "If I start letting my job impact me, then I'll want to put a gun in my mouth. You have to learn to compartmentalize. You can't take it this personally."

"You have to take it personally when people are getting murdered. When *children* are getting murdered." His eyes were blazing. With the scar running down his face, he looked even more threatening. "How does it not make you angry?"

She opened her mouth to pacify him but was distracted by an argument taking place on the other side of the curtain.

"You're unbelievable, you know that?" a man said, his voice dripping with contempt. "Can't you do a single thing right? Slipping in the bathroom like some idiot who doesn't know how to use his own legs."

An old man on a wheelchair flinched, his hands trembling slightly as they clutched the blanket. "I... I didn't mean to—"

"Didn't mean to!" the young man yelled. "That's what you always say, isn't it? Didn't mean to fall, didn't mean to screw up, didn't mean to ruin my goddamn day with your stupidity. Do you have any idea how sick I am of this? Of cleaning up your mess?"

The old man's eyes glistened with unshed tears, but he kept his head down. "I'm sorry... I really am..."

"Sorry?" he sneered. "You're sorry? Sorry doesn't fix anything, Dad. Sorry doesn't undo the hours I lost today because you can't even stay upright in your own bathroom. You're pathetic."

Staff arrived and swiftly ushered the pair into a room. Zoe stared at the man who was bullying his elderly father. Scott's words simmered inside her about how she could not be angry.

She was angry. The unfairness and injustice always got to her. She just had a different way of handling it.

The sound of Scott's phone ringing drew her back to the present.

"Hey, Dr. Wesley," he said, answering the phone with a sigh. "Yeah, I'm okay, I'm on my way out now. Thanks. What happened? Yeah, I remember... are you sure? Okay..." His eyes were bulging when he disconnected. "Remember the wire transfers to Logan Bennett's account from that shell company—Global Holdings Inc.?"

"Yeah."

"The court order went through with the bank." His smile was sly. "It is registered to Regina Warner."

THIRTY-THREE

The small park was tucked away, where the sea breeze carried a chill that clung to Zoe's skin. The sky above was a blanket of gray, heavy with clouds that threatened rain but held back, casting everything in a dull, muted light. The air smelled faintly of salt and wet earth, and the few trees lining the park's perimeter rustled quietly in the wind.

Zoe and Scott stood near a weathered wooden bench. Her coat was pulled tight against the cold. She looked down at her suede boots, caked with mud. Those were going to go down the dumpster. But she'd had no time to do any shopping. If she wasn't spending her time reading reports or witness statements, she was struggling in the kitchenette in her motel room trying to cook something healthy.

That was life on the road. A stray leaf blowing from one to another. But what roots could she put down when she didn't even know where she came from? When was she lying about who she was?

She watched the small group gathered in the center of the park—Regina, poised and polished, sitting on the edge of the stone fountain, speaking animatedly into the microphone held by a local reporter.

Scott stood quietly, hands stuffed in his pockets, eyes scanning the area with practiced caution. "Seems like everyone in this town has something to say," he muttered, his breath visible in the chilly air.

"Yeah, but not everyone's as good at spinning a story as Regina," Zoe replied, her eyes narrowing as she watched Regina gesture with her hands, her expression one of carefully crafted concern. "Let's hope she's in the mood to talk when she's done playing the saint. Did Terri find out how she knows Logan Bennett?"

He let out a small puff. "Five years ago, Logan Bennett was a consultant at EcoSolutions Group. She's trying to find a link between Regina or Global Holdings Inc. and that company."

The interview dragged on, the reporter nodding intently as Regina's voice carried on the wind, just out of earshot. Zoe's patience was wearing thin, her fingers tapping against her leg as she shifted her weight from one foot to the other. She spotted a man mimicking her impatience.

A medium-built man on the shorter side with styled, jet-black hair, and beady eyes stood at the periphery, his lips moving exactly like Regina's. He watched her with a burning ambition, analyzing every twist of her lips and flick of her hand, as if he was assessing how well his creation was doing.

Zoe immediately knew who it was—Regina's campaign manager, Connor.

Finally, the reporter lowered the microphone, offering Regina a polite smile as they exchanged a few final words. Zoe straightened, catching Scott's eye. "This is our shot. Let's go."

They started toward the fountain just as Regina stood up, her smile fading slightly when she noticed them approaching. Her eyes darted between Zoe and Scott, and for a split second, something that looked like annoyance flickered across her face. But it was gone as quickly as it had appeared, replaced by a pleasant but guarded expression.

"Detective Cohen and Agent Storm," Regina greeted them with a firm handshake. "I wasn't expecting to see you here. What happened to your face?"

Scott turned red.

"Ms. Warner," Zoe said. "We need to ask you a few questions."

Before Regina could respond, Connor, the omnipresent in Regina's life, jogged toward them. "I'm sorry, but now isn't a good time," he said, his voice clipped. "Ms. Warner has just finished an interview and needs a moment to herself."

Regina glanced at Connor, then back at Zoe, clearly uneasy. "Maybe we can do this another time? I'm sure you understand how draining these interviews can be."

Zoe wasn't having it. "This won't take long. It's important."

But Connor was already moving between them, subtly guiding Regina back toward the path that led out of the park. "I'm afraid you'll have to schedule something through her office," he said, his tone leaving no room for argument. "Right now, Ms. Warner has other commitments."

The reporter, still hovering nearby, raised an eyebrow, clearly intrigued by the interaction. Zoe clenched her jaw, not wanting to cause a scene but knowing they were being stonewalled.

"If you don't talk with us, I'll gladly tell the reporter what this is about," Scott said. Zoe eyed him and was surprised to find his eyes darkening. With the cut running down his face, still raw and fresh, he looked downright scary.

Connor flinched but his expression hardened. "Are you threatening us?"

"I have two dead girls and I'm running out of patience." He didn't take his eyes off Regina.

Regina sighed, her face troubled, and gave them a curt nod, gesturing them to move to a corner away from the hovering reporter. "How can I help?"

"Do you know Tara Bennett's father, Logan Bennett?" Zoe asked.

Regina drew a strangled breath and crossed her arms. "The name does sound familiar. Why?"

Connor stiffened. "We won't say a word without our lawyer. We know our rights."

"And I have the right to free speech." Scott turned on his heel to go to the reporter, but Connor blocked him.

"Fine. Fine." He chewed his lip and raised his hands in surrender. His cheeks tinged pink and Zoe noticed his hands were shaking.

"He worked at EcoSolutions Group. That name ring a bell?"

Connor licked his lips. "We did business with them. Many years ago."

"What kind of business?" Zoe said.

Regina opened her mouth but Connor spoke over her, his voice wavering. "The school for kids with special needs that Regina built around five years ago. They were one of the companies who were contracted to provide an environmental impact report before construction began."

"Then why are you still paying Logan five grand every month?"

"*I* am?" Regina cocked an eyebrow, her jaw locking.

"We traced it to a shell company called Global Holdings Inc., which is registered to you," Scott said. "It looks like bribe money. And now his daughter is dead. Do you see where we're going with this?"

"I'd be very careful about what you say next," Connor said, wagging his finger at them. "What would we gain from killing Logan's daughter?"

Zoe shrugged. "Maybe you're tired of paying him off. Maybe you need more cash to run an aggressive campaign."

"That is a very serious accusation, Agent Storm," Regina said.

"I've seen people kill for far less, Regina, and political aspiration is a big motive."

"Are you admitting that you are paying him off?" Scott asked.

"We are admitting to nothing." Connor tipped his chin up. "Whatever you found, it could have been a clerical error or maybe it's Hicks." His eyes gleamed with mischief. "Maybe he's actually worried that Regina is going to beat him, so he's using this case to plant false evidence to get rid of his competitor. I'm assuming you two are on his payroll."

"You have a lot of theories. Why don't I haul your ass to the station so that we can discuss this further?" Scott stepped forward.

"We have established a connection between you and Logan Bennett. It won't take us long to figure out what exactly you're paying him off for," Zoe said. "Perhaps then we can have a more civilized discussion."

"Until then," Connor said through gritted teeth, his eyes on Scott.

They glared at each other before Scott pulled back with a jerk. Zoe steered him away, back toward the car.

"You have to be tactful," she murmured. "She's powerful and if we go in too hostile, she'll make things harder for us."

"I've had my face cut in half today and then that chump has an attitude," Scott said. He pinched the bridge of his nose and sighed. "Sorry. It's a not good day."

"I get it." They reached the car. The wind picked up, ruffling her hair. "I'm sure if Terri digs deep enough, she'll find out why Regina has been paying off Logan."

"It's a strong enough motive." His eyes thinned, looking into the distance where mist shrouded their view of the ocean. "But what is their connection to Lily Baker?"

"Regina has had a long career and whatever happened with EcoSolutions and her school might just be the tip of the iceberg."

Zoe nodded. People like Regina with a henchman like Connor had several skeletons in their closet. Lily Baker might have been one of them. There was a man Lily had been "friends" with. Could that man have been Connor? She saw his temper flare today—a jarring contrast to the coolness and control of his employer.

"Something's nagging me though," he admitted. "If they are trying to erase their shady dealings, then why are they going about this in such a roundabout way? The messages and the ropes?"

"So that you ask that exact question. To deflect suspicion. Make people believe there's a new serial killer in town, get rid of the people who can expose your corruption and win the election." As Zoe finished her thought, the possibility marinated inside her. It wouldn't be the first time someone's ambition claimed innocent lives.

She wondered if that was what happened with Rachel.

A shiver rolled over her skin, sprouting goosebumps on her arms. Her eyes darted to Regina and Connor engaged in a heated, frantic discussion. A lot of hand waving, clenched jaws and scowls.

They were worried. Rightfully so. Zoe was encouraged that they had uncovered something that wasn't a dead end. This confrontation had rattled them. And she knew that rattled people made mistakes, they slipped in that frenzy of trying to salvage the situation and fix things that didn't need fixing.

But were Regina and Connor cruel and desperate enough to strangle two little girls and leave them in the woods?

Scott's phone pinged and his frown deepened as he stared at the screen.

"What is it?" Zoe asked.

"The rangers found a toy a few feet away from where Tara's body was found. A stuffed animal."

"Just like with Lily." The wheels in her brain turned.

THIRTY-FOUR

Zoe was wading through the dark with flailing arms. Someone was calling out her name. The voice echoed, like it was coming from the end of a tunnel.

"Zoe! Do you see her?"

Panic surged through Zoe. She didn't know where she was. The room was pitch black. Whenever she tried to memorize the layout based on the obstacles, they kept changing. A metallic smell hit her nostrils.

Blood.

Her heart rate skyrocketed. "Who is this?" she finally asked. And to her horror, the words made the darkness ripple like it was water. Something was amiss. She was stuck in a nightmare.

But who was the girl calling out to her?

"You have to see her! How do you not see her?" the girl whispered in her ear.

Zoe reeled back from the hot breath fanning her ear. Her back hit a wall, her breaths hot and sticky in her throat. Her hands blindly searched the wall for something—anything—a door, a window, a switch.

A switch. She flicked it.

The lights didn't turn on. Not at first. And then a white rod on the ceiling began flickering. The groan of the light hummed loudly in her ear. On. Off. On. Off. She was afraid she might have a seizure. She blinked through the lights that changed every second. The room was empty, reminding her of a basement with no windows.

Off.

On.

Lily stood a few feet in front of her. The marks on her neck visible. Her face gaunt and pale. Dressed in the same clothes she was wearing when they found her.

A scream clawed up Zoe's throat.

Off.

On.

Tara drew near as Lily disappeared. Her dark hair matted at the back. A more jagged bruising on her neck.

The lights went off again. This time they didn't come back on. Instead the keening groan from the rod grew louder and louder, until Zoe was crouching, covering her ears. Then the same voice of a girl whispered in her ear.

"Emily!"

Zoe woke up with a jolt. Her head was resting against the cool surface of the table. She adjusted her vision to the dancing dust particles before her eyes. It was a name she hadn't heard in a very long time. A name she had forgotten and buried deep within inside her. She hadn't recognized the voice until she finally did.

"How long was I out for?" Zoe rubbed her eyes.

"Just an hour." Aiden was sitting across from her, going through a thick file. "You looked beat so I didn't wake you."

She cracked her neck and stared at her laptop screen. "The motel mattress sucks. Haven't slept a wink since I got here."

"Now you get why I bought one." He winked.

"You still working on that video?" Scott said, appearing from behind her.

"Yeah. FBI is stretched thin on this one, unfortunately, so I'm trying to learn this software. There has to be *something* here. I refuse to believe we got nothing from this." Zoe let the irritation slip into her voice as she chewed on her fingernails.

Her phone buzzed. It was Simon.

S: *Sorry our conversation got interrupted last time. How's the case going?*

Z: *It would go better if IT weren't blocked.*

S: *My hands are tied, Z. There's a lot going on here.*

Z: *What happened?*

S: *Remember Bruce from counterterrorism? He was killed.*

Panic flared inside Zoe's chest. She wasn't close to Bruce but Simon was. They trained together back in Quantico.

She stepped out of the room to call him, with Aiden's watchful eye tracking her. Simon answered swiftly. "How are you doing?" she said.

"I don't know. I just don't know how to feel." His voice was heavy but muddled around the edges. Hadn't he slept?

"He had a family, right?"

"A wife and two kids."

She hung her head low, her teeth chewing on her weathered lips. "Do we know what went down?"

"Not yet. We've opened an investigation. Damn, Z. Sometimes I wonder if any of this is even worth it. Dying for your country when the only people who remember you are your family."

Family. The bonds that kept pieces of us strung together through the wear and tear of life. And Zoe had wronged her family—a promise made to her mother and that lifelong regret that festered inside her like an infected wound. A sharp thread of pain pulled through her as she thought of Rachel.

"It's not fair. None of this fair," he continued. "No one is going to know this man died for the greater good."

"I'm sorry. Nothing is fair, Simon. Fairness is a man-made construct. And that's why it's up to us to dispense it."

"Zoe Storm, the forever supporter of vigilante justice. Little Robin Hood."

Her stomach whirred with butterflies. It was the nickname he had given her all those years ago when they used to spend their nights tangled up in each other.

She stayed on the phone with him for a few more minutes while he composed himself before letting him go. When she hung up, she clutched the phone in her hand.

Somewhere she knew why Simon had reached out to *her*. But she refused to let the thought coalesce. It made her feel icky, like *she* was doing something wrong.

"What are you guys looking at?" Zoe asked, as she went back into the room.

"Trying to find a connection between Lily and Regina. Travis is working on filing a court order to get more access to Regina's finances. If her campaign is in financial trouble, then that strengthens our case." Scott sighed.

"But there's still a question mark hanging over Lily."

"Yeah." His face dropped. "The coroner sent us Tara's autopsy report." The door to Zoe's makeshift office pushed open with a creak and Terri popped her head in. "Logan Bennett is here."

"What is he doing here?" Zoe asked.

"I called him." Scott closed the file with a thud. "I figured I'd have another go at him now that we know about that bribe money. Maybe he'll spill something or know something about Lily."

"That's a good idea. Play your face card," Zoe suggested.

He paused, standing up. "My face card?"

"I saw his face when you were attacked. He didn't expect the violence. Seeing your face might make him feel more guilty."

"She's a got a point, boss," Terri said. "Or you can scare him with that face."

Scott shook his head and popped a Tylenol in his mouth.

Zoe busied herself with the autopsy reports that the coroner had sent. The cause of death was listed as strangulation just like Lily. Her blood toxicology reports showed traces of chloroform. The method was the same but the more Zoe studied the reports and pictures of the crime scene and Tara's body, the more she detected an aberration.

Maybe it was her nightmare that brought forward the observation sitting in her subconscious mind.

Aiden cleared his throat. "So, what did Simon want to talk about?"

She didn't miss the edge in his tone. "How did you know it was Simon?"

"A hunch." He shrugged, his eyes fixed on the file in his lap.

"Bruce died. From counterterrorism. He's taking it hard."

Something flickered on Aiden's face but he regained his composure and went back to the file.

"The marks on Tara's neck weren't as clean as Lily's. There were multiple areas of bruising on the neck as if the rope was repositioned and adjusted repeatedly. The overall pattern of the ligature marks followed an uneven path—the impressions overlapped and fluctuated between deeper and lighter," Zoe said, changing the subject. "Maybe you are right.

There are two killers. One is better at strangling than the other."

"Or the killer hesitated. After killing Lily in such a seamless fashion, why would strangling Tara be any harder for him? She had chloroform in her system, so she wouldn't have been able to struggle. Was it possible that killing another girl was beginning to take its toll on him? In his twisted mind, he didn't want to do this."

Another possibility came to her. "What if the killer *knew* Tara? What if he had a personal connection with her?"

Suddenly a loud voice punctured her thoughts. Followed by a gut-wrenching wailing.

Alarmed, she exited the room and hurried down the corridor into the main area where most of the desks, including the reception area, were. A couple of uniformed officers were standing around a hysterical woman, trying to placate her. She wore a green dress that was a little too tight, stilettos with straps that looked uncomfortable, and a large tote that was falling apart. Tears gushed down her cheeks, leaving mascara trails.

"Oh my God! Please do something!" she cried, clutching her unkempt red hair.

Zoe chalked it up to the woman being strung out. But before she could ask why no one was escorting her out of the station, the woman started howling and gasping, as if struggling to breathe.

"Where's Scott? I want Scott!" Her desperate eyes searched for him. "Scott!" she screamed. "Scott!"

The door to the interrogation room flung open and Scott came out, frowning. But when he saw the woman, he stopped in his tracks.

The woman rushed into his arms and sunk down to the floor. "She's gone! My Lucy is gone! He took Lucy!"

THIRTY-FIVE

Zoe had been in several tense situations in her life. She had attended briefings with powerful men and women. She had spent nights sleeping next to a predator undercover. But being in Travis' office with Scott and the woman who she had concluded was Scott's pseudo ex-girlfriend was the worst situation she had found herself in.

It vexed her how aloof Aiden was. He could probably sense the tension rolling off the townies more than she could. But where she was a sponge, absorbing everything, he was a shiny piece of metal, just reflecting it all.

The silence nicked by the woman's sniffles was stuffy. Zoe glanced at Scott who was leaning against the wall, his face eclipsed by worry.

The flappy door swung open and Travis entered, his boots squelching and water still dripping from his hat. "Imagine my surprise to get a call that there's chaos at my station *again* when I'm trying to convince Hicks that I got everything under control." He shed his coat. When he saw the woman next to Zoe, he did a double-take. "Carly?"

Carly.

"Lucy is missing," Scott said.

Carly sobbed into her hands. "Lucy... L-Lucy..."

Travis' eyebrows touched his forehead, his face ashen. He almost tripped as he fell into his chair that protested under his weight. But in the last few days, he had thinned to worrying levels. "When did this happen?"

"I was picking her up from her friend's place," Carly cried. "I just made a quick detour to buy some cigarettes before I got there so I was running a few minutes late. When I got there, her friend's mom told me she'd left already. But she never came home."

"What time did you get there?" Travis asked.

"Around five thirty."

"So thirty minutes ago. And what time did Lucy leave her friend's place?"

"F-four thirty." She lowered her gaze.

Travis paused. "Why the hell did it take you an hour to buy cigarettes?"

Carly's portly frame shivered. "I ran into one of my customers who hadn't paid up, we were arguing... I didn't realize the time."

Travis' eyes hardened. His hands gripped the edge of the table, knuckles white. The room felt like it was closing in, the air thick with tension.

"Carly," Travis said, his voice low and controlled, "why would Lucy leave her friend's place before you got there?"

Carly's lip trembled, and she looked down, unable to meet his gaze. "You don't know her. She's ten years old but feisty and independent and hardheaded. She... would get upset with me and do things on her own," she admitted, her voice barely audible.

"Let me guess. You neglect that girl so often that she was used to fending for herself and playing grown up," Travis said.

A tear rolled down Carly's face. Her shame hung in the air

like a heavy cloud. "Since the murders, I've been trying to be a better mom to her."

Scott, who had been standing silently in the corner, suddenly cursed under his breath. He started pacing back and forth, shaking his head in disbelief. "Unbelievable," he muttered. "Classic Carly. Every damn time..."

Zoe wanted to melt into her chair. It's like they had forgotten she was there. Whatever history they had was now spilling over for everyone to see.

Travis didn't take his eyes off Carly. "What did Lucy tell her friend's mom when she left? I doubt she would have let her just leave at a time like this."

"Lucy said I was outside waiting in the car. Look, you don't know her. That girl has forged my signature more than a couple of times just to go to field trips."

"You were running late because of your cigarettes and your... client," he said, the words dripping with disappointment. "Lucy was supposed to be home over an hour ago, and you were... what? Too busy feeding your addiction and chasing down clientele?"

Carly flinched at the accusation, her eyes flickering to Scott. The look she gave him was desperate, like she was seeking solace and only cared about his opinion.

"You just... you never change, do you?" Scott laughed in exasperation. "Why am I not surprised that you were too busy getting laid to care about your daughter?"

"Scott!" Travis jumped to his feet. "I'm warning you."

But Scott's eyes were locked on Carly. Zoe had never seen Scott like this—his edges so sharp and callous, his eyes burning with ruthlessness. There was not a tinge of empathy.

"Why?" Scott finally tore his eyes away from Carly and stared at Travis. "She knows what's happening in this town. Every parent is being careful. Are we really surprised, Travis? Don't we both *know* her very well?"

"Take a walk. *Now*."

Scott stormed out of the office so fast that Zoe felt a rush of air in his wake.

"I... I didn't realize the time, Travis. I know, I know it's my fault. B-but..." Carly gulped. "I don't know what to do."

"This is Agent Zoe Storm and Dr. Aiden Wesley from the FBI," Travis said, ignoring her last remark. "They will work closely with you. I think it's best to keep you and Scott away from each other."

Carly's teary eyes flitted to Zoe and Aiden in surprise, as if she hadn't noticed them until now.

"Carly, I'll do everything I can," Zoe said earnestly. "Have you noticed anyone suspicious around Lucy? A man being extra friendly or watching her?" Carly shook her head. "Did Lucy ever mention anything to you? A new friend?" She shook her head again.

Zoe wasn't surprised. There was a harebrained way in which Carly carried herself. A lack of conviction and control that she normally saw in parents. As she took her statement, Carly looked even more lost. A single mother who wasn't ready to be one. But there was an innocence in her eyes, like *she* was the child in this situation. Like she'd had Lucy because she needed someone.

"How often does Lucy go to her friend's place?"

"Every other day, same time. This is her picture." She pulled a small picture from her wallet and wiped away tears. "I thought... I thought you might need it."

"Definitely." Zoe brushed her finger over it. A mirror image of Carly.

Carly blinked, her mouth open like she was thinking of what to say. "What do I do now?"

Zoe couldn't reply. Her thoughts were tail spinning. Instead Travis escorted Carly out, assuring her that they would do everything to find her daughter.

When Travis returned, he sighed. "We can't be sure if Lucy was taken by the killer."

"What do you mean?"

"It's Carly." Travis shrugged. "She has a lot of clients. It's possible that Lucy was abducted by a jilted lover instead of the serial killer."

Or maybe Lucy was the final victim. The third girl for the third noose. The killer's final target before, in his words, *darkness falls*.

THIRTY-SIX

The rain pounded against the windshield, each drop a drumbeat. The wipers struggled to keep up, barely clearing Travis's view of the slick road ahead. His knuckles were white against the steering wheel, the pain in his chest a constant, gnawing reminder of the chaos unraveling.

What was he doing? When did that darkness engulf him? His mind and body were on different paths. There were times he would lose track of what was real and what wasn't. Dr. Melissa hadn't prescribed him any medication—yet. She wanted him to keep a journal of his thoughts and feelings. She thought the problem was him bottling everything up too much.

She had only scratched the surface.

But right now, there was something else that was bothering him—Ryan.

His son had been acting strangely—too quiet, disappearing for hours without explanation. It wasn't like him. And now, Travis was tailing Ryan through the rain-soaked streets, trying to keep his distance while the knot of dread tightened in his gut.

Up ahead, Ryan's car turned into a dimly lit alley, its taillights glowing like ominous red eyes in the night. Travis slowed, his heart hammering as he watched his son's car come to a stop in front of a run-down building. The kind of place that made Travis's stomach churn with foreboding.

What was he doing *here*? He was only seventeen.

Ryan stepped out of the car, his feet splashing through the puddles, hood up against the rain, and moved toward a group of shadowy figures huddled near the building.

"What the hell are you doing, Ryan?" Travis muttered, holding his breath.

He leaned forward, trying to see through the rain that blurred everything into a hazy nightmare. He could make out Ryan reaching into his pocket and handing something to the group—money, it had to be. One of the figures reached out, passing something back to Ryan in a swift, subtle motion. But the rain obscured it all, leaving Travis guessing at the exchange. Was it drugs? Weapons?

He scratched through his memories. Was Ryan into drugs? There was no smell of weed in the house. No physical signs of him using anything harder than that. But he rarely saw him anymore. Ryan was always dressed in hoodies and hauled up in his room. He could be using. And Travis was gutted that he didn't know what was happening in his own home despite being chief of Harborwood PD.

A chill ran down his spine, his worst fears tightening their grip on him. This wasn't supposed to happen. Not to Ryan.

Then, out of nowhere, a familiar, icy voice cut through the sound of the rain, freezing the blood in his veins. "You failed, Travis. And now look where it's gotten you. Where it's gotten him."

Travis's breath hitched, and he whipped his head to the side. In the passenger seat, where there should have been nothing but empty air, sat his mother. Her eyes were as cold and unyielding as he remembered, her lips curled into a cruel sneer.

"Mom?" The word was a whisper, barely audible over the storm raging outside.

Her expression didn't change, the venom in her voice unmistakable. "What have you done, boy?"

Travis blinked, his hands trembling on the wheel. *This isn't real. She's not here.*

The vision of his mother leaned closer, her voice a hiss in his ear. "I should have put you all down, like dogs."

Travis squeezed his eyes shut, trying to block out the voice, the image, the rising tide of panic that threatened to drown him. When he opened them again, the passenger seat was empty, the ghost of his mother gone, leaving only the echo of her words in his mind.

* * *

Benny wasn't answering her messages. She had sent three over the last couple days but had had no reply.

She needed another fight. The rage had been building up inside her like plaque. If she didn't release it in time, she was going to explode.

And there might be collateral damage.

So for now Zoe moved through the shadows of the dimly lit parking garage, her footsteps silent on the cold concrete. The low hum of fluorescent lights flickered intermittently, casting long, eerie shadows that stretched across the rows of parked cars. Her breath was steady, controlled, as she kept her eyes locked on the man ahead of her.

He was tall and wiry, his gait relaxed, almost too casual for someone who should have known better. He walked with an air of arrogance, like he owned the place, unaware of the predator stalking him just a few paces behind. Zoe had been tailing him for over an hour, watching as he moved through the city.

The man fumbled with his keys, the metallic jingle echoing

through the empty space. He was halfway to his car when Zoe imagined what she would do to him.

There were too many dead girls. Too much going wrong in Zoe's life and this case. And the grim possibility of something happening to Lucy loomed over her, snuffing out that light and cheer.

She had to get rid of it. She had to fix *something*.

She would strike him like a hammer. She wouldn't give him a chance to recover. A punch to the gut. She wouldn't care about his excuses or his pleas. All she saw was a pig in front of her, the man who had treated his elderly father like filth in public.

Another bad, bad person who was walking around freely.

Just like Rachel's killer.

She imagined what his blood would look like as it sprayed from his mouth, splattering across the concrete.

But she saw someone else. That faceless man who existed in her imagination. The one who had taken everything from her and her sister.

A hand landed on her shoulder, yanking her out of her fantasy. She spun on her heel, a scream of shock stuck in her throat—only to find Aiden.

"What are you doing, Storm?"

Was any of this real? She was still in a daze. The air seemed syrupy around her, rippling the edges of everything and making her vision sloppy. Aiden's probing eyes followed the man who was getting into his car and driving away. She blinked profusely and turned away from him, waiting for her nerves to stop fraying.

She was ready to snap, *so* close to revealing that violence resided inside her as if she had been boiling under the sun for eternity.

A deep breath. Another one.

"Were you following me?" Her voice shook when she faced him again, maintaining her composure.

His eyes widened behind his glasses. "Yeah, I was."

"Why?"

"Well, since you showed up with a bruise on your face that night and then you snuck out in this hoodie, you can't blame me for being curious." He gently guided her away. "What is going on with you? Do you know him?"

Shit. "I... I thought he might be a suspect."

"A suspect?" he said flatly. "Really?"

"Yeah, I saw him at the hospital and he was lingering and acting shady..." She scrambled for an excuse. "So I thought I should follow him." They stared at each other. She could tell he was waiting for her to come clean. But she just shrugged. "Do you want to leave? I think he's fine. I was desperate."

Aiden pulled a face. A sigh of resignation. But he didn't push her. Somewhere Zoe was relieved. What if he hadn't come? What if she had crossed that boundary and hurt someone?

As she followed him out, she looked over her shoulder. The man was gone. But she saw another figure lying on the ground—bruised and broken.

It was *her*. Only much younger. That teenager who was stupid enough to clean up a crime scene. Because she was just as responsible as the killer for justice evading them. Because she was weak and selfish.

THIRTY-SEVEN

Zoe leaned against the hood of her car, the early morning chill seeping through her jacket as she scrolled through her phone. She had decided not to think about what almost happened yesterday. How Aiden perhaps saw through her. If she pretended nothing happened, then maybe he'd forget all about it too.

A light mist clung to everything, beading on the leaves of the trees and the blades of grass. She could taste the salty tang of the ocean on her tongue. The sounds of the dock swaying with the tide and the gentle clatter of boats nudging each other in the harbor were becoming familiar.

She had gone back last night to assist Terri and the other officers canvass the neighbors and trace Lucy's movements.

Lucy's friend's house was only two rows away from her home. It should have taken her five minutes to get back home. She had left at 4:30 p.m., which was still early in the day. But no one saw anything. How was that possible?

Once again Zoe was back in the neighborhood, walking the path from the friend's house to Lucy's house. Did Lucy take a detour? There was only one street that led to her destination, and it weaved in between other homes. It would be harder for Lucy to be abducted if she took this path. In broad daylight when children were out playing, someone would have seen something.

Zoe spun round, scanning the neighborhood. Did someone lure her into one of these homes? And then her eyes caught sight of another path. A longer, twisted path that faced the backyards of a few houses and a stagnant pond on the other. She didn't know where this path led to. She jogged along it—it was narrow with just enough space for one car to squeeze through. The road vined into a curve that led to the path in between two houses—one of them Lucy's.

Could Lucy have taken this way home?

Zoe's eyes searched for any cameras but there were none. This dirt road could be accessed from the main street. Perhaps this is where Lucy was taken. Her phone rang. She hoped it was Scott but it was Terri.

"Hey, Terri. Have you heard from Scott?"

"Not yet, Agent Storm." Terri sounded concerned. She had been working under Scott for over four years. "Though I'm calling because neighbors reported a man called Sam Buster causing a scene outside Carly's house a few days ago. Yelling, threats, the whole nine yards."

"Sam Buster. Who is he?"

"Carly said he's a friend with a temper. Didn't give me much. But I know where he works."

"Great. Send me the address. Thanks."

When she hung up, she frowned, her thumb hovering over Scott's contact. She hesitated, knowing he was with Carly, but still thought she should update him.

Z: Sam Buster. Ring a bell? Neighbors say he caused a scene at Carly's place. I'm checking him out now.

No response. Scott was likely still tied up with Carly. Zoe sighed, sliding her phone into her pocket, before getting into her car and driving to the bar Terri had mentioned. Her phone rang again.

She glanced at the car's dashboard screen—it was an unknown number. She pressed the answer button on the steering wheel. "Hello?"

Silence.

"This is Zoe Storm. Hello?" she said again.

"T-this is Nancy."

For a moment, Zoe's mind went blank. "Nancy?"

"Yes, I know it's unusual for me to call but... I'm concerned about Simon. He hasn't been sleeping or eating or talking..."

"It must be Bruce's death," she replied, suddenly realizing who Nancy was. "He's been distraught over it."

There was a moment of silence but Zoe could feel the tension radiating through the phone. Her hands gripped the wheel.

"Right." Nancy's voice turned sharp and defensive. "Thanks, Zoe."

Before Zoe could reply, Nancy hung up. Her cheeks flamed —had Simon not told Nancy about Bruce?

She pushed the thought aside. The morning was still gray and damp, the sun barely breaking through the cloud cover, casting everything in a dull, washed-out light.

Zoe spotted Sam Buster before she even reached the bar. He was leaning against the wall, a cigarette dangling from his lips. He was big, bald, and had the kind of sneer that made Zoe's skin crawl. The kind of man who reveled in making others feel uncomfortable.

Zoe approached cautiously, her footsteps muffled by the damp pavement. "Sam Buster?"

He looked up, his eyes narrowing as he took her in. "Who's asking?" he muttered, his voice rough and gravelly.

"Zoe Storm from the FBI. I'm here to ask you a few questions about the other day. You were seen outside Carly's house, making a scene."

Sam snorted, a cruel grin spreading across his face. "That little tease? Yeah, I was there. Had a few things to say to her. She deserved it. Let me guess? Bitch cried rape."

Zoe's stomach churned. "And what exactly were you so upset about?"

His grin widened, and he took a long drag on his cigarette before answering. "She owes *me*, that's what. Told me she'd do more than just talk, if you know what I mean. I paid for more than what I got, and she backed out. Didn't like that, so I let her know."

Zoe's jaw tightened, but she forced herself to stay calm. "How long have you known her?"

"About two years."

"You know Lucy, her daughter?" She watched his reaction closely. A sick smile spread on his ruddy face.

"Yeah, I know her. Sassy like her mother." He took a puff and his eyes shone behind the smoke with a revolting glint. "Wonder if she'll look as hot as her mom when she grows up."

Zoe's blood frothed as searing disgust slashed through her. She picked up a stray brick lying on the ground and dropped it on his foot.

"Ah!" His body folded in half, the cigarette falling out of his grasp as he held his foot. "You bitch! You little—!"

Zoe twisted the collar of his jacket harshly and pulled his face closer. She ignored his rancid breath in her face, relishing the sight of his red face and watery eyes, as he writhed in pain. "Let me be blunt. I'm an FBI agent and you're a loser who has to pay women to get laid. Now tell me, without being gross, when was the last time you saw Lucy?"

"A few days ago!"

"And where were you yesterday evening?"

Sam didn't reply right away, locking his jaw in protest. His ego was too inflated so she twisted his ear, bending his body at an angle.

"At a job interview, if you must know. Got a job down at the scrapyard. You can check, but they'll tell you the same. Today's my last day here."

"Don't leave town."

Sam watched her, his sneer never fading. "Why you so interested, huh? You Carly's new watchdog?"

Lucy's disappearance was still under wraps. Harborwood PD was on the lookout, bordering patrols, and looping in the rangers and WSP but the media was still in the dark. Zoe wondered how long that was going to last.

Zoe ignored the jab, letting go of his ear. "Just doing my job. I'll be back if I find out you're lying."

She turned on her heel, eager to put some distance between herself and Sam Buster. He was still on the ground, nursing his foot. Maybe he had a hairline fracture. But she didn't care. The creepy smile that had crossed his face when talking about Lucy told her everything she needed to know.

As she walked back to her car, the morning fog seemed to thicken, wrapping around her like a shroud. She was almost at the driver's side door when she noticed a figure standing a few feet away, partially obscured by the mist.

Her heart skipped a beat as she reached for her phone, ready to call for backup if needed. As she closed the distance, she saw his face through the mist.

It was Keith.

"Hey, I didn't see you there," she said, slightly unnerved.

His face was grim, that steely resolve to not help her gone. "I thought you would look like her, but you don't. I think it's time we talked about your mother."

THIRTY-EIGHT

"My mother," Zoe said. "That's who I miss the most."

"How do you deal with her not being around?" Aiden asked.

"She lives on through my sister and her kids." Tears threatened to choke her, but she swallowed them. "It's always the small things that are left behind. Like how she had a habit of pulling down the corners of the bed sheet before getting into bed. Both Gina and I do that all the time without even realizing it."

She looked out the window at the snow carpeting the ground and the ice forming shapes against the window. Winter was Zoe's favorite season because snow was festive and pure and happy.

"I know what you're going through as I went through something similar myself," Aiden said softly.

"Did you lose your mother when you were young too?"

He didn't reply.

* * *

"Why?" Zoe blurted.

And then an inside voice chided her. *Don't scare him away.*

"Because..." He cracked a forlorn smile. "Your mother saved my life a very long time ago. The least I can do is tell her daughter the truth."

Her pulse fluttered in her throat as she waited for him to say the words she had been waiting for all these years. She was almost not ready to hear it. She had lived with that void inside her for too long, spent her life digging through old memories, latching on to words, turning them over in her head, refusing to let anything fade. Trying to salvage whatever pieces she had of her past to make sense. All to get to the truth.

That pesky thing that people took for granted. But it was the foundation for everything.

Her eyes glided over the ocean. The boats reminded her of herself—unmoored. But now everything was about to change.

Was she ready to hear it?

"Let's walk?" she suggested in a small voice.

And so they did, side by side, along the docks in the misty morning. The chill cooled her scalp, but under the layer of jacket she was sweating.

"I met your mother in the summer of 1977." He stared at his feet. "I had gotten a job as an executive assistant to this very rich VP at some insurance company who had a penchant for collecting art. Rachel was the receptionist there. She was... one of the most stunning women I'd ever met. There was this spark to her. She drew people in. And she drew me in too. Soon we became friends, even though there was always something more between us."

Zoe could imagine it all play in her mind's eye. Her heart refused to slow down. She was holding on to every word like it was treasure.

"Unfortunately, she was seeing someone at the time. So I didn't do anything. And either way, I was there for another purpose. That man, like I said, collected art. That's what I was after. An expensive painting he stored in his locker." His eyes met Zoe's, gauging her reaction.

"You were a thief?" she said.

"You can't arrest me now. The statute of limitations has passed," he added lightly. "It was all part of my plan to eventually get to the safe, steal the painting, and disappear. But being around Rachel was too tempting." He laughed. "And a three-month-long plan stretched to five months. Enough was enough. I decided to head to Rachel's and say goodbye to her. The plan was to disappear once I'd taken the painting."

"And then?"

"Her entire apartment was a mess." His eyes tapered at the memory. "Tables and chairs turned over, curtains ripped down, a vase shattered. I found her in the bedroom, huddled in a corner. She was catatonic and bruised. I was about to call 911 but she stopped me."

Zoe didn't believe it. "My mother stopped you? Why?"

He gestured her to sit on a bench, facing the calm waters. "She said she owed money to someone."

Zoe tried to imagine Rachel in the colors that he was painting her in. She knew Rachel had a past, something murky. "Why didn't she involve the police?"

His silver eyes bore into hers. "She said that whoever was after her was powerful. He had connections in the police. She didn't trust anyone."

"She never mentioned a name to you?"

A flurry of sounds took over—seagulls cowing overhead, a distant foghorn, waves slapping against the hulls of ships, and a bell signaling an arrival. Keith fidgeted, his gaze fixed on the flood of activities at the harbor, but his mind was somewhere else.

"You have no idea how many times I asked her." His voice became heavy. "But she was scared. Missing work. Always looking over her shoulder. Unable to sleep. And then I told her we should go away."

"What about your con?"

A dreamy look crossed his face. "I was in love. I didn't care about that anymore. I just wanted her to be happy again. And so we both quit and left for the west coast. Which is where that photo is from... things were good for a while but they didn't stay that way. One night, I saw her sneak out. I followed her and saw her meeting some man. She was buying a gun."

"A gun?" Zoe was still slotting together the information. Rachel always seemed hassled and worried. They never stayed in one place for too long so she never bothered to make friends. She spent most of her time at home, taking care of Zoe and Gina, telling them stories and making her own clothes. It was a lonely, quaint, and unglamorous existence of a woman on the run—but not a woman who bought a gun. "She must have gotten really desperate."

"That's not what shocked me. It was the fact that she knew guns a little too well."

Confusion muddled her mind. "What?"

"The man showed her a selection of guns and the way she handled them, to me it looked like she knew exactly what to do with them. She wasn't the Rachel I knew that night with that man. Gone was the terrified, demure woman. She was confident, the way she stood and walked. It was like she was a different person."

Her heart rose up her throat. "Did you confront her?"

"I did." His face was stoic and unreadable. "When she came back that night, she told me she was sick of living on the run and she had to confront her past. Again I tried to find out who she was running from, but she didn't give me a name. We decided to temporarily part ways. She needed a few months to sort out her shit. We planned to meet again in a year at this café we liked. I showed up, a year later, but she never did. And I never heard from her again."

"Was the person after her that powerful?"

Keith said nothing.

"But I'm an FBI agent. I can help," she insisted, sounding like a child. She was within reach of the complete picture. She could feel it in her fingertips, a relentless buzz as if that name was a physical object she could get her hands on.

Tears of frustration stabbed her eyes. She dug the heels of her hands into her eyes. The sight of finding Rachel's body was seared in her brain. But what crippled her was the aftermath. How she had got out the mop and wiped away evidence of muddy footprints and water on the bathroom floor. How she had closed the window to the fire escape. How she had even scrubbed the ledge of the window and the bathtub, while Rachel lay there dead, her eyes open, staring into nothing.

Keith's hand rested on her back. "She never gave me a name. She would often have these vivid nightmares and wake up in the middle of the night, sweating and screaming that the Viper will get to her. She was so scared of him that she was seeing snakes in her dreams. I'm sorry, kid. I wish I could help you more."

She nodded, her face still hidden in her hands. But she wasn't giving up. She had gotten this far.

Viper.

"I have no idea what happened to her. She had two kids, so I'm sure she found some happiness and normalcy before she passed. A part of me feared that the man had gotten to her. I looked for her but I didn't know enough to get anywhere."

Normalcy. The word tasted bitter in her mouth. She took a shuddering breath and threw him a glance. He looked almost pained, like he was aching for a piece of Rachel.

So Zoe gave it to him. "We spent almost a decade in witness protection."

THIRTY-NINE

Zoe blinked as she awoke, her eyes heavy with sleep, the remnants of her nap still clinging to her like a warm blanket. She stretched lazily, her small body sinking deeper into the couch where she'd dozed off.

As she rubbed the sleep from her eyes, the sound of hushed voices drifted in from the next room. Zoe frowned and her curiosity piqued. It wasn't likely to be her mother on the phone or chatting with a neighbor. Rachel lived an isolated life, not liking to mingle with anyone.

These voices were different—deeper, more serious. She sat up slowly, still groggy, and quietly slipped off the couch, padding barefoot toward the slightly ajar door that led to the living room.

Peeking through the crack, Zoe's eyes widened at the sight of two men in dark suits standing in the middle of the room. Their presence was imposing, their expressions stern. They wore matching badges clipped to their belts, and the way they held themselves, rigid and authoritative, sent a shiver down her spine. She didn't know much, but she knew these men were important.

Marshals. She'd seen men like them on TV, and they were always serious.

Rachel stood near them, her arms crossed tightly over her chest, her face drawn and tense. Zoe's heart sank at the sight of her mother looking so worried—Rachel was always so strong, so unflappable. But now, her eyes darted between the two men, her posture defensive, as if she were bracing herself for something bad to happen.

One of the Marshals, a tall man with a square jaw and closely cropped hair, spoke first, "Ms. Sullivan, we need to discuss some developments. We've received information that may require a change in your arrangements."

Rachel's eyes narrowed, her voice low and controlled. "What kind of developments? I thought everything was under control."

The second Marshal, slightly shorter but just as imposing, nodded. "We've had credible reports that your location might be compromised. It's possible someone's been asking questions—nothing concrete yet, but enough to raise concerns."

Zoe's heart skipped a beat. Compromised? What did that mean? She pressed closer to the door, her small fingers gripping the edge as she tried to make sense of what she was hearing.

Rachel's face tightened, her knuckles white as she clenched her fists at her sides. "You said we were safe here. That this place was secure."

The taller Marshal glanced at his partner before responding "We understand that, and we've taken every precaution. But we can't ignore the possibility that someone's looking for you. If you'd prefer, we can relocate you—keep you and your daughters safe."

Zoe felt her heart thump loudly in her chest at the mention of herself. Her eyes widened as she tried to process the gravity of the situation. Were they in danger? What was going on?

Her mother had never told her anything. Could this have something to do with those passports in the attic?

Rachel's gaze flicked toward the door for just a moment, but she quickly looked back at the Marshals. "No," she said firmly. "We're staying here. I'm not uprooting Zoe and Gina again. We've built a life here. I can't—won't—tear that apart."

The shorter Marshal exchanged a glance with his partner, then nodded. "We understand, but you need to be vigilant. If anything feels off, you contact us immediately. We'll have extra surveillance in the area, just to be sure."

Rachel exhaled slowly, her shoulders relaxing just a fraction. "Fine. But you'd better be right about this."

The Marshals nodded, their expressions unchanging as they turned to leave. As they moved toward the door, Zoe quickly stepped back, pressing herself against the wall in the hallway, her heart racing. She watched as the men passed by, their presence like a dark cloud hanging in the air, before they exited the house, the door clicking shut behind them.

Rachel stood in the living room for a moment, her back to the hallway, her posture still tense. Zoe hesitated, not sure if she should reveal that she had been listening. But something in her mother's stance made her step forward, her small voice breaking the silence. "Mom?"

Rachel turned, her eyes softening when she saw Zoe standing there. "Hey, sweetie. You're awake."

Zoe nodded, biting her lip. "Who were those men? Why were they here?"

Rachel hesitated, then walked over to Zoe, kneeling down so they were at eye level. "They're just... making sure we're safe, honey. Everything's fine, okay?"

Zoe wasn't convinced. "Are we in trouble?"

Rachel shook her head, forcing a smile. "No, we're not in trouble. We're just being careful, that's all. I promise, everything's going to be okay."

But as Rachel pulled Zoe into a reassuring hug, Zoe couldn't shake the feeling that something was wrong—something big that her mother wasn't telling her.

Zoe stood under the scalding spray of the shower, letting the hot water pound against her skin. Steam filled the small bathroom, curling around her like a warm, protective blanket, but it did little to ease the knot of tension that had taken up permanent residence between her shoulder blades since she arrived at Harborwood. She pressed her palms against the cool tiles, bowing her head, trying to let the heat wash away the frustration and helplessness. But no matter how hard she tried, the thoughts kept circling, relentless and sharp.

Her mind drifted to her conversation with Keith and the little pieces of information he had given her.

Now it made sense. Rachel had pissed someone off big-time and she must have testified against him or provided some information, which is why she went under witness protection. Perhaps it was because she got pregnant with Zoe that she didn't go back to Keith.

Heaviness pressed into her chest.

The motel's showerhead sputtered slightly, the water pressure faltering for a moment before resuming its steady flow. Zoe sighed, rolling her neck to work out the stiffness. Just as she began to relax, a sharp knock echoed through the room.

Zoe's eyes snapped open, her heart rate spiking as she quickly turned off the water. She stood still for a moment, listening, her senses suddenly on high alert.

Another knock.

It was urgent, insistent. She wasn't expecting anyone, especially not at this hour—it was midnight. Her mind raced, running through possibilities, none of them good.

Zoe stepped out of the shower, gasping as the cool air hit her wet skin. She grabbed a towel and wrapped it tightly around her body, droplets of water still clinging to her as she moved quickly through the room. The knocks came again, more impatient this time.

She reached for the Glock she kept on the nightstand. Holding the gun low but ready, she approached the door, her bare feet soundless on the worn carpet. She took a deep breath, her grip tightening on the handle as she cracked the door open just enough to see who was there.

It was Scott.

He was leaning heavily against the doorframe. His eyes were bloodshot, half-lidded, and his clothes were disheveled. The stench of alcohol hit her immediately—strong, sour, and overpowering.

"Scott?" Zoe's voice was low, cautious. "What the hell are you doing here?"

He swayed slightly, his hand slipping off the frame as he tried to focus on her. "Zoe... I... I needed to see you."

She scanned the hallway behind him, ensuring he hadn't been followed, then opened the door wider, stepping back to let him in. Scott stumbled forward, almost falling over before Zoe quickly reached out to steady him.

He was a mess, his body sagging with the weight of whatever had driven him here. He smelled like cheap whiskey and sweat, clinging to him like a second skin.

"Jesus, Scott," she muttered, guiding him toward the bed. "You're drunk as hell."

He collapsed onto the bed with a groan, his head lolling to one side as he stared up at the ceiling. Zoe kept her distance, unsure of what to do or say.

"Lucy..." Scott's voice was slurred, thick with emotion. "Lucy... she's..."

Zoe froze, her blood running cold at the mention of Carly's

daughter. "I know. I'm sorry."

She could tell from their interaction at the station that they had a history. The guilt of this unsolved case reaching someone he knew must have driven him to have a breakdown. But then he said something that disrupted her train of thoughts, sending them wayward.

His eyes glassy, unfocused. "She's mine, Zoe... Carly just told me... She's my daughter."

The words hit Zoe like a physical blow. "What? Are you sure?"

Scott let out a bitter laugh, his eyes welling with tears. "Yeah... I'm sure. Carly's known all along but was so bitter about me leaving her that she didn't tell... until just now. I couldn't stop myself. I went to a bar and I—"

"Scott..." she began, struggling to find the right words, but he cut her off, his voice cracking.

"I didn't know, Zoe... I didn't know," he mumbled, his body sinking further into the bed, his hand coming up to cover his eyes. "What the hell am I supposed to do now?"

Zoe stood there, towel still wrapped around her, the Glock hanging loosely at her side.

"Just... just get some rest, Scott," she finally said. "We'll deal with this in the morning."

Scott didn't respond, his breathing already slowing as the alcohol took its final toll, dragging him into unconsciousness. Zoe watched him for a moment longer, her mind racing, before she quietly set the Glock back on the nightstand.

This was too much even for her. Another girl was missing. The biological daughter of the lead detective on the case. But her thoughts were too mushy and shapeless. She couldn't think straight. She was about to call him a cab but the sound of him snoring soon joined the sound of crickets. She was thinking about crashing on the couch when there was another knock on the door.

Her mind was too preoccupied with Scott being Lucy's father so she opened the door without thinking. Alarm ghosted down her spine. It was Simon's wife—Nancy.

"Nancy!" Zoe's eyes widened. "What are you doing *here*?"

Nancy's hold on her bag tightened. "It wasn't hard to figure out where you're staying. I just had to look into my husband's phone. We need to talk."

Her brain short-circuited, still trying to absorb the sight of her. "About what?"

Nancy pressed her teeth together, breathing hard and bubbling with frazzled energy. She opened and closed her mouth like a fish before finally spitting out the words, "Stay out of my marriage."

"Huh?"

"I've seen you and Simon at work always laughing and teasing. And then he tells you about his friend dying but not his wife?" Her eyes brimmed with tears. "I checked his phone the other day. He was talking to you and not *Dale*—"

"It *is* work, Nancy. We only talk about work."

"Then why did he say your name in his sleep yesterday?" Her voice cracked, her face creased with desperation and hatred.

A sharp, throbbing pain began blossoming in the center of her forehead. "I don't know what to tell you, Nancy. But I'm not having an affair with your husband."

Her nose turned red, flaring as she took quick breaths. Then her eyes looked past Zoe into the bedroom, widening at Scott snoring away on her bed. A mirthless chuckle left her. "You're such a slut. God knows whose husband you're banging now. You'll burn in hell one day."

FORTY

Rain hammered against the windows as Regina slipped into the darkened office, the wind howling through the narrow gaps in the old building's frame. The lights had gone out minutes earlier, leaving her in near-total darkness, but she couldn't wait. There was too much at stake.

There was a low rumble of thunder, like a warning, as she fumbled through the desk drawers with shaking hands. Her flashlight cast an eerie, narrow beam, illuminating papers strewn across the desk, files haphazardly stacked, and the occasional coffee-stained document.

She pulled out a manila folder, its label barely legible in the dim light: Financial Projections—Q4. Flipping it open, she found spreadsheets, profit and loss statements, and funding forecasts. Her breath caught in her throat as she scanned the figures. Red ink everywhere. The numbers were dire. The campaign was hemorrhaging money—way more than she had been led to believe.

Guilt flooded her. She was their leader, the boss. She should have known about this instead of trusting Connor with everything.

Next, she found a stack of loan applications, each neatly bound with rejection letters stapled to them. One after another, banks and private lenders had turned them down. "Insufficient collateral," "high risk," "no credit history"—the reasons varied, but the result was the same. The campaign was on the brink of financial collapse, and no one had bothered to tell her.

A flash of lightning lit up the room, the sudden brightness throwing the papers into sharp relief. For a moment, she stood still, the realization of their impending doom sinking in. They were out of time, out of options.

But then, just as quickly, darkness swallowed the room again, and in the afterglow of the lightning, her eyes caught something else. Something hidden under the desk, barely visible beneath a pile of old newspapers—a duffel bag.

Regina's heart galloped as she knelt down, pulling the bag out into the open. It was heavy, the zipper straining against whatever was inside. With a trembling hand, she slowly unzipped it.

Another burst of lightning flashed through the window, just as she peeled the bag open. Inside were neat stacks of cash, tightly bound with rubber bands, the sight of which left her confused if anything. Was Connor stealing money from the campaign and building his own nest? But there was no time to be angry about that. There was something else that made her blood run cold.

Nestled beside the cash were several unmarked black envelopes and, most terrifying of all, a gun—its cold, metallic surface glinting in the brief light.

FORTY-ONE

Zoe was never the villain in anyone's life. She was fairly well-liked. That skip in her step, that endless positivity, the chirpy tilt of her voice and always armed with something sweet, she was nobody's idea of what an FBI agent looked like. She wasn't jaded and weary like most of her coworkers. It was an ardent effort to not have a chip on her shoulder.

But last night she had been the villain. To Nancy, her ex-boyfriend's wife who he met years after their breakup. How was Zoe still a shadow looming over their marriage? She swiveled on her chair, capping and uncapping her pen, her mind ticking over Nancy's spiteful words.

It gave birth to a nub of shame inside her. Did she still have feelings for Simon? Was Nancy picking up on something neither of them was brave nor astute enough to admit?

Lucy's picture stared back at her, a haunting reminder. The weight of the investigation was pressing down on her, and she could feel the tension building in her shoulders. No other girl had gone missing. She was inclined to believe that Lucy had been taken by the killer they were hunting.

The news that Lucy Robinson was missing broke in the wee

hours of the morning. The news cycle was thrilled to find another enthralling story other than just the elections. They not only regurgitated the fears of Harborwood and Zoe but also inflated them, painting a gruesome picture that made Zoe queasy.

Is Lucy hanging in the woods waiting to be discovered?

None of the victims had been founding *hanging* in the woods. But there had been nooses, and the press found it shockingly easy to mold them into a lie.

Zoe clicked her pen incessantly; the repetitive sound tethered her. On the big television screen at the station, Mayor Hicks was being interviewed. But the volume had been muted. Lucy had disappeared without a trace. Despite the number of emails and phone calls from the sheriff's office and WSP, they had no news. The rangers had been tracking the woods but hadn't discovered anything.

The hope of finding Lucy had been dwindling and so was that plucky positivity she carried through cases like this.

Zoe had barricaded herself at the station away from the chaos, swimming in thoughts of worst-case scenarios. Her eyes searched the office for Scott—she hadn't heard from him since last night.

"Chief!" she called when Travis appeared around the corner, his phone pressed to his ear. She approached him hurriedly but he raised a finger, gesturing her to keep quiet. She rocked on her heels, waiting for his conversation to finish. "Yes, yes, I'll be there. Maybe tomorrow. Okay." He hung up. "Sorry, that was Hicks."

"Where's Detective Cohen? I haven't heard from him."

He winced. "You haven't heard?"

"Heard what?" Her heartbeat slowed.

"My buddy saw Scott drinking at the bar. Said he got shit-faced drunk. I don't know if you know about his past..." he added warily.

"I do." Zoe looked down at her feet.

"He is too closely connected to the case and with him relapsing, I'm keeping him away. It's an unofficial suspension. Excuse me, I got a few fires to put out."

She nodded in understanding just as Aiden rounded the corner. "Did you hear? About Scott?"

"Yeah..." He pursed his lips in a thin line. "That's where I was. Hunter wanted me in the room when he broke the news to Scott."

"What happened?"

"He seemed to be in shock... like there were other things on his mind." His eyes narrowed. "Do you know something?"

"He showed up at my room drunk and told me that Carly confessed to him that Lucy was his child."

Aiden's lips parted. "Interesting."

She checked her phone again, hoping to hear something from Scott. But there were no notifications. New town, an unknown terrain, and a killer who was too good at leaving clean crime scenes.

"I'm working with Terri going through social media to see if there are any hints there. I think we might have something." Aiden hitched his thumb over his shoulder.

She returned to her desk, trying to wrap her head around Scott's suspension and the weight of it all resting on her shoulders. The only relief she had was that she had finally figured out how to use the dated software at the station to analyze the CCTV footage found at the bakery. Her eyes still ached from the hours she had spent glaring at it without any breaks. The hustle and bustle of the station and the uneasy noise in her own head evaporated as she watched the video frame by frame.

Based on the dimensions of the counter, the height of the culprit was extrapolated to be between 1.78 to 1.83 meters. It was an average height and someone that tall could very well have a shoe size of ten. The display case was made of glass. She zoomed in and cleared the image, trying to capture a reflection of his face in the display case as he cleaned out desserts to feed his victims.

Her eyes narrowed, clicking the button again and again, but she was sure she could see a dark mark on the face. Irritation slashed through her. The killer was wearing a mask, hiding the lower part of his face. With his hoodie on, she couldn't even capture the color of his hair.

But there had to be something. The need to salvage anything from the footage clawed at her.

And then she noticed it. In the reflection of his hoodie on the display case, there was something white. She focused on its shape—was it a logo? It was nothing familiar. Perhaps a local brand? But when she zoomed in on it, the shape of it was too haphazard with no definitive symbol or word on it.

A stain. That's what it was, she concluded. Most likely bleach.

"A killer with a bleach-stained hoodie and a genetic disorder," she repeated to herself. Outside the bright light weaved uninhibited through the branches crisscrossing the skies. Her mind drifted to Rachel, Keith, and the con that had changed everything.

The door to her office rattled open and Aiden popped his head in.

"Please give me some good news," Zoe groaned, throwing her head back. "And get me some M&Ms from the vending machine so that I can think."

"We found something." He showed his laptop and placed it in front of Zoe, shoving hers aside with a sweep of an arm. "I had asked Terri to keep tabs and join those Facebook groups."

With a few clicks, she opened a page of amateur sleuths in town discussing the case in a series of posts.

> Detective Scott Cohen was drinking at a pub. He doesn't care!
>
> Lucy's mother is a prostitute. I think she was abducted by the wife of some client she banged.
>
> I made a map of where Lily's and Tara's bodies were found. I extrapolated where Lucy will be found and it forms an Illuminati symbol.

"This is a very active page." Zoe kept scrolling over conspiracy theories that ranged from children being kidnapped for government experiments to blood sacrifice in the woods following some occult tradition.

"This is the most interesting thing to have happened to Harborwood. It's a classic response to the traumatic breach of their sociocultural equilibrium caused by the violent crime, so the townspeople engage in collective projection and mass psychogenic hypervigilance. They spin conspiracy theories and become amateur sleuths to alleviate cognitive dissonance and reassert control over their disrupted reality."

She stared at him blankly. "Was that in English?"

He bit his lip, hiding a smile, and highlighted a post. "We found this."

As Zoe read the words, her blood curdled.

> Anyone looking for pictures of Lily, Tara, and Lucy not known to public. Contact me.
>
> Got unseen pictures of Lily, Tara, and Lucy. DM me for price.

"What the hell is this?" Zoe clicked on the name of the person who had made the post. Not only was the name John Doe, but there was no profile picture and the profile was locked.

"And this isn't the only post he made."

John Doe had posted on several groups all over social media offering to sell people "exclusive" pictures of the three girls. Two weeks ago, it was only of Lily but after Tara was found dead his list had grown. And now it included Lucy.

Zoe looked like she'd seen a ghost. "What does he mean by unseen and exclusive pictures?"

Her stomach roiled but she fought the urge to do more than just retch. "What does this mean, Aiden?"

He pinched the bridge of his nose, thinking hard. "Voyeurism, desensitization to violence, objectification of victims..." He placed his hands on the table, leaning forward. "The profile diverges from what we are looking at—someone who has a childhood regression and is recreating something."

Her eyes widened. "But there's a possibility of two killers. So this might be one of them. I'll get the FBI to track down the IP address."

"Think they'll move fast?"

"Simon better." She grabbed her keys, ignoring Aiden's lingering gaze.

FORTY-TWO

Silhouettes of birds tapered across the sky. The blue color was melting into a dark gray. Zoe listened to music to drown out the perpetual hum of the city. She swung the grocery bag back and forth, walking past identical-looking blocks of concrete with peeling posters and amateur graffiti. It was a sketchy patch outside downtown. But it was Chicago—she knew this city.

Plus it wasn't like Zoe hadn't taken this path before.

Singing along, her steps matched the beat of the music. She was too preoccupied to notice a figure emerge from the shadows. She almost jumped back.

It was a middle-aged man wearing a coat on a hot summer day. His skin was blotchy, his eyes weary. He extended his hand. "You got change?"

She removed her earphones and looked around. No sign of anyone. She hesitated but figured it was better to help him. "Yeah, sure."

Zoe took out her wallet from her pocket and discreetly opened it, away from his prying eyes. Her hands trembled. She had a lot of cash, expecting to buy more groceries, but the shop was out of stock in a lot of things.

The man's eyes flashed. He gripped her hand and pulled her closer.

An involuntary scream escaping Zoe's throat was abruptly cut off. Her heart pounded hard. The bag slipped from her hands and all the groceries rolled out.

She tried wrestling her way out of his unyielding hold. But one arm was around her waist almost crushing her ribs. His other hand was on her mouth. It was difficult to breathe. The scent of something metallic and rotten assaulted her nose.

He was pulling her into the alley with him. Away from the street. Further into darkness and isolation.

I'm going to die. He's going to touch me and then kill me.

Because the fear of just losing her life wasn't cruel enough.

We have to tell our daughters to be careful, because no one tells their sons to behave. Be careful, Zoe. Her mother had given her strict instructions when she had moved to the city. Zoe cried and grappled; a sense of doom overcoming her. Suddenly, she froze. She realized why the man was wearing a coat. His shirt was covered in blood.

She bit into his hand and as he released his grip in pain, she shouted, "Help!"

"Bitch!" He smacked her in the jaw and threw her to the ground. Climbing on top of her, he immobilized her legs. He was so heavy. Tears fell down her face. He grabbed her wrists with one hand and pinned them above her head.

No. No. Please. No.

"Get off her!" she heard someone growl. Before Zoe could register anything, someone flew at them, slamming into the man and rolled away with him.

Finally she could breathe. Everything happened so quickly. She heard a siren. A cop car had pulled up. An officer was rushing toward her and calling for help. The fading adrenaline left her with shivers. She could hear grunting and crunches.

She looked over her shoulder and saw a woman raining punches on the man.

After a few minutes, she stopped and stood up, panting. "Cuff this asshole! Now!"

The officer obeyed. The woman wasn't in uniform. She was wearing an impressive pantsuit. Her dark face contorted in fury. Her long and straight hair was pulled in a high ponytail. She was tall and imposing and downright terrifying.

Zoe almost recoiled when the woman laid eyes on her.

"It's okay," she said softly, taking out her badge. "I'm Detective Taylor from the Chicago PD. You're safe now."

And Zoe did feel safe. She glanced at the revolting man who had tried to hurt her. He had already hurt someone else. That much blood on his shirt couldn't have been his own if he was still able to walk around and attack her. But this woman had saved her. She had done something incredible, monumental, and she had probably done it so many times that she didn't even realize the enormity of it.

Zoe stared at her in awe. And right then and there, she found her way to the truth. She knew what to do.

Zoe had driven like a maniac. It had taken her five hours. She wasn't distracted by the scenic views of the Olympic National Park when driving on the 101 South or flustered by the traffic on WA-305. She had zipped through the unfamiliar roads in a frenzy, her blood pressure hovering at an all-time high.

She parked haphazardly and marched into the FBI's Seattle office, past some familiar faces who tried greeting her and were surprised at her attitude. Zoe was rarely in a bad mood. She made it a point to smile, to joke like she had stepped straight out of a romantic comedy.

But today she wore her rage like a badge.

She climbed the stairs and found Simon in a conference room with one of the assistant directors. Two suited men engaged in a somber discussion with thick stacks of paper in front of them. Her hands fisted around the printouts she was carrying, and she burst into the room.

"Zoe!" Simon's eyes widened in shock and he stammered for an introduction. "You know Campbell from counterintelligence. This is Special Agent Zoe Storm."

"Of course I know her!" The stocky man shook Zoe's sweaty hand but didn't seem to mind. "She sends my family chocolates every Christmas."

"Sorry, but do you mind if I have a moment with Simon?" Zoe asked Campbell nicely. "It's an emergency."

"Sure, no problem." He stood up with his hands in the air. "I gotta take a leak and then a smoke."

Once he left the room, Simon watched her like she had grown two heads. "What's going on? How's Wesley?"

"I need tech support."

He rolled his eyes. "We've been over this, Z. You know my hands are tied—"

She shoved the papers in his chest. "I *need* tech support, Simon. Read this and tell me you can't help."

Simon sighed in exasperation but once he began reading the printouts of all the posts made by John Doe that Zoe that consolidated, the color drained from his face. His nostrils flared and a muscle in his jaw ticked. "I see."

"Campbell is here. He likes me. He's counterintelligence. Convince him to loan you more resources or—"

"The guys will work overtime on this tonight," Simon said, his tone flipping suddenly from annoyed to purposeful. "You're looking for an IP address, I'm assuming?"

"Y-yes." Zoe crossed her arms, suddenly unsure of what to do. She had been preparing to make a whole speech and threatening to quit if needed. "I'll send you the information. That's it? You just agreed?"

He sucked in a sharp breath through his teeth. "Is that how little you think of me? That I won't help with something like this?"

For a moment, Zoe was catapulted back to her time at the academy. The first time she felt a little tug for Simon in her chest. He had given a passionate lecture on a case he had recently solved. She saw that same passion and fury now, not a man whose hands were tied by paperwork and corporate red tape.

"Thank you. I should head back." The energy simmering inside her was finally settling down. "Can you get back in forty-eight hours?"

"I promise."

She turned to leave and hesitated. A meandering thought suddenly crystallized. "Can you do me another favor? A personal one?"

"Depends on what it is." His eyes narrowed.

"There's no time limit on this. Can you look into the name Keith Gordon? He owns a bar in Harborwood."

"Sure. Why?"

"A favor for a friend." She gave a noncommittal shrug and walked away, her stomach in knots.

* * *

Scott reread Zoe's message.

> Z: Have a lead on creep who has been posting things about victims online. FBI is helping find the IP address.

His face burned. Her niceness was a machete to the gut. He gripped the steering wheel and punched the button to speed-dial Travis. As he waited for Travis to answer, he bobbed his knee and rubbed his lips.

"How long is this *unofficial* suspension going to last?" he demanded as soon as Travis picked up.

A sigh. "Scott, I gave you a chance to control yourself. Instead, you got drunk. I can't risk this investigation."

He caught a reflection of his face in the side mirror. The angry scar that ran down his face was still far from healing or turning white and there was mild swelling on his right temple. He looked like a monster; he felt like one too. "I made a mistake. It won't happen again. But the big picture is this case. You can use me. You're wasting a resource—"

"You have become a liability," he said sternly. "And you have a personal connection to the case with your history with Carly!"

"She's mine! Lucy's mine!" he growled.

Silence. A thick, pregnant silence.

"What?" Travis asked.

Scott rested his head back, exhausted by Carly's lies and drama. "She didn't tell me until Lucy went missing. But the timing makes sense."

"Holy crap."

He felt like a fool. Once again Carly had caught him in his drama, and this time it was by keeping his kid away from him. "Come on, Travis. Are you really that surprised? You were with her too. You know what she's capable of."

"I wasn't until now," he admitted softly. "But I'm sorry, Scott. This doesn't change the fact that your behavior has been erratic. In fact, you're even more involved now. You're off this case but you can report to duty next week."

Scott gritted his teeth when the line went dead. A sharp spike in anger and he slapped the steering wheel with the palm of his hand. It throbbed, turning red. He threw the phone on the passenger seat and floored the gas, peeling out of his driveway.

He was on a mission. He didn't care that he didn't have Travis's permission. This was his case. This was his kid. He was going to solve it. He had told Terri to get a few patrol officers to keep an eye on Bella—Lily's defensive, drug-addicted sister who knew the dealer they'd found at that abandoned building.

There was a loose end there. He could feel it in his gut. It didn't take him long to find Bella at her high school. She was a senior and hanging out in the parking lot with some friends.

Scott observed her from a distance, trying to memorize the faces she was talking to. None of them looked suspicious. They just looked like kids. She got into her red truck—a clear hand-me-down—that had peeled paint and an engine that coughed loudly when it roared to life. She peeled out of the parking lot and got on the main street.

And then Scott followed her. He had tailed people before—mostly Carly when she used to lie about where she was going. He maintained a distance and he wasn't surprised when she didn't go home and instead headed to one of the town squares. With her backpack slung over her shoulder, she walked to the pharmacy. He killed the engine and followed her in.

Scott blended into the few people milling about inside the pharmacy just as Bella approached the counter. The conversation was quiet, muffled by the ambient noise of the store.

The pharmacist handed over a small paper bag, and Bella mumbled a quick thanks before turning to leave. As she did, the bag tipped slightly and fell from her grasp, spilling a bottle with the familiar logo of Tylenol. Scott frowned. It was over-the-counter stuff, nothing unusual. But something wasn't right.

Once Bella left, he approached the pharmacist. He knew the old, stout woman with round glasses and graying hair. Luckily, it wasn't hard to make friends in a small town like Harborwood.

"Hey, Liz, how's it going?" He placed his hands on the counter, giving her a crooked smile.

Liz looked up from her notepad, her eyes widening both in surprise and then concern. "Scott! Oh my goodness. I saw the news. That crowd did a number on you."

He touched the scar. He'd forgotten it was there because his mind was too crowded with more important things. But now he realized, a patch of his face was in pain. "Yeah..."

"You want anything for that face, honey? A cream to prevent scarring or extra strength Tylenol?" She jumped into her mamma bear mode, ruffling through the shelves of bottles and tubes. "Ah, darn it! Bella took the last Tylenol I had. I'm going to have to place an order." She shook her head, flustered, and went to the computer. "How do you work these things?"

"Is Bella okay? You know, considering..."

"She is as good as can be expected." Liz pressed a hand to her chest and clicked her tongue. "She's being more responsible. Her mother used to pick up the kidney medication, but Bella tells me that Mary doesn't want to leave the house anymore. Worst nightmare for a parent, Scott. Worst one." Her gazed fixated on the screen. "Now, how should I place an order?"

Scott helped Liz place the order. But what she just said left him with jangled nerves.

FORTY-THREE

The room was plunged into darkness, the only light coming from the occasional flash of lightning that briefly illuminated the space, casting long, eerie shadows on the walls. The storm outside raged with ferocity, rain pelting against the windows and thunder rumbling ominously in the distance. Regina sat in a chair near the corner, her hand wrapped around a glass of Scotch.

It was her late father's preferred drink. She turned the glass around in her hands, the liquid glimmering at different angles. Today she needed her father's cruelty—she'd despised it growing up. She'd always been looked down upon because he had wanted a son. Only men had the stomach to live with hard decisions, or so he had often told her.

Her nose wrinkled in distaste at the memory. If only he was still alive to see her and everything she had achieved.

The front door creaked open, and Connor stepped inside, shaking off the rain from his coat.

"What are you doing here?" Connor demanded, flicking the light switch only to find the power was out. He grumbled and tossed his coat onto a chair. "Did you see my notes for your debate tomorrow? You're gonna need them."

Regina steeled herself for this moment. "I didn't look at your notes, Connor. I don't need them. Because you're fired."

Connor froze. The rain pelted like stones against the windows running along the side of the room. Then he threw his head back and let out a booming laugh that cleaved through the room. "Fired? You can't fire me, Regina. I'm your campaign manager, your ticket to the big leagues."

"I don't need you anymore." She leveled her voice. "There are other people who can take your place. I've lined up a few interviews for tomorrow."

Lightning flashed, illuminating his face. The trees in the garden swished and sashayed in the wind causing the shadows to dance on his face. He looked menacing, almost evil, reminding Regina of the villains she watched in Hitchcock movies.

"You can't do that to me. I've worked very hard to get you where you are," he said coldly, his voice devoid of emotion.

"And I think the money that you've been siphoning from my campaign has more than compensated for those efforts." She let her words sink in. "Yes, I know, Connor."

Connor closed his eyes, his mouth tightening. "You have no idea what I've done for you, Regina."

"Why? Why are you *so* hellbent on me winning, Connor? You can join Hicks or anyone else."

He cupped his mouth with his hands, turning away to face the window. His silhouette was half concealed in the shadows. "I got involved with some bad people."

"What people?"

"Let's just say some important people want you to win and not Hicks."

Regina's mind ticked over the kind of dealings Connor

could be embroiled in and then it struck her. "That casino owner."

He nodded. "Hicks is shutting it down. I made a deal with him that I'd convince you to keep it open if you won. If you don't then... let's just say I might lose my legs."

"The money you've been stealing is in case I lose and you have to disappear?"

Connor's face tightened, anger flashing in his eyes. But he forced a smirk. "Okay, so what if I did? I have to look out for myself. Yeah, I did something stupid, big deal. But you're no saint either."

"*You* convinced me to sign off on that environmental report and pay off Logan." Her voice trembled in anger. Another fork of lightning slashed the sky and the rain intensified like white noise.

"It is still your signature, *your* culpability. So let me make this clear, Regina. We work together, we both win. You try to take me down and I'll drag you to hell with me."

For a moment Regina thought he would hurt her. His ambition and sense of self-preservation knew no boundaries. She downed her drink, giving her the push she needed.

"Not anymore," she said quietly, her hand slipping into her pocket. In the next instant, she pulled out Connor's gun. The metal gleamed in the brief flickers of lightning, the barrel steady in her grip.

Connor's bravado faltered as he stared at the weapon in disbelief. "What the hell, Regina? Where did you get that from?"

"I found this in your things," Regina said, her voice calm, almost detached. "It seems you were planning for every possibility, weren't you? Well, here's how it's going to go: you're going to leave, and you're not going to come back. Because if you do, I have no problem getting rid of you, Connor."

His eyes darted from the gun to her face, searching for any

sign of hesitation, but there was none. He raised his hands slowly, taking a step back. "All right, all right, let's not do anything stupid here, Regina. Just... put the gun down. Come on... you're not going to kill me."

Her eyes locked onto his. The alcohol swimming in her veins emboldened her. "Oh, I can. I can do a lot of things. I can shoot you and then lie that it was in self-defense and I couldn't see it was you in the dark. I can cut the same deal you did with that casino guy and make sure you are redundant."

Panic took over. "I'll tell everyone! I'll go to the media!"

She clicked off the safety of the gun, the sound sharp and piercing. "You try doing that. I dare you."

Connor began backing away, his lips twisted. "You're going to regret this, Regina! Mark my words, you're going to regret this!"

"I don't give a damn."

FORTY-FOUR

"Is there any emotion in your job that makes you curious?" Aiden asked.

Zoe sipped her chocolate milk and curled her legs underneath her. This couch was getting too comfortable. And so was his company. "Curious? I don't know..."

"For me, it's that conflict between the predator who wants to kill and then the morality construct that killing is wrong and how some of us succumb to the former," he offered.

"That's interesting, I suppose. For me, it's the aftermath."

"Aftermath of what?"

"Of doing something wrong." Her mind began to float away as Rachel's face transpired in her mind. "Guilt. How people deal with guilt. Even though I'm not around for that part, but I always wonder."

"Not all killers you catch lack a conscience..."

"Exactly."

He scribbled something down—the only thing that annoyed her. "Do you wonder what you would do in their situation?"

"Yes."

"And what would you do?"

She lifted her eyes, smiling coyly. "Guilt is a private affair, Dr. Wesley. There are some emotions that I don't share with anyone."

* * *

"Terri!" Zoe called over the middle-aged woman with a prominent mole on her cheek. "Did you get a chance to check Sam Buster's alibi?"

"I did. He did have a job interview at three thirty but he left it an hour later."

"Four thirty, eh? That falls within our window." Zoe crossed her arms. "How long would it take for him to reach Lucy's place?"

"Ten minutes." She shrugged. "I'm still digging into where he allegedly went after that."

Zoe was surrounded by stacks of case files and a series of crime scene photos spread out before her. The harsh fluorescent lights overhead flickered slightly, casting a cold, sterile glow on the room. She picked up one of the photos, her eyes narrowing as she focused on the image of a small stuffed animal lying on the ground a few feet away from the crime scene hidden in the ferns. It had been recovered days later.

Why was the killer leaving toys? It was a symbol of innocence. The stuffed animals didn't belong to the victims. Did they belong to the killer? They had no prints. Why would this be left at such a grisly crime scene? She closed her eyes, casting her mind back to the crime scene.

The ancient trees with gnarled trunk and knotty roots that looked like tentacles. Trees that looked like witches lived there. The ropes hanging ominously. It all meant something to the killer. Every little detail.

"That's a rare find," Terri said casually, preoccupied with something on her phone.

Zoe looked up at her. "The bear?"

Terri nodded, stepping closer to get a better look. "Yeah, it's an antique. Not the kind of thing you'd see just lying around. My mom had one like it when she was a kid. They don't make them anymore."

Her interest piqued. "Are they easy to come by?"

"Not really," Terri replied, rubbing her chin. "I tried to buy one for my kid a few years ago. Thought it'd be cool for grandmother and granddaughter to have the same toy but I couldn't find one. No store has it. This must belong to the killer."

Zoe's gaze returned to the photo, her eyes scrutinizing the toy. Something didn't add up. The bear didn't look old. There were no signs of wear and tear, no discoloration in the fabric. In fact, it looked like it had been well preserved, almost as if it had been kept safe for years. Not something that had been used or played with. "This doesn't look like it's been around for decades. If it's new, then maybe we can trace where it's from."

"Let me do a quick search. If it's an antique piece, then maybe some collectors sell it." She tapped away on her phone. "No stores are selling this model, but... there was a buyer on eBay. The seller listed it as sold two weeks ago."

"Contact the buyer. We need to find out who purchased that bear."

Her phone buzzed. She glanced at the screen and saw her sister Gina's name flashing. A small smile tugged at the corner of her mouth. She could use a break.

"Hey, Gina!" Zoe answered, trying to inject some cheer into her voice.

"Zoe, it's about time you picked up!" Gina's voice bubbled through the line, as lively and warm as ever. "I've been trying to get a hold of you for days! Are you buried in work again?"

"Guilty as charged," Zoe admitted, leaning back in her chair and closing her eyes for a moment. "It's been a rough week."

"Well, you need to come up for air every now and then, sis.

Life's too short to be all work and no play. Speaking of which, guess who's been asking about you nonstop?"

Before Zoe could answer, she heard a little voice in the background, followed by the sound of the phone being passed around.

"Aunt Zoe!" her nephew's excited voice came through, loud and clear. "It's me, Danny!"

"Danny! Hey, buddy!" Zoe said, her smile widening. "How's my favorite nephew doing?"

"I'm good! We're learning cool stuff in school. I wanted to tell you!" Danny's enthusiasm was contagious, and Zoe felt her spirits lifting just hearing the excitement in his voice.

"Oh yeah? What cool stuff are you learning about?"

"Biology!" Danny exclaimed. "We talked about recessive traits, like how some things get passed down from our parents, but they don't always show up unless both parents have them. Like, if someone has blue eyes, it's because both their parents have the recessive gene for blue eyes."

Zoe's eyebrows shot up, impressed. She was glad that at least one person in the family was interested in science. "Wow, Danny, that's awesome! You're really getting into this science stuff, huh? What other traits did you learn about?"

"Um, we talked about hair color too. Like, if both parents have brown hair but carry the gene for blonde hair, their kid could have blonde hair if they both pass on that gene. And dimples! Dimples are a dominant trait, so if one parent has them, the kid probably will too."

"That's really cool, Danny. Sounds like you're going to be the family scientist in no time."

"I wanna be!" Danny said, enthusiastically. "I like figuring out how things work."

Zoe chuckled. "You're going to do great things, Danny, I just know it."

"Thanks, Aunt Zoe! Mom says I have to finish my homework now, but I'll call you later, okay?"

"Deal. You be good for your mom, all right? I'll talk to you soon."

"Okay! Bye, Aunt Zoe!"

"Bye, Danny."

The line went quiet, and Zoe's smile lingered for a few moments longer. She had almost forgotten that she was neck-deep in a case where someone was leaving dead girls in the woods. Her stomach recoiled at the thought of someone hurting Danny.

She picked up Lucy's picture and studied it. Could it be that Sam Buster took her? He was a crass man, a brute. She could imagine him hurting Lucy. Especially the way he leered at the thought of her.

But then she noticed something. How Lucy had attached earlobes. Exactly like Carly. It was Danny's words that made her search the Internet for dominant and recessive traits. Attached earlobes were a recessive trait just like Lucy's blue eyes. But Scott had brown eyes and free earlobes.

The possibility ricocheted through her, making her queasy. Was it possible that Scott wasn't Lucy's father? Had Carly lied?

FORTY-FIVE

Zoe pushed open the heavy wooden door of the dimly lit bar, her eyes scanning the room until they landed on Scott. He was slumped over the counter, nursing a glass of whiskey, his posture a portrait of defeat. She had made a wild guess that he was at a bar. This was the second one she had tried. She felt a pang of sympathy but steeled herself.

She approached him quietly, sliding onto the stool next to him. The clink of glass on wood as she set her bag down was the only sound between them for a moment. She knew he had noticed her and waited for him to break the silence. But he didn't.

"Scott," she began softly, trying to find the right words. "We need to talk."

He finally turned to face her, his eyes red-rimmed. "I'm sorry about yesterday. It was very unprofessional of me to show up like that."

Zoe swallowed, waving her hand dismissively. "Don't worry about that. Look, I know this is the worst time, but it's important. It's about Lucy."

Scott stiffened. "What about Lucy?" His voice was rough, as if he already feared the worst.

Zoe hesitated. The words were lodged in her throat. "Scott, there's something you need to know. I've been looking into a few things, and... I think you need to consider the possibility that Lucy might not be your biological daughter."

The color drained from Scott's face and, for a moment, Zoe thought he might pass out. He stared at her, uncomprehending. "What are you talking about? That's... that's..."

She felt a wave of pity for him. He had gone through a ringer this past week. "I'm so sorry, Scott. I don't want to hurt you, but I found some things that don't add up. It could be nothing, but considering your past with Carly and her ability to play with your head, I think you should do a paternity test. Just to be sure."

Scott's hand trembled as he set down his glass. He looked lost, like a man suddenly cut adrift in a storm. "How... how could this happen? Why now? Why would you even look into this?"

Zoe sighed, wishing she could take away his pain. "I didn't want to believe it either, but there were things that didn't make sense. Lucy's physical traits—it raised questions. I thought it was better to know the truth now than to live with uncertainty. And I don't know how much you trust Carly to just believe her word."

Scott buried his face in his hands, his shoulders shaking. "Shit." He looked up at her, his eyes glistening with tears. "Why would Carly lie?"

Zoe squeezed his arm gently. "I'm not saying that she's lying. But you've been through a lot and the last thing I want you to do is deal with this life-changing news without confirmation. Just talk to Carly and get a paternity test, okay?"

Scott stared at her for a long moment, before finally nodding. "You're right."

. . .

Scott's lungs were burning. He stumbled out of the cab, his legs feeling like jelly, his blinks lazy. But his mind was as sharp as a tick. He wasn't drunk—well, he wasn't *that* drunk. The perks of being an alcoholic was that his tolerance was way higher. And despite what that they say, that was a skill that was never unlearned.

His hand gripped the railing as he climbed up the stairs and knocked on the door. His whiskey-infused breath cut through the cool night air. He swayed, his eyes catching sight of the dense woods across the street. Was Lucy lying in the woods somewhere? The air was choked with moisture and darkness. He was used to these kinds of nights. As a kid, he would hike into the woods at night and camp there.

It was Harborwood. No one expected to stumble upon dead bodies.

The door opened and Carly's tear-stained face appeared. "Scott! Did you find her? Any news?"

The moment he saw her his anger flared. He barreled past her into the small, cluttered living room that was dimly lit.

"No more lies, Carly," he growled.

She tightened her night-robe around her and took a step back. "You're drunk again."

"Don't you dare judge me!"

"Hell, I will!" she hollered, surging ahead. Flaky and messy Carly was what he was used to. But this one was feral. Shadows danced on her face from the flickering fire. "Lucy is missing and you're drinking at a bar? What's wrong with you?"

"Is she mine?"

She gasped. "What?"

"Is she actually mine or is this one of your many lies?"

Her back pressed against the wall as she tried to compose herself. "No," she whispered, her voice breaking.

He ran a hand through his disheveled hair, as he paced around the room. It was like someone had torched him and filled him with poisonous gas. He just wanted to slice open his skin and crawl out of it. "Why the hell would you lie about that?" he suddenly shouted, making her flinch. "Are you out of your mind?"

"I thought you would take the case more seriously if you thought she was your daughter," she whined. "I didn't plan it. I'm so scared. So terrified. I can't breathe."

"Why would you think I wouldn't take Lucy's disappearance seriously?"

"Because two girls are dead, Scott! And I thought you could use some incentive to find the third one alive."

Her words were a punch to his gut. It took the air out of him. Silence descended between them; the only sound was of the fire crackling. "You think I don't know how to do my job?"

"That's not what I meant—"

"So you thought it was fair to put me through hell—"

"I'm going through hell!" She beat her chest, her wild hair cascading down her shoulders. "*Me*. She's my daughter!"

"And I thought she was mine too but you're such a manipulative bitch!"

"I think you should leave," she said, wringing her hands. "You're drunk and I don't feel comfortable—"

"This is classic. So typical." Scott fell to his knees. Suddenly everything was spinning. He'd thought that perhaps Zoe was mistaken, that Carly wouldn't lie to him about something as important as this. But the shred of doubt wouldn't leave him. "Why do you keep ruining my life?"

"You're the one who keeps coming back," she snapped, despite the tears forming in her eyes.

"Because I look at you and still see that girl I fell in love with back in senior year." He sniffled. "All that shit you put me through for years with your jealousies, insecurities, and then your… infidelities!" He let out a sarcastic laugh. "With my boss of all people. Chief Travis, who I report to."

"You dumped me, remember? You only come here to get some and use me. Why are you complaining, Scott? We both use each other."

"Because it never feels enough." His fingers clenched in tight fists. Anger fueled him. "No matter how much I hate you, it's never enough. You knew what this case was doing to me. And then you decided to throw it in my face that I fathered a child I didn't know about, a child who is missing, and then I find out you *lied* about that too. You're the devil."

Carly stood up. Scott's breath was heavy and rancid. His eyes were wild, bloodshot, and fixated on Carly, who backed into a corner, her hands trembling. The long, jagged scar ran down his face, still pink and healing. It twisted his features. He stared at her, and all the lies she had ever told bubbled in his mind.

All those years he'd spent working hard to make money for them, only for her to blow it all on drugs. All the times he'd heard from people in town that she was sleeping with other men and he ignored it, choosing to trust her. The number of people she'd forced him to cut out of his life because she wanted him for herself.

He'd forgiven her time and time again. But this time he snapped. This time Carly had stooped too low.

He lunged at her, the rage he had been holding back finally unleashed. His hand shot out, ready to strike, the scar on his face twisting as his mouth curled into a snarl.

Carly gasped, her instincts kicking in. She ducked, just in time, as his fist missed her by inches. Desperation took over, and her hand shot out, grabbing the lamp. Without thinking, she swung it with all her strength, the base crashing into the side of his head.

The sound was sickening—bone and metal colliding, followed by a sharp crack.

He swayed for a moment, then crumpled to the floor. His anger drained away and underneath the pain, there was the blood-curdling realization of what he'd done.

Had he actually attacked Carly?

* * *

Zoe watched her shadow stretch out in the moonlight as the hours went by. The thick forest surrounding the station cast deep shadows under the dim glow of streetlights. Inside, the station was eerily quiet, the kind of silence that made every creak and rustle seem amplified. She sat at her desk, the evidence files spread out in front of her, the harsh fluorescent light above buzzing faintly.

"Thank you, Agent Storm," a young patrol officer said from her cubicle a few feet away from the desk Zoe had taken. "I love sunflowers!"

Zoe smiled at the bouquet of flowers she had ordered for the patrol officer. "You're welcome, and congratulations!"

She'd overheard that the young woman had recently gotten engaged but wasn't telling anyone about it at work because of the cases they were entangled in. But Zoe wouldn't have survived these years ignoring the good things that happened—she knew bursts of good were sparse in life. Her heart ballooned as she watched the woman beam at the flowers. At least it was a fleeting moment of joy in this season of gloom in Harborwood.

Zoe went back to work, running her fingers through her hair, pushing it back from her face, eyes scanning the same report for what felt like the hundredth time. Next to her, the trash bin contained three empty plastic bags of candy. She made a mental note to hit the gym to offset all this sugar. Idly, she wondered if diabetes ran in the family. There was no way for her to be sure as she didn't know who her father was.

Her current focus was the difference between the two crimes. The MO was the same. Girls propped against the tree trunks. The cause of death strangulation. Ropes hanging from the trees, the ends curled into nooses. A picture tied to one of the nooses with a note scribbled on the back.

But why was Lily's handwritten and Tara's printed? Something didn't add up. Why change the method? She leaned back in her chair, the wheels squeaking as she did. Then there were the hesitation marks. They were prominent in Tara's case but none were found in Lily's. The toy too—Lily's toy looked like it had been used but the toy left next to Tara looked brand-new.

There could be an explanation. Maybe killing was taking its toll. Maybe the killer had grown more attached to Tara during her captivity. Maybe he was afraid his handwriting might give him away. It could be a simple case of him learning to perfect his crimes.

But he'd left his DNA, albeit partial, on the ropes. That was a serious blunder.

Her phone buzzed, jolting her from her thoughts. She grabbed it, only to feel a wave of disappointment wash over her. No updates from Simon. "Come on, Simon," she muttered to herself, scrolling through their last messages.

"Did Simon get back to you?" Aiden asked, offering her coffee, which she accepted.

"Not yet. But he will." She slurped on the hot liquid. "He was asking about you. You don't give him updates?"

Aiden stiffened. "No... I figured you would."

She blanched at his comment but decided to ignore it. "Anything from WSP or the sheriff's office on Lucy?"

"Nothing. I believe she's still in town considering how they have been patrolling the borders. Not a lot of missing kids in the area at the moment."

Zoe scratched through all the information. What were they missing? "Lucy means... light. His note said when the darkness falls."

Aiden was visibly irritated at their lack of progress. "Yeah, I don't understand the connection between Lily, Tara, and now Lucy. They didn't know each other—no common friends, or classes or babysitters or family. But there's something there."

A man walked in through the main doors. It was 10 p.m. and the station was mostly empty. The minute Zoe saw him, her pulse quickened.

It was Benny.

His face was bruised and movements deliberate. An arm in a sling. What the hell was he doing here?

"What is it?" Aiden's eyes bounced between her and Benny. "You know him?"

"No. But I should help."

Benny approached one of the desks where a uniformed officer sat. "I need to file a report."

"I'll take this!" Zoe jumped up from her chair and rushed to him, signaling the cop to stay seated. "I'm Agent Storm from the FBI. You are?"

Benny's eyes widened, his mouth falling open. "You're in the FBI?"

Her heart slammed against her ribs. But she pretended to take notes. "Just shut up, Benny. What happened? What are you doing in Harborwood?"

"My grandmother lives here so I was visiting," he said, rubbing his jaw where the bruise was darkest. "A bastard took a shot at me."

"Betting gone wrong?"

He was still staring at her like she had grown two heads. "You're FBI? What the hell, Z?"

A pause. Her eyes darted to Aiden who was watching their interaction like a hawk, surely prying open the cracks. "Who I am at your club and who I am outside are totally unrelated. Okay?" He didn't look convinced so she smiled sweetly. "You've known me at least a couple years, Benny. If I wanted to harm your business, I would have done so already. I see crazy shit at this job and need a space to let out my frustrations so I do it at your club. Don't overthink it, okay? Just give me the details and don't tell anyone here. I got a rep to maintain."

He grunted. "All right."

She made a note of the details. Luckily, it wasn't anything that could be traced back to her. Her eyes bore into his. "Why have you been ignoring my messages? I need a fight."

"I was busy with this. In a few days. I need time to recover," he said, avoiding eye contact. "I'll be in touch. Just don't come after me. I'm a businessman and I pay taxes." He was backtracking and before Zoe could respond, he was exiting the station, almost stumbling on his way out.

She was about to leave when she saw Travis, his face contorted.

"Everything okay?"

He clenched his jaw. "I was just at Carly's. Scott showed up drunk and almost attacked her."

"*What?*" Her knees knocked into each other.

"Turns out Carly lied to Scott about him being Lucy's father because she thought we'd take the case more seriously," he said tartly.

Zoe bit her tongue. She shouldn't have said anything to Scott, especially knowing that he had relapsed and was unpredictable. "What happens now?"

"I called some guys to take Scott home so that he can sleep it off. Carly isn't pressing any charges. But Scott's suspension just got official."

FORTY-SIX

Travis had always felt a gnawing unease when it came to Ryan. The late-night phone calls, the secretive behavior, the friends he never introduced to his father—everything about Ryan screamed trouble. But Travis had always chalked it up to teenage rebellion, a phase that would pass with time. He was refusing to believe the worst, secretly hoping that if they didn't look at that bad thing it would go away. But he couldn't do that anymore.

Tonight that unease had turned into a full-blown knot of dread in his stomach, and he couldn't shake the feeling that something was very wrong.

It was just past midnight when Travis crept up the stairs to Ryan's room, his heart thudding in his chest. Ryan was out. Again. He had no idea where he was. Again.

The door creaked open with an eerie slowness. There was a faint smell of sweat in the room, and something else—something metallic and unsettling. Travis hesitated for a moment—he didn't want to invade Ryan's privacy. But the worry swallowed that hesitation whole.

He started with his desk, rifling through drawers filled with scribbled notes, broken pencils, and other random things that offered no clues. But then, behind a stack of old comic books, he found it: a small, battered shoebox with the lid slightly askew.

Travis pulled it out, his hands trembling as he pried the lid off. Inside were photographs—dozens of them, haphazardly thrown together. As he started flipping through them, his breath caught in his throat. He couldn't breathe. This couldn't be happening.

He plopped on a squeaky chair, blinking at the pictures, refusing to believe they were real. His mind raced, trying to make sense of what he was seeing, but all he could feel was a wave of terror crashing over him.

Questions clamored in his head, making it hurt. How did Ryan... *Why*? If anyone found out about this, then everything would be ruined. Travis would lose everything.

The room suddenly felt suffocating, the walls closing in. He began to shake violently, his mind screaming for him to do something—anything—to make it all go away. He stumbled out of the room, his breath coming in ragged gasps as he made his way downstairs to the kitchen.

There, in a moment of panicked clarity, he grabbed a pack of matches from a drawer. He barely registered what he was doing as he picked up the box of photographs and went out to the backyard, his fingers fumbling as he struck the first match. It flared to life, and without hesitation, Travis dropped it into the box. The photographs caught fire immediately, the flames licking up the edges of the images that had haunted him just moments before.

He watched in grim silence as the fire consumed the box, the faces in the photos curling and blackening until there was nothing left but ashes.

FORTY-SEVEN

Scott was going to spend the rest of his life trying to erase the night before. What kind of a man had he become?

Had he actually tried to hit a woman?

He gnashed his teeth together as a rancid taste flooded his mouth. He had to quit drinking. Again. The irony was that the first time he started drinking was the first time Carly had cheated on him. It all boiled down to that woman—years and years of her lies and infidelity and the foolish mockery she made of him, while he was that wimp who stayed at home cleaning the house for her.

And now he felt like a fool again for believing Lucy was his. She wasn't and it oddly felt like a loss.

His muscles cramped around his bones; his head felt bulky. But he steeled himself. This was still his case. Even if Lucy wasn't his, this felt personal. Like it was his mess to solve.

He stood on the worn front steps of Lily's house. He wasn't supposed to be here. If Travis found out, he'd be in real trouble. He took a deep breath and knocked on the door, the sound echoing in the quiet, still air.

After a few moments, the door creaked open, and Tim

stared at Scott. He looked as though he hadn't slept in days—his eyes hollow, his shoulders slumped. He was a well-built man, working a rigorous job at the processing plant. In the last two weeks, he seemed to have lost half of his body weight.

"Detective Cohen," he mumbled, his voice rough and tired. "You find anything yet?"

It was the question Scott hated the most. Especially when he had to say *no*. "We have multiple leads. How's your wife, Mary?"

A tingling silence.

Tim's eyes darkened, and he glanced behind him at the hallway, his lips tightening into a thin line. "She doesn't leave her room anymore," he muttered, his voice barely above a whisper. "She's... she's not well."

He nodded, not pressing for more. "I have to check Lily's room again. Would that be okay?"

Tim nodded and let him in. His feet dragged heavily. Despite Scott being taller and bigger, he felt dwarfed under Tim's shadow. It was so looming and the grief spilled out of him, engulfing him.

Upon reaching Lily's room, Tim stopped and his empty eyes welled with fresh tears. "I... I can't go in."

"It's okay. I won't take long," Scott said gently.

Lily's room looked untouched—a time capsule of a child's life that had been abruptly cut short. Toys were scattered across the floor, a half-finished puzzle lay on the table in the corner. The bed was neatly made, but the blankets still carried the imprint of a small body that had once curled up there.

His eyes were drawn to a small, cluttered table by the bed. On it sat a large, well-worn medical box, the kind that was usually reserved for someone with chronic health issues. Scott stepped closer, his breath catching as he flipped open the lid. Inside were dozens of bottles, some labeled, some not, all jumbled together in a chaotic mess. He sifted through them—

ibuprofen, cough syrup, Tylenol, antiallergics… he recalled Andy's statement about how Lily was regularly sick, especially in the days leading up to her abduction, and Bella's insinuation that Mary was an obsessed, helicopter parent.

And then he saw it—a bottle tucked in the back, almost hidden among the others. He pulled it out, his eyes narrowing as he read the label. It was a prescription diuretic; just like the pharmacist had mentioned. But what caught his attention was the name on the label—it wasn't Lily's. It was prescribed to Mary Ellen.

Was Mary on kidney medication? Did it end up in Lily's room by mistake?

"Mr. Baker," he asked Tim who stood at the threshold, "is your wife taking kidney medication?"

"No." He frowned. "Her mother used to be. My mother-in-law."

A chill ran down Scott's spine, as he turned the bottle over in his hands. "Mary Ellen?"

"Yeah. She passed away about six years ago."

Scott's heart pounded. If Mary Ellen had been dead for six years then why was Mary still picking up her kidney medication? What was it doing in Lily's room? But he already knew the answer and the cold realization settled in his gut.

FORTY-EIGHT

Zoe noticed Aiden's socks when the hem of his pants rode up a little. Minions. She decided he officially had her seal of approval. Who would have thought that the seemingly uptight psychologist liked to wear socks with cartoon characters? And the last few days had told her that he wasn't as bad.

"What's your favorite book?" Zoe asked with a smile.

He looked up at her. "When did I become the patient?"

"Pfff, we are almost friends now." She waved her hand dismissively.

His shoulders sagged, a bright smile sparking on his face. A rare sight. "Let me think. Okay, well, not a book, but a play—Hamlet."

"That was... overbearing." She scrunched her nose. "Why?"

"The madness, the insanity, the doubt whether it was psychosis or manipulation. One of the greatest literary puzzles. Your turn."

Zoe didn't have to think for long. "The Scarlet Letter."

Something flickered across his face. His fingers holding the pen shook as his eyes did a calculation. "It's an interesting study of how people approach redemption differently. Why do *you like it? Because the reverend seeks pain to deal with his guilt?"*

Her breath stopped. "What?"

"Is that what draws you to the book? Is that something you do as well?"

A slap to the face. A whiplash that sucked all the oxygen from her lungs. How did he know?

The parking lot of the run-down motel was nearly empty, just a few scattered cars and a flickering neon sign casting a dim, sickly light over the cracked pavement. The air was thick with the dampness of the Pacific Northwest night, the scent of pine and rain lingering in the cool breeze. Zoe and Aiden parked in a spot near the back, the headlights cutting through the mist before she killed the engine.

He had been trying to question her about Benny and she was dodging him. But she was getting tired. This is why she didn't like working with a partner.

"Is that Scott?" Aiden said, squinting.

Scott was leaning against his car, arms crossed, his silhouette tense under the motel's faint lights. Her heart skittered.

"Scott, where the hell have you been?" she asked, stepping out of the car. "I left you messages."

Scott pushed off his car and met her halfway, his movements agitated. The gravel crunched beneath his boots as he closed the distance between them. "I know, I'm sorry. For everything. But I found something."

He wasn't supposed to be here, wasn't supposed to be on this case at all, but there he was—riled up and impatient, the fire in his eyes unmistakable.

"You should be laying low. You're off the case," Aiden reminded him.

"I don't care about that," he shot back.

"You should!" Her eyes bulged. "Look, I'm so sorry for everything you've been through this last week with the pressure from this case and your toxic ex but you're out of control. I have to agree with Travis and Aiden—"

"I found a connection between Lily and Lucy. I couldn't just sit on it."

He brandished his phone and Zoe and Aiden were hooked. The answer to that one question that had been evading them since the beginning—it finally cracked and the truth was bursting through it.

The motel's sign buzzed faintly. "All right," she said, caving in to the urgency in him. "Tell me what you've got."

He didn't waste any time and showed them the pictures of medicinal bottles on his phone. "This is diuretic found in Lily's room."

"You went to Lily's place?" She was aghast. "You're on suspension."

He stared at her. "What's important is that diuretic wasn't prescribed to Lily. It was prescribed to Mary Ellen."

Aiden frowned. "Mary? She left it in Lily's room by accident?"

He shook his head, a glint flashing in his eyes. "Mary Ellen is Lily's maternal grandmother who has been dead for six years but according to the pharmacist, Mary has been getting refills. I guess the names are the same so it's easier."

"Diuretic... that's for kidneys. Lily had kidney damage in her autopsy report." Zoe began to stitch together the pieces into an image that revolted her.

"We thought it was due to some environmental toxin or the result of her being in captivity but the damage could be from this." Aiden nodded. "We do know Mary was a helicopter parent and Lily wasn't keeping well. What about Lucy?"

There was an edge to Scott's voice. "I went to Carly's place, but when she wasn't home."

"So you broke into her place?" Zoe was appalled.

"No." He sighed. "I was going to but I was circling her property looking for a way in when I found this." He showed her more pictures.

Zoe looked at a picture that was of one of the garden beds on the side of the house, her eyes narrowing as she recognized the tall, feathery stems topped with clusters of pale flowers. "She's growing valerians," she noted, almost to herself. "Is she into gardening?"

"No. And this is the only thing she's growing. In small doses, the valerian root helps with anxiety and in large doses, it causes sleepiness and lethargy."

Zoe's heart began to race as she processed what he was saying. "Is it possible that Carly was using this for herself?"

"She's got Xanax and a whole stash of pills in her bathroom for her anxiety," he replied flatly.

"What about Tara?" Aiden asked.

He held the sides of his waist and shuffled his feet. "That's what I was doing yesterday. I haven't been able to find anything on Tara being poisoned or hurt by her father. But that's also because he doesn't want to talk. He's still livid."

"He's going to feel like that for a long time," she muttered. "But that doesn't mean he wasn't. There could be anything in that house he could have been using."

"Think this is enough for a warrant?" His eyes were hopeful as he watched them.

"I can try. But are we sure this is the connection?" Zoe said.

"What else could it be?" He spread his arms and looked around. "Munchausen by proxy, Zoe. These kids were being hurt by their parents." He waved his hands animatedly, leaning into her. "Our killer targets them, feeds them desserts and lots of nice things in the days leading up to their death and then *gently* kills them. What do you think, Dr. Wesley?"

Aiden's face was ashen. "In his head, he's rescuing them by taking their lives. Maybe those toys he leaves is ceremonial. Like he's sending them off to a better place."

Scott's eyes glistened with hope. "Now you see where I'm going with this."

"The question is who would know about this." Zoe bit her lip and began pacing. "This is intimate knowledge about three families who share no common friends or babysitters or anything like that."

"There is one person who can help us corroborate this," Aiden said.

"Bella. But you can't come with me. You are still on suspension, Scott," Zoe said.

He conceded. "Fair enough. But we are onto something."

A sinking feeling exploded in her chest—if kids weren't safe in their own homes with their families, then what chance did they stand in the outside world?

FORTY-NINE

Zoe leaned against the side of her car, her eyes fixed on the entrance of the high school. The afternoon sun hung low, casting long shadows across the parking lot. She tapped her foot, impatience gnawing at her, but she knew better than to rush this.

"Munchausen by proxy." She popped a gum into her mouth. "Makes me shiver."

Aiden stood next to her, dark circles lining his eyes. The only blemish in his otherwise steely and spotless armor. She relished to see he was human. "There are many reason for this illness. Lacking a stable identity, they find purpose through the victim's fabricated illness. Could be a need for validation and attention. Or an anxious attachment style, where they subconsciously depend on that relationship to feel secure—"

"How do you do this?" she snapped.

"Do what?"

"Talk about something so disturbing without feeling any emotions. This is disgusting. Parental love morphing into selfishness."

He seemed to be taken aback by her words, his hands flinching around his coffee. "It's a unique mental illness."

"Don't say *illness*. Illness takes away personal accountability," she argued hotly. "It's a crime."

"It's both. It being a crime doesn't mean it isn't an illness."

She rolled her eyes. "Great. Everyone's a damn victim. Including a parent poisoning their child. So Mary was abusing Lily and Carly was abusing Lucy?"

"Different root causes. Carly's stems from avoidance of personal issues and neglect, and for Mary, I would say role fulfillment."

"And what about Tara? What was your take on Logan?"

He was stumped. "I don't know. Logan has severe anger issues... but it's hard to box him into a category. I've filed a request to look into his background more."

Evil manifested in the strangest forms and this one was the most ruthless one. Zoe wondered what ugly shapes love could take, how something powerful meant it was unstoppable.

Finally, the doors swung open, and students spilled out, laughing, talking, eager to leave the confines of school behind. They spotted Bella almost immediately. She walked with a group, her dark hair falling carelessly over her shoulders, her expression a mix of boredom and defiance. The kind of girl who wore her armor well, but Zoe could see the weight behind her eyes.

Bella noticed them too. Her eyes flickered with recognition, then annoyance, before she rolled them dramatically, signaling her disdain. She broke away from her friends, who threw curious glances at Zoe, and strolled over.

"What do you want?" Bella asked, her voice flat, as if she was already over this conversation before it even started.

Zoe didn't flinch. She had dealt with tougher girls than Bella before. "I need to ask you something. About your mother."

Bella raised an eyebrow, feigning ignorance. "My mom? What about her?"

"Did she ever try to hurt you?" Zoe's tone was steady, probing.

Bella snorted, playing dumb. "What are you talking about?"

Aiden stepped closer, lowering his voice. "Did she ever try to keep you sick? Give you medicines you didn't need?"

For a moment, something flickered across Bella's face, a crack in her armor, but she recovered quickly. Her expression hardened as she turned on her heel. "I'm done here."

She started to walk away, her pace quick, but Zoe called out, "Bella, we found evidence."

Bella froze mid-step. The wind picked up, tousling her hair. Slowly, she turned back around, her eyes wide, the defiance slipping away to reveal the raw fear. "What evidence?"

"Lily. Your mother was giving Lily medication she didn't need, which is why she fell sick so often. It was damaging her kidneys."

Bella's lower lip jutted out. "I don't know what to say."

"I'm assuming she did that to you too when you were younger? Is that why she began neglecting you and turned her attention to Lily?" Aiden asked.

"I'm a horrible sister." She shook her head, her face tortured.

"You can trust us," he said.

"Trust *you*?" she barked. "I can't trust anyone. I can't trust my own mother. And Lily... when you found her dead, for a second I was relieved. When you told me that she wasn't... hurt in any other way, I thought it was a good thing she got away from our mother. Because either our mother was going to inadvertently kill her, or she was going to end up damaged goods like me."

That's where the false bravado stemmed from. Bella felt unsafe at home and unable to trust her mother, so she had to craft this harsh, insensitive armor to keep everyone at bay. But inside she was hollow. True strength came from love and not loneliness, Zoe thought.

"When did you realize what your mom was doing?" Zoe asked.

"When she started doing it to Lily. That's when I started drawing parallels to how she used to do the same thing to me. And it all made sense."

"Did you confront her about it?"

"I couldn't." Her chest deflated. "I can't. I just... I know what she has, Agent Storm. I'm not stupid, I looked it up. But it's just too much to talk about it. All I want to do is graduate high school and leave this town."

"Why didn't you tell the police, Bella?" Zoe's words came out sharper than she intended. "If you knew she was doing the same to your baby sister, why didn't you call CPS?"

"Because she's my *mom!*" she cried, her voice breaking. Tears welled up, and for a second, she looked like a little girl, lost and hurt. "I don't expect you to understand. But just because I want to get away from her and I'm mad at her *all* the time doesn't mean I want to see her behind bars. I still love her. Even if she's incapable of loving me back. Now please, leave me alone. I can't help you."

Zoe curled her hands into a tight fist. She had to alert CPS, even if Bella didn't want the authorities involved. A message popped up on her phone and she exhaled a tense breath.

S: *Here is that creep John Doe's IP address and location.*

* * *

The towering evergreens created a thick canopy that blocked out much of the weak morning light. Zoe led the way, her boots sinking slightly into the damp, moss-covered ground with each step. The cold, wet air clung to their skin, the scent of pine and earth heavy in the mist that hung between the trees.

The team followed closely behind, their movements silent and deliberate. Travis was next to her, his boots squelching in the muddy forest floor and cold drizzle slicking his hair to his forehead.

"We're about twenty-five feet away." Zoe checked her phone as they closed in on the red dot. "Do you know these woods?"

Travis was eagerly scanning the rain-soaked, dripping branches. "Not as well as the rangers do. But I'm surprised something is happening here. Must be a new operation."

Zoe's breath fogged in front of her as she scanned the terrain, her sharp eyes searching for any sign of movement. "We need to interview Carly again."

His foot snapped a twig. "Why?"

"Scott found evidence of Munchausen by proxy."

"Scott?" he snapped. "What the hell is he doing working on this case? Defying orders?"

"This was before he was suspended." A white lie.

Travis narrowed his eyes but didn't push.

The shed loomed out of the mist, a dark silhouette against the towering pines, barely visible through the tangle of branches and fog. It looked ordinary enough at first glance, the tangle of wires snaking from beneath the structure and the faint glow of monitors inside, leading to a small satellite dish perched precariously on the roof.

She motioned with a gloved hand, signaling a halt. The team froze, crouching low behind the cover of a fallen log. They were close now. Her sharp eyes scanned the perimeter, catching the faint glimmer of lights through a cracked window. She gestured with two fingers, pointing at the entrance, then flicked her hand in a circular motion, directing the team to spread out and surround the shed.

After a brief moment, she nodded, and they moved again, slipping through the trees like shadows, the morning mist swallowing them whole as they advanced toward their destination. They spread out, each member taking up their position around the structure. Zoe crept up to the window, the glass fogged and streaked with dirt, and peered inside. Three men were hunched over a cluster of computers, their faces lit by the eerie blue glow of multiple screens. The room was a mess of wires, keyboards, and blinking lights, wires sprawled across the floor like vines, connecting to various machines she couldn't identify from her angle.

Her fingers tightened on her gun. No time to lose.

With a swift, powerful kick, she blasted the door open, splinters flying as the wood cracked under the impact. "Hands up! Now!" she barked, her voice cutting through the electronic hum like a whip. "Step away from the computers!"

For a fraction of a second, there was silence and stillness. And then the room exploded into chaos.

Before Zoe had time to register any faces, one of them withdrew a gun from his jacket and aimed it at her. A deafening shot rang out right next to her, striking the wiry man straight in the chest. He dropped to the floor.

Another man tried to climb out the window and make a run for it. Travis and the team converged on him and that's when the third man, who was in the corner, lunged at Zoe with a snarl, his body a blur of motion. Zoe barely had time to react before he slammed into her, driving her back into the wall. The impact knocked the wind out of her, but she didn't lose her grip. She twisted her body, throwing him off balance, and they crashed into a table, sending equipment clattering to the floor.

He came at her again, swinging wild punches, but she was faster. She ducked under his arm, landing a quick jab to his ribs, then followed up with an elbow to his jaw. He staggered, but only for a moment—then he was back, trying to grab her gun.

They struggled, locked in a brutal grapple, muscles straining as they fought for control.

Zoe felt his hand close around her wrist, trying to twist the gun from her grip. She gritted her teeth, slamming her knee into his gut with all the force she could muster. He grunted, doubling over, and she seized the moment. With a fierce yank, she freed her arm and spun him around, slamming his face into the wall. He groaned, stunned, and she didn't hesitate—she pinned him there, her gun pressed to the back of his head.

"Stay down!" she ordered, her voice ice-cold. He stopped struggling, breathing hard against the wall. "Gather up all the equipment!" she instructed the team.

With a harsh grip, she yanked his head back and looked at his face. Now that the adrenaline had receded, the familiar face triggered the recognition.

Sam Buster. One of Carly's Johns.

FIFTY

Sam Buster already had a criminal record but nothing in his rap sheet was as disturbing as his current crime. The brute of a man was pumped full of steroids and fury because deep down he knew he was scum.

He'd been charged in the past with battery, assault with a deadly weapon, and resisting arrest. His violent outbursts had landed him in prison more than once—three years for aggravated assault, two years for illegal firearms possession, and a few shorter stints for parole violations. The charges stacked up over the years: domestic violence, disturbing the peace, even one count of witness intimidation that had mysteriously been dropped.

Zoe pressed an ice pack to her jaw. Luckily she hadn't broken it.

"He's a ticking time bomb." Aiden appeared by her side, looking at him in the interrogation room.

"Did we get anything from the computers?"

"Terri is still looking into it but Sam Buster is John Doe. We found evidence of that. Travis is working on the other guy you captured, but it seems like Buster was the leader. Need me in there?"

"Nah. He's a punk. I got this."

As Zoe barged into the interrogation room, she caught a reflection of her face in the two-way mirror. It wasn't the bruise on the right side of her jaw that startled her—it was her expression. Hard eyes, stone-faced and *so done*.

"How's that jaw doing?" Sam sneered, revealing his chipped tooth.

She sat back, nonchalant. "Do you know what people do to people like you in prison?"

He locked his jaw. "I don't hurt children if that's what you're insinuating."

"We know you are John Doe offering to sell pictures of the victims to people. Your associate is with the chief of Harborwood PD right now giving his statement."

Sam stroked his jaw. "Like I said, I don't hurt children."

"Then what exclusive, unseen pictures are you selling?"

"It's not that!" He sat back in his chair, appalled.

There was a sharp knock on the door. Terri strolled in and handed Zoe a file, whispering in her ear, "We just started retrieving some of the images from their computers."

When she left, Zoe braced herself and cleaved out whatever emotions were stirring inside her. It was better to rip off the Band-Aid and get this over with. She flipped through the file until she came to the collection of pictures.

"What's this?" she said.

"See?" Sam said. "I told you, you got this all wrong!"

The pictures were of Lily, Tara, and Lucy. Their bodies arranged in different poses in different locations. One picture had zombies in it and one was in a submarine with sharks. "The hell is this?"

Sam brooded and crossed his arms. Zoe could sense he

didn't like being bossed around, but she didn't have time for this.

"Pictures don't have to be sexual for their distribution to be illegal. Violent pictures such as these violate many laws include obscenity laws." She forced him to look at them. "And since your subject matter are underage girls, I can guarantee you'll be going to jail for a long time."

He wiped his nose. "There's a market for people on the dark web who are fascinated by people, especially kids who are either dead or gone missing, and enjoy violence. For them, it's art. Since they're dead it's not harassment or defamation—"

"It still is, you asshole," she hissed. "They have families."

He took a strained breath, controlling his anger. "Like I said, no one was harmed. We just create pictures using AI that will sell."

"You're going away for a long time." She closed the file and pushed the chair back.

"Wait."

"What?"

"I know something." He licked his lips. "About Carly and Lucy that can help your case."

She drummed her fingers on the table, pretending to consider what he was saying. Was he lying to get out of this? But he was close to Carly. "What is it?"

"First promise me leniency." He pointed a finger at her.

She suppressed a grin. "Sure, I promise."

He assessed her but she kept a straight face before he gave in with a sigh. "Now Carly doesn't want to be a mom, okay? Whenever I was over, Carly would make sure Lucy wasn't in the house. But there were a lot of times she couldn't. And Lucy... is a chatty, active, and nosy kid. Always asking questions. Always running around. Never sitting still in a room. You can't just place her in front of a television and hope she'll be busy for the hour. Carly used to complain to me that her... business was suffering."

"Her prostitution business."

"That's right. She couldn't always go to her client's place because who would she leave Lucy with? She can't afford babysitters and she doesn't have any family. So she would always have clients over at her house. It was easier that way too. But most clients aren't comfortable with a loud and curious child when they're there to bang her mother. Also Lucy was at that stage where she's needy and full of energy and Carly just didn't have the bandwidth to handle her. One time Lucy was sick. She had the flu so she was in bed for a few days. Carly told me those days were the best days of her life."

A hollowness opened inside Zoe's chest. She knew what Carly had been doing. But the confirmation still made her ears want to bleed.

"She said it would be great if... Lucy stayed sick most of the time. She told me she was giving her this tea that kept Lucy at low energy most of the time."

"Did she say anything else about this tea? What was in it?"

He puckered his lips and shrugged. "No. But I remember her taking her to the hospital because Lucy was getting *really* sick. She told me it was because she was giving her too much of that tea... Now can I leave? This information has to be worth something, right? She was poisoning her own kid!"

It was something else that Zoe had latched on to. Carly had taken Lucy to the hospital.

"You can't leave. You're under arrest."

"We had a deal!" he screeched in protest, his bulky body shaking in ragged breaths.

"I lied and you're an idiot." She left the room, still buzzing with the revelation.

What if Lily and Tara had been taken to the hospital too? That could be the connection they had been searching for. Someone at the hospital would know—someone who decided to take matters into their own hands and dispense his twisted sense of justice.

* * *

The automatic doors whooshed closed behind her as Zoe approached the front desk, where a tired-looking receptionist tapped away at her computer.

"I'm looking for three patients who might have been brought in recently. Lily Baker, Tara Bennett, and Lucy Robinson," Zoe said.

The receptionist looked up, her fingers still hovering over the keyboard. "I'm sorry, ma'am, but I can't give out patient information unless you're family."

Zoe flattened her mouth. She didn't have time for court orders. She leaned in slightly, lowering her voice. "I'm with the FBI. I need to know if they were brought in and when."

The receptionist hesitated, her eyes flicking to Zoe's badge, which she held out just long enough to confirm her credentials. Reluctantly, the woman began typing again, her eyes scanning the screen. After a moment, she nodded. "The names... it's those girls, isn't it?" Her eyes turned glassy. "The dead ones in the woods."

"Yes, that's why this is important. Please help us."

She nodded, understanding. "There is no record of Tara Bennett checking in, at least in the last six months, but Lily Baker came in about three months ago and Lucy Robinson a month ago. They were both assigned to the same doctor—Dr. Parsons."

Zoe's heart skipped a beat. She remembered Dr. Parsons from when Scott was admitted after being attacked outside the police station. He was well into his seventies, with a raspy smoker's voice that somehow didn't match his kind, grandfatherly demeanor.

"Where can I find Dr. Parsons?" she asked, a slight edge to her voice.

The receptionist pointed down the hall. "He should be making his rounds in the east wing."

Zoe didn't waste a second. She turned on her heel and marched down the corridor, her eyes scanning the sea of white coats. Finally, she spotted him—a stooped man with thinning white hair, talking softly to a nurse. His hands moved gently, guiding the nurse's attention to a chart.

"Dr. Parsons," Zoe called out.

He looked up, and a warm smile spread across his weathered face. "Oh, I remember you. The girl who likes hospitals. How's your friend doing? Scott, that was his name, wasn't it?"

Zoe forced a polite smile. "He's doing great even though someone injured his face *again*. But I need to talk to you about Lily and Lucy. The names are familiar to you?"

Dr. Parsons's smile faded slightly, and he glanced around as if to ensure no one else was listening. "Yes... those girls were in the news. Lily was killed, right?"

"Do you remember why they were brought in?"

He scratched his head, digging through his memory. "Lucy was more recent. She had presented with nausea and diarrhea. Her mother said she had bad takeout so we just put her on electrolytes and sent her away. But Lily..." He blinked vehemently, his mouth moving even though no words came out.

"What about Lily?"

"She had an electrolyte imbalance. We treated her but we found diuretic in her system. Her mother said Lily had accidentally consumed them but..." His voice trailed off.

"But what?"

"Something felt wrong. I don't know what. Call it an instinct but it just felt off."

"How?"

His hand clasped the railing of the staircase to balance himself. "It just reminded me of something that happened a long time ago, kid. I'm seventy-four years old. I've seen a lot of things in this hospital."

"What was it?" she pressed, softening her voice.

Horror crossed his face. "It was over forty years ago. I was in residency. But there was a case that I was on. Two kids presented on different occasions with symptoms ranging from hallucinations and mood swings to diarrhea and respiratory distress. Although of varying ages, they were all under ten years old. It raised a red flag because they were siblings. It made me suspect that something was happening in their home."

"Munchausen by proxy."

He nodded grimly. "I talked to the doctor in charge and she agreed. There was enough evidence for us to call the authorities."

"And did you?"

"We did." His voice cracked and he coughed like a broken engine until Zoe had to pat his back to soothe him. "We shouldn't have."

"Why?"

"Because they were found dead, hanging from the ceiling. The parents killed them as soon as they realized that they were being investigated."

Zoe was stunned. The image tried to force itself into her head but she pushed it away, erecting a giant wall around her sanity. "They *killed* them."

"Maybe that's why somewhere along the line I stopped questioning as much. Maybe subconsciously I look away when I shouldn't." Parsons's lips quivered. "Did I fail Lily? Should I have reported that? Would she still be alive if I had?"

She touched his arm lightly and lied. "No, there's nothing you could have done."

He seemed to believe it, perhaps it was easier that way. He took out a handkerchief from his pocket and dabbed his forehead as pink spots dotted all over his skin.

"Who knows about that story?" Zoe asked.

"A lot of people. Almost everyone in the hospital at the time. People talk. I probably told some of my friends and family about it over the years."

"Is there anyone who has been asking about this or Munchausen syndrome lately?"

He shrugged helplessly. "Not that I know of. It's been a while since I recounted this story. Not an easy thing to talk about."

When his pager started beeping, he excused himself, almost bumping into a bonsai tree on his way. Zoe watched his aged, frail frame disappear around the corner, taking away the hope that was barely flickering inside her.

Her mind raced. Lily's and Lucy's paths intersected at this very hospital. She scanned the workers around her—not just doctors and nurses but also janitors and administrative staff. These were the people who saw death every day, watched families get ripped apart, heard soul-shredding tears. Zoe knew the discipline it took to keep the ugliness of the world at bay. How it spread like a nasty infection, killing morals first and empathy next.

Or maybe it was another patient. Someone who had come into the hospital to get treated for hereditary hemochromatosis.

Zoe got a call from Aiden. "Any news?"

"Terri tracked down the buyer of that toy from the seller on eBay. It's Connor, Regina's campaign manager."

FIFTY-ONE

"You've been a little different these past couple of sessions," Aiden noted.

She shrugged. "I... don't think so."

They stared at each other. A battle of his scrutinizing gaze and her rehearsed cheerfulness.

"You've been smiling too much," he said accusingly.

"I'm a happy person."

Aiden sighed and closed his notepad. "Storm, if I did anything to... offend or hurt you, I apologize. But please just be honest with me. There's no need for a show."

She ground her molars despite keeping her voice light. "I'm being honest. You did nothing wrong. I'm just in a good place and want to get through this."

His eyes lingered on her for the longest time, but she was too good at this. He didn't believe her. "Okay... we're almost done, we don't have much more to go over."

"Let's do it." She smiled as she rued the day she opened up enough to give him a peek of the carnage of her past that she carried inside her.

* * *

Zoe had never lived in a nice house. All those years hopping around with Rachel, they lived in modest homes in remote neighborhoods. Rachel used to love greenery and storms and the ocean. But they always lived in dry, desert towns.

The next day, Zoe went to pay Regina a visit at her home. Regina lived in a two-story house with a warm beige exterior surrounded by a lush garden bursting with color. The large windows were framed by dark shutters, and the front door was painted a deep navy blue. Zoe had a dream that one day she would retire in a house like this. One day she would put down roots and not just own a place but be owned by it.

She knocked on the door, and a rattled, overworked intern who hadn't combed his hair and had an earpiece answered. "Is Connor here? FBI." She flashed her badge.

The man's eyes widened and he sighed. "He isn't here anymore. Why do you think this place is going down the dumps?"

"Who is it?" Regina bellowed, and the intern startled like a rabbit caught in headlights. "Oh, Agent Storm!" Regina appeared in the doorway, not a single hair out of place and not a single wrinkle on her purple pantsuit. "Postpone the next interview," she ordered the intern, who hurried away.

Behind Regina, Zoe could see the whirlwind of activity—people shouting and moving rapidly, dodging each other, phones ringing and keyboards clattering.

"How can I help you?" Regina shut the door behind her, cutting off the sound of chaos. "Some quiet feels good. Easier to chat here."

"I'm looking for Connor. Is he not here?"

Regina pulled back her shoulders. "No. I fired him."

"What? Why?"

She forced a polite smile but it was too tight. "Many

reasons. Biggest being that he was doing things behind my back. I couldn't trust him anymore so I got rid of him. It's why we are in a flux right now. But we'll manage. I'm interviewing some promising candidates for the position."

"What did he do exactly?"

"He was siphoning money from my accounts," she said. "I shouldn't have given him that much control over my affairs."

Zoe mulled it over—Regina was born for public office, always composed and quick on her feet. But whatever she was saying wasn't beyond the realms of disbelief. Connor had a temper, and there was a callousness to him. "We are looking for him. Do you know where he is? He wasn't home."

She shrugged. "No idea. The last thing he told me was that he'd gotten involved with some shady casino owner, which was why he was stealing money from me. Why are you looking for him?"

"He might have some information for us. Do you know where he might have gone? Any place he mentioned?"

Regina thought for a moment and then said, "He used to mention something about an old family cottage. I haven't been there but maybe he's up there?"

* * *

"Do you ever have a day where everything just feels weird?" Zoe asked Scott as they parked at the edge of the woods. His suspension was finally over. The forest was so choked with trees that no vehicle could enter.

"No... should I?" Scott asked, baffled.

Zoe killed the engine and sucked the last remnants of her milkshake. But it didn't taste the same. And she had a theory—something bad was going to happen if milkshakes tasted off. It was a complicated, long-winded link between her instincts and taste buds.

"Maybe it's anxiety. The case is coming to an end." Scott's breaths formed little clouds as they ventured into the woods.

There was a harsher chill in the air. The trees loomed over them, their branches heavy with water, creating a gloomy canopy that seemed to absorb the fading daylight.

"So Connor has motive to kill Tara. Not only would it get Logan Bennett off his back but it would also create a controversy he could leverage against Mayor Hicks and cast Regina as the hero this town needs," Zoe summarized.

"And he targeted Lucy and Lily, two victims who had nothing to do with him and Regina, to deflect any suspicion. He created the whole thing with the ropes and the notes so that we'd think we were dealing with a serial killer."

The wind whipped through the trees, sending cold droplets splashing onto their faces. Zoe's boots sunk into the mire as she hopped forward, trying to avoid the tangled roots and slush of leaves and mud.

"But it can't be a coincidence that Lucy and Lily were both victims of Munchausen by proxy." He smacked a branch out of the way as they pushed through the maze of crowded trees.

"He must have figured it out from the hospital. Might be related to someone who works there who told him about Lucy and Lily."

The cottage came into view. The towering pines began to thin, revealing a faint glow in the distance. The structure appeared old and weather-beaten, its wooden shingles darkened by years of exposure to the elements, the windows fogged up from the cold.

"Think he's been squatting here?" Scott asked.

"It's his family cottage. No one has heard from Connor and his phone has been switched off."

"It's also the perfect place to keep Lucy captive."

Zoe knocked firmly on the front door, the sound muffled by the pelting rain. She prayed that Connor was there. What if that casino owner he owed money to had gotten to him first?

After a tense moment, Connor opened the door. His face was gaunt and pallid, like he had been surviving on sparse amounts of food.

"Connor!" Scott said firmly. "We need to talk."

Connor was like a scared animal. There was a mad desperation in his eyes, like he would bite anyone who came close. For a fraction of a second, fear flashed in his eyes and then he attempted to slam the door shut.

Zoe's hand shot out, catching the door just in time. "Connor, don't do this!"

"Not so fast!" Scott said, forcing the door open wider, as they pushed their way inside.

Panic-stricken, Connor fled, bumping into old furniture and antiques that cluttered the space. He flung open the back door, and a blast of cold wind and rain surged into the room. He stumbled into the storm, slipping on the slick ground as he tried to escape.

The forest outside was now a dark, swirling mass of shadows and rain. Zoe hesitated for a moment. She was never one to be scared of the elements but the wilderness of this place had gotten under her skin. When Scott shot past her, she followed suit, ignoring her fears.

Her vision was blurry in the downpour. She could make out the faint outline of Scott ahead of her, weaving through the drooping branches that were blowing in their faces. He reached out, grabbing Connor's jacket and yanking him back into the mud. Connor fought back, swinging an arm wildly, but Scott ducked and tackled him to the ground. They crashed into the muck, mud splattering everywhere.

Connor tried to wriggle free. He slammed his head into Scott's who fell back. Zoe lunged at him, but he picked up a rock and swung it into the side of Zoe's head. She ducked but wasn't quick enough—he wasn't able to knock her out but he drew blood. Her knees softened and she also dropped on the ground, mildly disoriented. He ran past them back to the cottage.

"Are you okay?" Scott asked.

Zoe was on all fours. She brought her hand to her temple and inspected it. It was covered in blood, but the rain fell on it with such speed and force that it quickly washed away, mingling with the soil underneath. "Go after him. I'm fine. He's heading back to the cottage."

He hesitated just for a moment and then hurried away. She called after him to be careful but her voice was drowned out by the thunder.

Zoe got to her feet slowly and steadied herself. Did she have a concussion? Her vision rippled and she blinked several times against the battering rain for it to return to normal. Her hair was matted to her scalp and she was chilled to the bone, barely able to feel her face. When her vision stabilized, she spotted something in the shadows. Another figure in the distance. Lightning lit up her surroundings and she saw Rachel.

A blink of the eye and she was gone.

But it propelled Zoe to head back to find Connor and Scott. When she reached the cottage, the back door was wide open. She withdrew her Glock from her waistband and cautiously entered, trying not to slip.

It was eerily silent and still. She squinted for a better view but the only light came from a dying fire in the fireplace and the occasional flash of lightning. She moved her arm, aiming the gun in the dark corners. For a moment she thought she was alone.

But then a bullet whizzed past her and a hand came around her ankle, yanking her down.

"He's got a gun." Scott was taking cover behind a sofa, his

hands secured around a gun. "I only have one bullet left and by my count he has two."

"I got a full round." Zoe breathed hard. "Can we call for backup?"

"No reception."

"You won't pin this on me!" Connor yelled from across the room, hiding behind an armchair.

Zoe thought fast. They could avoid bloodshed. "Connor, we know you bought the toy from eBay that was found close to Tara's crime scene. You can't deny this anymore."

"Regina made me do it!" Connor cried out, desperate. "I'll testify against her. She wanted to cut off Logan Bennett after the campaign money started to dry up."

"Regina has given us evidence of how you were siphoning off money from the campaign, and we found your communications with that casino owner," Scott retorted.

"But if you have a different version of events, we're willing to listen. But not like this," Zoe countered. Turning to Scott, she whispered, "We have to make him feel safe."

"I don't trust you!" Connor's voice broke, like he was crying.

"Where is Lucy, Connor? Hand her back to us and we can talk about a deal," Zoe said.

"I don't have Lucy! I didn't take her! I didn't want to kill Tara. But... I couldn't see any other way." He started wailing.

Zoe and Scott exchanged a puzzled glance. "What do you mean, Connor? You didn't take Lucy?"

"No! I didn't kill Lily either. When the news broke that Lily had been found in the woods, it was the perfect opportunity for me to use that to make Regina win. We needed to get rid of Logan so it was killing two birds with one stone."

"How did you replicate the crime scene and MO with such accuracy?" Scott said. "We didn't release the details to the public."

"I have a source! A uniform. Terri Walters. She fed me enough information."

"Damn it," Zoe hissed under her breath. Scott shook his head in disappointment. She connected the dots—that's why there were so many hesitation marks around Tara's case, why the note was printed instead of handwritten and why the stuffed animal was brand-new—details he got right but not completely right. "Okay, Connor. I'm going to stand up, all right? Don't shoot me. Let's talk face to face."

Scott gripped her arm. "What are you doing?"

"We need this stalemate to end." She tucked the gun back into her jeans but turned off the safety in case she needed it. Her knees shaking, she stood up with her hands in the air and her heart in her throat.

Connor peeked from over the armchair, the top of his head visible. "Tell your partner to drop his gun too."

"I can't do that, Connor."

"Are you going to arrest me?"

"Connor, we'll take you to the station and take your statement and then after that—"

"No! No! No!" he cried. "I'm not going anywhere. You need to let me disappear."

"We can make sure that that casino owner doesn't bother you again. I'm offering you the chance to do the right thing. I know you feel guilty for killing that little girl." Zoe's courage was faltering the longer she stood like this in a vulnerable position. "Isn't that better than living your life on the run always looking over your shoulder?"

Something flashed in his eyes. A cruelty. "But it's better than going to prison."

In a swift motion, his arm reached over the top of the armchair, gun in hand. He pulled the trigger, a deafening blast filling the room. Zoe's hand instinctively went for her weapon, but before she could react, Scott shoved her aside, throwing her to the floor.

He loomed above her but his hands had gone slack next to him, his mouth slightly parted, his eyes rolling to the back of his head.

"Scott!" Her voice tore through the night.

He collapsed on the floor just as she sprang to her feet. There was a noise, squelching footsteps, grazing armchair and the door opening. Connor was running away. Without hesitating for a second, she pulled out her gun and shot him in the back of the head.

He stilled for a second and then slumped down the door.

But Zoe didn't care about him. She attended to Scott who lay on the floor motionless. Blood oozed out of his chest, turning his white shirt dark.

"Scott!" She shook him, opened his eyes. "Can you hear me?" Tears raced down her cheeks unchecked, her heart drumming against her ribs. "Scott!"

She checked his pulse. It was thready. His eyes fluttered open, a glimmer of hope sparking within her. But then, with a labored breath, he slipped away into the darkness.

Zoe froze, her mind struggling to process the reality. The thunder roared around her relentlessly. Scott was gone.

FIFTY-TWO

Zoe had no idea how she got here. She stumbled through the darkened woods as the rain pounded against the canopy of trees, each drop like a drumbeat on her skin. The wind howled, twisting the trees into grotesque shapes that seemed to reach out for her.

She could hear it—an ominous presence—breathing heavily, chasing her. The shadow moved silently between the trees, its shape barely discernible but ever-present, closing in with each passing second. Panic surged through her as she tried to navigate through the swirling darkness, her heart pounding in her chest.

She burst through the underbrush into a small clearing and froze in terror, almost bumping into someone. There was just enough moonlight to reveal who it was.

Scott.

He was drenched, his face lacking the brutal scar that ran down the middle. He looked exactly like he did when she first met him. Back when she had no idea that this is how their story would end, how he was destined to die in front of her.

"Scott!" She ran to him, realizing it was a dream. A terrible

dream designed to twist that knife deeper into her heart, until all she felt was guilt.

Scott's gaze met hers, his eyes filled with a profound sadness. "Zoe, we've been betrayed."

Before she could respond, Zoe felt herself being yanked from behind. And then she was plunged into a different scene so quickly that she got whiplash.

She found herself in a familiar place—her old house, bathed in the soft, warm light of a late afternoon sun. The storm was gone, leaving behind dripping leaves. She was standing by the window, looking out. It was rare for it to storm like this here.

A reflection appeared in the window—Rachel stood behind her, holding a dish rag. Zoe felt like she was drowning. She couldn't breathe. But she didn't turn round either. This was a memory.

"Too bad that it stopped raining." Rachel's lips twisted in regret.

"You like storms," Zoe said.

She smiled. "So much so that I wish I could name myself after them."

* * *

Zoe dragged her feet into the station with a throbbing headache. Aiden was right behind her. It had been a few hours since she'd managed to call for backup in the woods and was escorted to the hospital. She stood in the center, observing everyone—patrol officers and uniform cops all standing subdued, unsure of what to say. She swore the walls were closing in, having absorbed the tragedy and buckling under its weight.

Aiden had driven her back from the hospital. It was a quiet ride. She could sense he was trying to say something but would never have guessed that even shrinks could be speechless. She almost bumped into the corner of a desk and Aiden's hands came around her, freezing before they could make contact.

"I'm not fragile," she said tightly.

"No, but you just watched someone who was like a friend get killed," he murmured.

There it was. Scott was dead. Each time she blinked, she saw red liquid fanning out, dousing his clothes and skin before he was lost somewhere in it.

Her eyes scanned the despondent faces, looking for that one face. But when her eyes landed on Scott, her heart sank in her chest. He was talking to a patrol officer, giving him instructions from the looks of it. When he saw Zoe approaching, he raised a hand to wave at her.

She raised her hand as well. But just as she was about to make contact, a figure brushed past her, momentarily blocking her view. As the person moved away, Zoe realized that it was Travis speaking with the patrol officer, not Scott.

She turned to Aiden. "Look. You were right. There were two killers. The message left with Tara and the hesitation marks. Except the two killers weren't acting in collusion; one was a copycat. I know you probably want to go all shrink-y on me and talk about this. But now's not the time. I'm not in the mood."

"I'm not asking anything from you, Storm." His smile was forlorn.

She headed toward her office. As she neared, she saw Terri hunched over her desk, talking to someone on the phone.

Zoe stared at her—an earnest, hardworking woman who had been working with Scott for years. She waited to feel anger and spite, remembering Connor's words about how she was his source, feeding him information from the inside. But Zoe was too tired, too numb. It was like the grief was tugging at her skin, pulling it down.

"Terri," Zoe said, her voice breaking the silence with a sharp edge. "We need to talk."

Terri looked up, her eyes swollen and red from crying. "Agent Storm," she said, her voice quivering.

Her gaze was hard and unyielding. "Were you slipping information to Connor?" When Terri opened her mouth, Zoe raised a hand to interrupt her. "Don't even think about lying. Connor told us before he died."

Terri's face fell further, and she took a ragged breath. "I— I didn't think it would come to this," she sobbed. "I just needed the money."

"He *murdered* a girl."

Tears streamed down her cheeks as she struggled to find the words. "I didn't know that! I swear!" Her outburst drew some looks. "He told me he just needed to stay ahead of the other news channels for strategy. For Regina's campaign. He would just ask for details. I didn't think anything of it."

Zoe's anger flared. "And when Tara went missing and was found dead, you didn't think anything of it then?"

"I didn't. Please believe me." The corners of her mouth pulled down. "I have a kid too. I would never... The note at the first crime scene suggested there would be more victims. I thought it was the killer."

"And the differences between the crime scenes? That didn't ring a bell?" Zoe's voice climbed up a notch.

She flinched, looking down at her feet. "I... I didn't make the connection, Agent Storm. Like you said, I thought it was the killer improving."

She broke down in tears, but Zoe didn't budge. There were too many people dead, people who now only existed in photographs and memories. "I had made it clear to everyone not to leak details outside. *This* is why. How do you plan to live with yourself? Because of you, Scott is dead!"

Travis quickly interrupted them. "What's going on? Agent Storm?"

But Zoe's eyes were pinned on Terri, undeterred by her crying. "Terri leaked case details to Connor in exchange for money. That's why Connor was able to stage the crime scene and leave that note when he murdered Tara."

A series of gasps. Eyes filled with accusation and disbelief.

The shock on Travis's face was palpable. He cleared his throat. "Terri, is this true?"

Terri nodded solemnly. But Zoe kept glaring at her. It didn't feel enough. No matter how many tears Terri shed and how red she turned, it wasn't enough for Zoe. Her right eye twitched. An itch grew stronger. The desire to scratch it ran up her body. The carnal need to right a wrong, to dispense justice.

Terri's hands trembled as she tried to compose herself. "I swear, Chief, I didn't want anyone to get hurt," she said, her voice breaking. "Connor made it sound harmless. He just needed some inside info to boost Regina's image. I never imagined this is what his plan was all along."

"When did this start?"

"He contacted me a few weeks ago," she said. "He offered me a lot of money, and I—I was desperate. I didn't think it would go beyond PR stunts. I just gave him some details about the ongoing investigations. I messed up. I didn't see the bigger picture. Connor seemed so convincing, and I needed the money. I never imagined it would lead to this. Please, you have to believe me. I didn't want Scott or anyone to get hurt."

Travis sighed. "Terri, come into my office. We need to discuss your future. And Agent Storm," he said, looking at Zoe who was still quaking with rage, "focus on finding Lucy. The clock is ticking."

Before Terri followed Travis into his office, she turned back to Zoe. "Scott was important to me. He was like a brother. What

I did is going to mess me up for life, but if there's anything I can do to help, tell me. I don't care about anything anymore but atonement. Please." With that, she went into Travis's office.

Zoe didn't want to think about Terri. Loneliness was cold and brutal. With Scott dead and Terri rightfully fired, it dawned on her that she lacked allies in a new town. She shrugged off her jacket and recruited more patrol officers to update her on the latest reports from the rangers and anonymous tips.

Hours bled into each other and Zoe felt like a rock was sitting on her chest. Lucy's picture was pinned to her desk. Where was she?

In the waiting area, Carly sat with her knee bobbing and shredded lips. She chewed on her jagged nails and glanced around waiting for some news. She came in every day and left after sunset. Her throat worked overtime, always swallowing and taking strained breaths. She was losing it. Every day that insanity inside her became a little more visible. Zoe watched her from a distance, thinking back to what Bella had said about still loving her mother.

The CPS had been alerted after Sam Buster's statement. But with Lucy still missing, the CPS were on hold, ready to swoop in when she was found alive and well.

If.

Zoe took a break from reading one bad report after another. The suspicious man who Lily recognized was still a mystery. And Lucy's friends and neighbors hadn't reported any man lurking or Lucy mentioning anyone.

She went to get some water and paused next to Scott's desk. It still hadn't been cleared. Her throat closed as her fingers grazed his chair. His desk was sparse, only the things he needed—things still covered in him. One coffee mug with a sailor on it. A true resident of Harborwood. A rueful smile curled up her lips as she flipped open a diary. He had scribbled notes in there—reminders of leads to follow up, affidavits to write, and random ideas.

Her hand hovered over a page.

Lucy. Check dumpster contents.

Zoe frowned. He hadn't mentioned this to her. Was this a random train of thought? Did he get around to it?

She asked a patrol officer she recognized as assisting in the case. "Were there dumpsters where Lucy was taken? Communal ones."

He contemplated her question. "Yes, ma'am. They are maintained by the municipal waste management services."

"Was anything collected from them when Lucy went missing?"

"Yes, Detective Cohen told us to. It was a surprising request, but he was being thorough. It's in the evidence room. Not sure if anyone has looked into it."

"Take me to it."

He led Zoe down a narrow, dimly lit hallway with low ceilings and walls adorned with yellowing posters warning against various misdemeanors. The sound of their footsteps echoed on the cold concrete floor as they approached a heavy, metal door at the end of the corridor.

The patrol officer unlocked the door and pushed it open, revealing the evidence room. It was a cramped, windowless space filled with metal shelves stacked with brown evidence boxes and a few locked cabinets along the walls. The air inside was stale, with a faint scent of dust and old paper that tickled the insides of Zoe's nose.

"Here we are, ma'am," the officer said, moving toward a corner where several large, black trash bags were piled up haphazardly. He reached down and grabbed two of the bags, hoisting them up with a grunt. "These are the ones you asked for."

Zoe slipped on her gloves. The weight of them suggested they were full, and as she set them down on the nearest table, the distinct, unpleasant smell of rotting garbage began to waft from the seams.

"Would you like some assistance?" he asked.

"No, thank you." She wasn't in the mood. She needed to be left alone today.

She pulled open the first bag, and the stench hit her—an overpowering mix of decaying food, sour milk, and the acrid tang of something chemical. She wrinkled her nose but didn't hesitate, plunging her gloved hands into the bag. The contents were a chaotic jumble: crumpled fast food wrappers, soggy coffee grounds, and bits of unidentifiable sludge that stuck to her gloves. She turned over each piece, inspecting it carefully, ignoring the way the slimy, putrid mess clung to her fingers.

Anything that would stand out. She wanted Scott's instincts to turn out to be right. It made her proud how extra careful he was. He didn't deserve to die, not like that, and he certainly didn't deserve the train wreck of his last few days.

Zoe reached deeper into the bag, sifting through more debris—broken glass, twisted metal, a tangle of hair that made her grimace. Nothing seemed out of the ordinary, just the usual filth one would expect from a dumpster.

She wasn't ready to give up. Not yet. Her hand pulled out what looked like an empty package. It was hollow but Zoe stopped, noticing something on it. It was a phlebotomy kit. The outer packaging contained information on what to expect inside —needles, collection tubes, alcohol swabs. She studied it for any information on the recipient name or address but the package had been torn. Stuck to it was a manual with details on how to draw blood.

The supplier information was on it though. *Harborwood Central Pharmacy*.

Zoe's mind raced. Phlebotomy kit. This was something that

could be used for the treatment of hereditary hemochromatosis. Was this a coincidence? What if the killer had discarded this? What if he lived near Lucy?

FIFTY-THREE

Zoe could feel the dampness of the night clinging to her skin, her clothes sticking uncomfortably to her body. The sky was a deep, inky black, with only a few stars peeking through. The neighborhood was quiet, save for the constant chorus of crickets chirping from the overgrown lawns that lined the narrow, cracked sidewalk. The houses here were old, their paint peeling and rusted bikes leaning against sagging porches.

She paused for a moment at the foot of the steps, glancing around the empty street, then climbed the steps to the front door. Was this the best idea? She was still livid, feeling that wrath coursing through her body.

She knocked thrice. For a moment, there was no response, just the persistent chirping of the crickets and the faint rustle of leaves in the distance. Then, the door creaked open, and Terri appeared in the doorway, her face lit by the weak glow from inside.

She looked different out of uniform. Her hair, usually in a tight bun, cascaded around her shoulders. "Agent Storm? What are you doing here?"

"I heard you lost your job."

Her nostrils flared. "Yeah. Can't say I didn't deserve it. Internal Affairs might get involved."

"Did you mean it when you said you would do anything to redeem yourself?"

"Yes." A spark of hope. "Please give me chance."

Zoe had taken a few hours to cool down before deciding that Terri's remorse was genuine and she had been truly naïve in her dealings with Connor. Zoe needed someone to step out of line for this one. "The outer packaging of a phlebotomy kit was retrieved from a communal dumpster in Lucy's neighborhood." She showed Terri a picture of it on her phone. "It doesn't contain the recipient's name and address but it does have information on the supplier."

Terri nodded. "You think someone in the neighborhood is using phlebotomy kits to treat their condition?"

"Possibly. It could be nothing. But it needs to be followed up on. Now privacy laws and HIPAA are a bitch to get around. If I file a court order to get a list of all the people who have been ordering this kit from that pharmacy, the chances of a judge signing that are slim, especially considering phlebotomy kits can be used for other cases than the specific genetic condition we're looking for."

"And with Lucy's life hanging in the balance we don't have time to test out that theory."

"Exactly." Zoe locked eyes with her. "Now it would be great if someone could get into the pharmacy's records to get the recipient's name and address. Someone on the outside who is willing to take a risk and doesn't have much to lose."

Terri squared her shoulders. "I understand." Zoe turned to walk away when Terri called out, "Are you going to the funeral?"

Her chest tightened. "Yes. You?"

"No, I think I just found a better way to honor Scott."

* * *

The sky wept as mourners gathered beneath a canopy of dark clouds, the steady drizzle soaking through their black coats. The cemetery was a sea of glistening headstones, the rain drumming softly against the polished granite, merging with the tears of those gathered to say their final goodbyes.

Zoe and Aiden stood at the edge of the crowd. Her hands clenched around a small bouquet of white lilies. The flowers drooped under the weight of the rain, their petals slick and fragile. She didn't even know if he liked lilies, or any flowers. It filled her with sadness that she didn't know much about him and yet she was there for the worst moments of his life.

Aiden's hands were clasped in front of him. He hung his head low, his eyes closed. Was he saying a prayer?

She stared at the closed casket and an indescribable feeling overcame her.

She looked at Travis standing on the other side of the casket. His eyes were bloodshot, the edges smeared with tears as he stared at the casket with a mix of horror and disbelief. Next to him was Carly, sitting on a chair, her eyes downcast and face devoid of any expression. Zoe didn't recognize anyone else. But Scott was a born and bred Harborwood resident and despite the backlash the police were getting for handling the case, several people had shown up, including Mayor Hicks and Regina.

The rabbi's voice carried over the sound of the rain as he recited some words of comfort.

Zoe had lost count of how many times she'd heard those words, how many funerals she had attended over the years.

The casket was a simple, elegant box of dark wood, now streaked with rain. She didn't know Scott very well but she knew he would like this design—simple and no nonsense, like him. It rested above the open grave, a final resting place, soon to be hidden from the world. The pallbearers, their faces drawn with grief, waited for the signal to lower it, their hands gripping the straps that would guide it down.

A gust of wind whipped through the cemetery, tugging at the edges of the mourners' coats. She pulled her coat tighter around herself, but the cold seemed to seep into her bones. The memory of Scott bleeding to death transpired in her mind. She stared at her fingers, clenching and unclenching them, still feeling his gooey, sticky blood on them.

The family followed suit, each dropping a handful of earth, the soft thud of soil on wood blending with the rain.

"I'm going to stay behind and pay my respects to his family," Aiden whispered. "Do you want to say anything to them?"

Her eyes flickered to the aging man with a walking stick, probably thinking it should be him in a casket, not his son, and a young woman sniffling next to him—Scott's sister. The thought of talking to them made her chest contract.

"I can't. I'm sorry. I... can we just stay here for a minute?"

"Y-yeah." He couldn't hide his surprise.

Zoe was too tired and stifled from the heaviness. She dropped her head to his shoulder, just resting there, not caring if this was crossing some professional boundary. Vaguely, she heard his breath hitch, like he wasn't expecting this. But then he relaxed and shuffled closer, leaning into her. She closed her eyes and let the contact comfort her, let the sadness wash over her like water, trying not to drown in it.

They didn't say anything to each other. And after a minute or so, Zoe walked away.

She trudged across the rain-slicked parking lot, her heels sloshing through the puddles that had formed in the wake of the morning's deluge. She barely noticed the icy bite of the rain against her cheeks.

Scott was trying. He made mistakes but they all did. This case was the biggest he'd ever worked on. Even for Zoe, who had the experience he lacked, it had left her with sleepless nights and intrusive thoughts that encroached on her sanity.

And it had killed him.

She reached her car and fumbled with the keys, her hands trembling slightly. Finally, she managed to unlock the door and slip inside, grateful for the warmth of the car. She slammed the door shut behind her, cutting off the relentless roar of the hailstorm.

Sinking into the driver's seat, she allowed herself a moment, the rain's rhythm against the windows a distant, almost soothing sound. Her composure cracked, and she began to cry silently. Whatever control she may have had suddenly snapped and it all poured out. She pushed her thumbs into her eyes, trying to avoid the image of Scott dying in front of her.

After what felt like an eternity, she took a shaky breath and glanced up, catching a reflection in the rearview mirror.

"What the hell?" She whirled around, her heart leaping into her throat.

Keith was sitting in the back seat. "I'm sorry, Zoe. About what happened to your colleague." His voice was strained.

"Have you just been sitting there while I was crying?"

He shrugged weakly.

She rolled her eyes and wiped her face. "What are you doing here and how?"

"I know I shouldn't have broken into your car, but old habits die hard. I had to see you. I—" He faltered, his gaze dropping to his hands. "I'm sorry about Scott. I really am. I know this isn't the best time, and I didn't want to do this, but..." He paused, struggling to find the words. "I'm leaving town. I can't stay here any longer. I just... I needed to see you before I left."

Zoe's breath hitched as she processed his words. A sigh escaped her lips; suddenly she felt heavy like the weight of a big rock was strapped to her feet and pulling her down. "Why?" she finally managed to ask, her voice barely above a whisper. "What happened?"

He was kind enough to show remorse. "I thought I was safe after all these years. But I'm being threatened again."

"Who is it? That man you and Rachel ran away from?"

"Yes. Somehow you being here raised some flags. I have no idea why."

Zoe bit her tongue. Was it possible she was being watched? Outside the car, their surroundings were a blur of white. Icy pellets crashed on the ground, creating a frenzied dance of shimmering white. The streetlights struggled, their beams barely penetrating the dense curtain of hail. Her stomach dropped. There was a danger to wilderness. It shrouded predators and secrets alike. And then another realization smacked her. Simon. She had asked Simon to look into Keith. He must have entered the name somewhere. That would have raised flags.

"If you're in danger, then the FBI can protect..." She didn't finish.

Keith gave her a knowing smile. "We both know that Rachel wouldn't have killed herself, Zoe. Especially when she had two kids that needed her. Someone got to her."

Zoe nodded, her neck stiff. Rachel was murdered while she was in witness protection. "They did."

"And now I have to disappear before they get to me. Maybe they've been keeping tabs on you too. Just a heads-up."

Why did it feel like she was losing a piece of her past again? The one tangible connection she had found to Rachel, to why and who killed her, and it was slipping away. "Is there no other way?" she pleaded. "Please... I just..." Tears collected in her eyes. "I just can't lose everything."

"I'm sorry, Zoe. But there is one thing I can do for you." He retrieved a key from his coat. Its brass surface was tarnished to a deep, uneven patina, featured elaborate engravings, with swirling patterns. "Your mother gave something to me when she left." He gripped the bow of the key. "She said this was my insurance policy in case they came after me. This key opens a safety deposit box in Chicago."

Chicago. A surreal feeling swept through her. All those years she had spent in the windy city and all the while it contained something she had been searching for.

"The safety deposit box contains something important to that man who was after her. I want you to have it."

Zoe swallowed. With a trembling hand, she took the key from him. Keith released a breath, his eyes lingering on the key.

"Why are you giving it to me? You'll need it if you're going to be on the run."

"Because this is the least I can do for Rachel." His brows pulled together, a wan smile spreading on his lips. "I can take care of myself but if they come after you or Gina, then you have leverage."

She turned the key between her fingers. "What does the deposit box contain?"

"You'll see for yourself. Hopefully, you'll be able to understand it because I couldn't." He clicked the door open. "I hope one day our paths cross again. Take care, Zoe."

He exited the car with the collar of his coat up, chin tucked in and hands stuffed into his pockets. Zoe watched him disappear through the frosted window as she pondered what he'd just told her.

Anticipation built inside her as she studied the key. Keith might be gone, but this was his parting gift to her. She clasped her fingers around it, and the tapered edge of the key dug into her skin. One step closer to the truth.

Her phone buzzed with a message. It was Terri.

T: The recipient of the phlebotomy kit is John Smith. Larkspur Greenhouse, 1120 Cedar Hollow Road.

FIFTY-FOUR

A quick search of the Larkspur Greenhouse on the Internet yielded no information. It was a private property—not registered or run by any organization. But that wasn't what stood out to her like a giant, loud red sign.

It was John Smith.

Why would anyone ordering a phlebotomy kit online give the name *John Smith*? It was because he had something to hide. He didn't want his identity known.

She dropped a quick message to Aiden, letting him know where she was headed.

The greenhouse was nestled in a small clearing, surrounded by towering evergreens that seemed to close in on all sides. The glass structure was dimly lit by the last rays of twilight with ivy creeping up its sides and moss gathering at its base. There was no sign of life, no other buildings, no distant hum of civilization —just the greenhouse.

Zoe moved quickly but quietly, scanning the area for any signs of surveillance or recent activity. She noticed the heavy padlock on the door. It was old but sturdy, the kind of lock that wasn't meant to be easily tampered with. Without hesitation, she pulled out a small set of tools from her jacket, quickly working the lock until it gave way with a soft click.

The door creaked open, and she slipped inside. The interior was almost completely dark, save for the faintest glow filtering through the glass walls. Her eyes adjusted, revealing rows of plants on long tables, their leaves casting strange, elongated shadows across the floor. The air inside was thick and humid, carrying the earthy scent of soil and the sharp tang of fertilizer. The walls were lined with shelves, stacked with gardening tools, pots, and various bags of soil amendments.

"Hello? Is anyone here?" Zoe shouted out, her voice bouncing around the greenhouse. She knew there was no one around but it didn't hurt to try. The scent of *greenery* was overwhelming and she searched for a power switch to turn on the lights but to no avail.

Her heart thudded slowly in her chest and her skin tingled.

She inspected the plants closely—varieties she didn't immediately recognize, some of them rare or exotic, their leaves glistening in the dim light.

She could dig into property records and figure out who owned this place but she was hoping this approach would be quicker. An isolated private greenhouse was also a perfect place to hide a child. Perhaps this is where Lily had encountered devil's club and got an allergic reaction. Zoe approached a table and rifled through the few papers—seed catalogs, plant care guides—from decades ago.

Confusion flared. There was no information on the owner, and only old plant guides, and yet it appeared from the plants that someone was maintaining the greenhouse at *some* capacity.

Then something caught her eye near the back of the greenhouse. A small section of the floor looked different—less worn, the dirt not as compacted. She knelt down and ran her hand over the area, her fingers brushing against a metallic edge hidden beneath the dirt. She carefully cleared the soil away, revealing a hidden latch.

Zoe paused, her instincts on high alert. An energy cackled through her. She gripped the latch, her knuckles white with tension, and pulled. The floor gave way with a low groan, revealing a narrow staircase leading down into the darkness.

Using her phone's flashlight, she went down the staircase. She hated the dark and had never got over that childish fear that something would reach out and yank her in. Her labored breathing echoed in her ears. She waved the flashlight around until it landed on a metallic door covered in rust in front of her.

She checked her Glock, safely tucked in her waistband. As she padded softly toward the door, she could hear muffled voices coming from the other side. Fear clawed up her skin, making her shiver. Her toes curled in her boots.

The door wasn't entirely closed. She took a breath and pushed it open.

"FBI!" she shouted, her gun pointed ahead.

The room was bathed in warm, yellow light. Sparse furniture. Stone walls. A carton of bottled water and sandwiches piled on the side of the room. But it was the sight in front of her that made her stop.

There was a small cot. Lucy was sitting on it, eating an ice cream. Next to her, a young man was standing with his arms crossed, leaning against the wall. Their faces snapped in Zoe's direction.

The man's eyes flashed with fear. He licked his lips, eyes darting around for an escape route, but the only way was through Zoe who had a gun. He was wearing faded jeans and a black hoodie with a big bleach stain on the front.

Her scalp prickled.

The same hoodie she'd seen in the CCTV footage of the burglary at the bakery.

"Lucy, honey." Zoe kept the gun aimed at the man. "Why don't you come with me? Do you want to go home?"

Lucy nodded with her mouth full. She put down the ice cream and ran toward Zoe, wrapping her arms around her legs. The relief Zoe felt nearly knocked her off balance.

"Please try to understand!" the boy who couldn't be a day over twenty begged. "This isn't what—"

"Save it!" she hissed and he cowered, crouching on the floor. "On your knees, hands behind your head."

He did as she said. Zoe pulled out the handcuffs from her back pocket and secured his hands behind his back. He kept his head down, his shoulders drooping. She didn't put her gun away yet—not until she had backup. But she ran her eyes all over Lucy, whose face looked thinner but there wasn't a single blemish on her.

Relief flooded her. She had found Lucy alive. Lucy was fine. This was over.

"What's your name, kid?" she asked.

"Ryan Hunter."

FIFTY-FIVE

Ryan Hunter.

Zoe repeated his name over and over in her head. She was afraid to ask the question that was sitting on the tip of her tongue.

Are you related to Travis Hunter?

She didn't need to. The resemblance was unmistakable. She knew Travis had a son but she didn't know his name.

The ambulance and squad car lights cast colored beams all over their faces and on the greenhouse, their sirens piercing the still air. Lucy was being lifted into an ambulance with two patrol officers on guard. Two more squad cars were parked. One of the patrols was talking to Ryan who stood defiantly, his face crumpled somewhere between annoyance and pain. A group of officers were whispering among themselves. The locals must recognize him.

"How did you know to bring the cavalry?" Zoe asked, seeing Aiden round the corner. He was out of breath, his face twinged with confusion as he searched the space for someone. "What happened?"

"I looked up the address and it was in the middle of

nowhere, and at this time of night I was worried." His face fell when his eyes landed on a handcuffed Ryan.

"I need to talk to him." Aiden shouldered past her, but she was right behind him.

Ryan shifted uncomfortably and averted his gaze. He didn't want to talk to them. He kept blinking like he was fighting back tears.

"Is Travis your dad?" she asked.

Silence.

She sighed and leaned her elbow on the roof of the car. "You have to cooperate, kid. You were caught with a missing girl in a basement. What did you expect me to do?"

Ryan looked at her. "I didn't hurt her."

"I haven't told your father, but I bet someone here made the call." She hitched her thumb at the clusters of people surrounding them. The news was going to spread like wildfire. But for just one moment, Zoe wanted to focus on the lightness coursing through her body.

They had saved Lucy. Reality washed over her, loosening all those tightly wound muscles.

"Why did you do it?" Aiden finally asked. All this time he had been watching Ryan, like he was trying to figure out what would be the best way to cut him open.

Ryan's eyebrows pulled together like he was deep in thought. There was a cut on his lip. Zoe tried a different approach. "Who does the greenhouse belong to? Your dad?"

"My mom. She passed away a few years ago, so no one really takes care of it. I come here from time to time."

"We have you on video stealing desserts from that bakery. There's no way out of this."

He opened his mouth but then an officer interjected. "Agent Storm? The victim is crying. Do you think you can help?"

"Stay with him," Zoe muttered to Aiden and went to the

ambulance where Lucy was strapped to a gurney with tears streaming down her face. She looked so tiny, Zoe just wanted to cradle her. "Lucy, I'm here. You're safe now."

"Where's Mommy?" she asked, hiccups jolting her body.

"We have let her know, and she's coming straight to the hospital." Zoe ran a hand over her head, soothing her.

"I just want to go home."

"You will." Tears bubbled in Zoe's eyes as she realized that the home Lucy would return to was about to change forever. Now that she was found alive, Zoe was obligated to inform the CPS of Carly's crimes against her own daughter.

"We have to take you to the hospital to make sure you're okay and that boy didn't hurt you."

"He didn't hurt me." Lucy was fading away, her blood pressure dropping.

"What's happening to her?" Zoe asked the paramedic.

"She's okay, it's exhaustion and mental duress." The paramedics checked her vitals. "But we should take her to the hospital right away."

Zoe gave them the go-ahead. She hopped off the ambulance when she saw Aiden approaching. "What was Lucy doing with Ryan when you found them?" he asked.

"She was eating ice cream and he was just standing there. Why?"

He licked his lips and ran a hand through his hair. "Was she scared? At all?"

"Not until I pulled out the gun. For a moment. But why? We know he feeds them well and takes care of them before it's lights out. That's what he did with Lily."

"Storm, Lucy is eleven years old." Aiden's voice was thick with frustration. "Even if she's given all the toys and candy in the world, she's not going to be relaxed in an underground bunker away from everything she knows. And there's no way that that boy matches the profile."

Zoe was puzzled. "I don't understand what you're saying."

Aiden hesitated and then said something that made Zoe's blood pound in her ears.

* * *

Zoe stared at the doors to Travis's office. She still remembered the first time she'd burst through them. She almost expected to Scott to be in there again too. But in the last few days, the entire landscape of Harborwood PD had shifted.

And one last piece of the puzzle was yet to be slotted into place.

Travis Hunter was sitting at his desk. Behind him it was pitch black outside, no sign of rain or thunder or wind. Like a still painting. His desk was clean—all the clutter cleared out. Only one thing remained—a glass of whiskey.

Zoe and Aiden moved forward to sit across from him. The air was soupy and viscous. She felt like this space existed in another plane. Travis didn't look at them. As he stared into empty space, he picked up the glass and took a sip from it.

With bated breath, she waited for him to puncture the silence with words. But the silence stretched between them, filling it with a tension that could be cut with a knife. There was a peace to this moment, like the calm before the storm or those seconds before a vase comes crashing down. The truth hung between them; Zoe could feel it. But without acknowledging it, she could pretend for a few more seconds that it wasn't there.

She waited for Aiden to say something. But he was too absorbed, observing Travis's apparent calmness.

"Do you know your son was arrested after being found with Lucy in the basement of a greenhouse?" Zoe said.

He nodded, his expression unchanged. "One of my guys called me."

"He refuses to cooperate without a lawyer. I confronted him but he didn't deny anything," she said.

Travis's eyes flitted to Zoe, a zing of confusion. "He didn't?"

"No. I thought it was him. He was wearing that hoodie from the video, which now I realize you could have easily borrowed. Lucy told me that she'd never met him before today and that he was trying to help her escape."

She didn't want to ask him if there was even a faint possibility that this was a mistake.

"He's trying to protect someone he loves but doesn't understand." Aiden leaned forward, pinning him with a hard look.

"My mother had it." Travis finally gave in, his hand swirling the glass in which the burgundy liquid sloshed. "Munchausen by proxy. She liked to keep us sick. Not my father. But he was a weak man. He just did what my mother told him to do. After a while, I think he... lied to himself and pretended that everything was fine. My mother was a vicious woman. Unhinged. Thought we were the devils but still loved us. Someone found out and reported them." His gaze drifted into empty space, taking him somewhere else. "She panicked. I remember coming home after school one day to find her force-feeding my sisters milk. She ordered me to drink it too. I knew what it was, probably something that would give us an upset stomach or make us drowsy. It was easier to do as she said rather than resist. It made her worse if I argued. Except this time I was wrong." A lone tear trickled down his cheek. He took a big gulp of whiskey. "My sisters passed out first. I was tired but still half-conscious. I watched my mother prepare three ropes, curling their ends into nooses and hanging them from the ceiling fan. My eyes were closing, my energy fading as she took my sisters and placed them in the nooses. I couldn't move. And then it was my turn."

Zoe recalled the story Dr. Parsons had told her at the hospital.

"She did the same with me. I didn't resist; I guess I was too afraid, too shocked. She left the room. The door clicked shut. I remember that very well. That door clicking shut and somehow how I found my strength again. As soon as she left the room, I felt this last speckle of strength surge through me. And that's when I escaped from my noose. Something that morning told me to grab a pocket knife and hide it up my sleeve. But it was too late for my sisters. I checked. They were younger than me and much smaller in size. My mother must not have accounted for that when she roofied us so it didn't hit me as hard. I had enough strength to crawl out the window and never look back." He finished his drink, his hand trembling as he wiped his lips. He finally gazed at Zoe. "I was thirteen. I took a bus to my aunt's place. She never liked my mother but was fond of us kids. I never told her about the things Mother did to us. She raised me and gave me her name. It was so long ago. With time, it felt unreal. Has that ever happened to you? A part of your life so different and immensely confusing that it feels like a distant dream?"

Zoe didn't respond but her face gave it away.

"You do know. It's okay, that's your story. I forgot about mine with time. Locked it away somewhere deep inside." He pounded his chest and winced. "That is until I was at the hospital one time for my symptoms. You see they come and go. I hallucinate sometimes. I see my dead sisters and mother. I never really dealt with what happened so they still exist somewhere inside me and come out from time to time. I overheard Parsons talking about Lily to someone on the phone. He was crying, saying it reminded him of that case all those years ago."

That was the pivot Travis's life took. That one nudge that had sent him back down the path he had managed to avoid.

"That's when I started seeing them again more often." His eyes glazed past them. "My sisters and my mother. They're standing behind you, Agent Storm and Dr. Wesley."

Zoe went cold inside.

"But you won't see them," he said calmly. "Only I do. Thank God, Ryan doesn't. I was worried about him, worried that he was like me, seeing things he shouldn't. I even followed him once. Turned his room upside down. But I found pictures... pictures of me talking to Lily." He laughed without humor. "He knew. He knew what I'd done and that's why he hated me. But he didn't say anything. And I said nothing too."

"Ryan went to the greenhouse to save Lucy," Aiden said.

A smile that made his eyes twinkle. "I'm proud of my boy. I'm so proud. He's not like me. He's like his mother. It's a powerful bond. No matter how much we hate our parents, it's hard to turn on them. He didn't turn on me; the same way I couldn't turn on my mother. But he tried to do the right thing. He must have figured out where I was keeping Lucy."

"What was your endgame, Travis?" Zoe's tone was caustic, her mind still ticking over his words.

He looked past her at the ghosts of his dead family. "Because I left them. I abandoned my sisters when I was supposed to die with them. I was their older brother; I should have protected them. Instead, I climbed out of that window and left them hanging." The corner of his mouth curled into a sneer filled with self-loathing. "And when I found out about Lily, it all came flooding back. I needed to die with them. This time."

"The three nooses. Lily and Lucy to represent your two sisters. The third noose... was for you," Aiden stated.

He nodded. "I was always the third victim. But when Tara went missing, it threw me off. I had no idea that Connor would exploit this for his political gain. She wasn't supposed to die."

"But Lily and Lucy were?" Zoe argued hotly. "How could you do this to them?"

He played with the phantom ring on his ring finger. "Their mothers would have killed them either way. I just got there first. But I was very gentle. Isn't it better to die at the hands of a stranger than your mother?"

Zoe didn't know how to feel. She was drowning in everything. Travis's confession settled over her but there was no clarity. It filled her with a sense of hopelessness. Were people really forever slaves to their trauma? She knew she was—it was why she hunted for pain in illegal, underground fights.

"You could have ended the cycle, Travis." Aiden couldn't hide the disappointment in his voice. "You were raising a good son, you were doing good for the community. Why didn't you just open an investigation into Lily's parents? You aren't that little boy anymore—"

"But I am!" His voice bubbled with lodged tears in his throat. "I'm still that little boy and I always will be. We don't shed our childhood when we grow up. We grow around it. It's our core. And I knew what Lily's future was—dark and guilt-ridden. She was going to grow up to be like me. Dysfunctional and messed up. Maybe she would have been better at hiding it but there would always be something rotten living inside her. She was born to be ill-fated. They both were."

"Why didn't you kill Lucy? You held her captive for longer than Lily."

"When Scott told me that he wasn't the father... I suspected I might be. Carly and I got involved around then. But I'll never know." Travis stood up and cleared his throat. "I'm turning myself in. I won't need a lawyer. I'll sign my confession." There was an air of serenity around him.

"Do you feel guilty?" Zoe asked.

"No." And then his voice cracked. "I feel nothing."

EPILOGUE

"Well, I'm happy to report that you get a clean chit from me to resume your duty at the FBI." Aiden signed a form with a flourish.

"Lucky me." She threw her head back. The last couple hours had been painful to wade through.

"I hope we get to work again soon," he said seriously.

Zoe's eyes narrowed into slits as she mentally imagined how it would feel to peel his brain. *"I hope not."*

He blinked, almost hurt. *"Sorry?"*

He'd snaked his way into getting her to like him, but it was only so he could psychoanalyze her, a trick to get her guard down, while she, like an idiot, thought they could be friends.

"Because I don't trust you, Dr. Wesley."

* * *

"Good morning, Harborwood!" Regina stood at the podium, looking and feeling radiant. This was the moment she had been preparing for, the moment she was afraid of losing. The moment she wished her father saw. "I want to begin by expressing how incredibly honored and grateful I am to serve as your new mayor. This town has been my home for many years, and I am committed to working tirelessly to ensure a brighter future for all of us."

A round of applause, and cameras flashed. Regina basked in the glory of the compliments and the praise, shaking many hands and posing for several pictures.

"However, I know that recent events have cast a shadow over this victory. It has come to light that my former campaign manager was involved in criminal activities. This revelation has been deeply shocking and disappointing, not just to me, but to everyone who believed in our campaign."

The room fell silent, the tension palpable as Regina addressed the scandal head-on. "I want to make it clear that I had no knowledge of these actions. The trust you placed in me is something I take very seriously, and I understand that that trust has been shaken. But when I became aware of the situation, I did what was necessary. I cooperated fully with the police, providing them with the information they needed to bring this individual to justice. While this has been a difficult chapter, I believe it's also an opportunity for us to come together as a community. We must hold each other accountable, and I promise to lead with integrity and transparency. Together, we can move forward and build a better future for our town."

* * *

Zoe's stint at Harborwood PD was officially over. She sat on a wooden bench at the docks, gazing into the endless blue ocean. Boats of all sizes were moored along the piers, their masts swaying gently with the movement of the tide. The sunlight danced on the water's surface, creating a shimmering path.

She was going to miss this. That perpetual salty tang in the air, the scent of brine, and the sound of waves lapping against the shore.

Her hands were curled around a cup of strawberry milkshake. The last time she'd had one was the day Scott died. Now that she was leaving Harborwood behind her, it felt it was time for her to get reacquainted with her favorite drink. She took a sip, relishing the sugary, fruity taste coating her tongue and that rich texture sliding down her food pipe.

A smile spread on her lips. Everything was going to be fine. Zoe didn't have many things, but her superpower was her endless positivity. A renewable source that resided inside her.

Her phone rang. It was Simon.

"Hey," she answered.

"Just wanted to check on you now that the case is over. When are you coming back?"

Zoe felt the key Keith had given her in her pocket. "I'm thinking of taking a few days off."

"Zoe Storm is taking time off?" He chuckled. "Did the case impact that you much?"

"Yes." A moment of honesty. "But it isn't that. I just want to visit a few friends in Chicago."

"Fair enough. We'll survive without you."

"You can try," she sang-song.

"Another thing. You should know... Nancy and I are separating."

Zoe's breath hitched. A seagull's cried echoed. A couple of fishermen called out to each other. "Why?"

"Things have been rough." He sighed. "We'll see it how it goes. Just wanted you to know. It's not about you, though," he added quickly, with a tinge of awkwardness.

"Okay." What choice did Zoe have but to believe him? "Anyway, I'll see you soon."

"See you."

Zoe hung up. She had never told him about Nancy confronting her. It felt unnecessary to get even more entangled in their drama when she was being dragged into it already. But she pushed the thought of Simon away. There was something more important waiting for her.

She was just unlocking the door to her room when Aiden staggered at the end of the hallway, dragging his luggage. "Hey. Heading back?"

"Yeah." He pushed his glasses up. "I'm heading to San Diego for a friend's wedding."

"Sounds fun. What about your mattress?"

He laughed. "I've decided to donate it to the motel." Then his eyes assessed her. "How are you doing, Storm?"

A shiver rolled through her. Although the case was now closed, it had been picking away at her insides. "It is what it is. Just move on to the next one."

"That's a good attitude. You have my number if you need to give me a call."

"Sure. It wasn't too bad working with you. And as much as I hate to admit it, we wouldn't have been able to solve this without you."

He raised his eyebrows. "Really?"

She looked at her feet. "You were right about many things, two killers, unresolved childhood trauma. I think we make a good team."

"I'm sorry, I'm not used to you being nice to me." He frowned, humor dancing in his eyes.

She rolled her eyes. "I'm a rainbow, you're the problem here. But still. It wasn't too bad."

"No, it wasn't." His eyes twinkled. "I'll see you around."

"Will you?"

"Absolutely."

She watched his large frame grow smaller as he walked away and then disappeared around the corner. Despite that hot spurt of shame from Aiden coming so close to knowing her other side, a watery smile tugged on her lips.

She stumbled into her motel room, ready to pack up. She had a sore back—one thing she wasn't going to miss was the soft mattress.

The room seemed unusually quiet, the kind of stillness that made her skin prickle. Zoe scanned the room, but her weariness made her dismiss the feeling of unease. She moved toward the bed, her hand reaching for the lamp to shed some light.

Before she could react, the closet door burst open behind her with a violent bang. A figure surged forward from the shadows, a blur of motion that left her no time to prepare. He struck her—his fist connecting squarely with the small of her back. Zoe's breath exploded out of her in a harsh gasp, the pain radiating through her torso like fire.

Instinctively, she tried to fight back. She spun round, aiming a sharp elbow to his midsection, but he anticipated her move. His hand shot out, grabbing her arm and twisting it painfully behind her back. She cried out, her body jerking as she struggled to break free.

He slammed her against the wall with a powerful shove, disorienting her. Her head hit the hard surface, and the room seemed to tilt. Before she could regain her footing, he drove his knee into her side, sending her crashing to the floor.

Her head exploded in pain as she hit the ground. Dazed, she tried to push herself up, but his heavy boot was already on her chest, pinning her down. She swung her legs, aiming a desperate kick at his shin, but he was faster and brought his fist down in a punishing blow to her stomach.

Zoe's vision swam. The room spun as she fought to stay conscious. Her mouth was flooded with the taste of metallic blood. He searched her pockets and found Keith's key. She fumbled, trying to get a hold of it. For a moment, she had it in her grasp—but he ripped it away with such force that it sliced her palm open. Blood trickled out of her hand but her heart was bursting at the seams.

Not the key. Not that piece of her mother.

"No... please, no."

He stood over her. "Stop looking into Rachel. Or Viper will have you killed too."

Zoe lay on the floor, the side of her head pressed into the carpet. Her body felt like lead. Her vision blurred as she followed the shoes of the retreating figure making his way out of the room.

Her eyes rolled back in her head as she tried desperately to hold on, but the walls weren't just closing in, they were blackening. The edges of her vision searing like burned paper. The door burst open again and this time Aiden ran in.

"Storm!" He crouched down, his worried face hovering over hers. "Storm! Stay with me!"

And then she catapulted into another nightmare.

She was running through the woods, the trees twisting and closing in around her, their branches clawing at her as she pushed forward. The air was thick with mist, making it hard to see, but she couldn't stop. A young girl's voice echoed through the darkness, pleading for help.

"Help! Please, help me!"

Zoe's heart raced as she followed the voice, her feet barely touching the ground. The sound led her to a small clearing where an old, moss-covered well stood. The voice was coming from inside.

"I'm here! Please, help me!"

Zoe leaned over the edge, peering into the blackness below. She could just make out the faint outline of a small figure, huddled at the bottom, hidden in the shadows.

"I'm going to get you out," Zoe called, trying to keep her voice steady.

"Please, hurry. I'm so scared," the girl cried, her voice barely audible now.

Zoe reached out, but the darkness seemed endless, the well impossibly deep. She leaned further, straining to reach the girl, but suddenly the ground beneath her gave way. She felt herself falling, the world spinning as the darkness swallowed her whole.

"Emily!"

A LETTER FROM RUHI

Dear reader,

I want to say a huge thank you for choosing to read *The Hanging Dolls*. If you did enjoy it, and want to keep up to date with all my latest releases, just sign up at the following link. Your email address will never be shared and you can unsubscribe at any time.

www.bookouture.com/ruhi-choudhary

I would be very grateful if you could write a review. I'd love to hear what you think, and it makes such a difference helping new readers to discover one of my books for the first time.

I love hearing from my readers – you can get in touch through Twitter or Goodreads.

Thanks,

Ruhi

𝕏 x.com/RuhiSChoudhary

ACKNOWLEDGMENTS

Writing is a lonely job, but publishing is all about teamwork. I'm extremely grateful to my editor Nina Winters for her passion, hard work and commitment. She has truly been a partner in creating this new character and series.

Big thanks to editors Anna Paterson and Shirley Khan, cover designer Head Design Ltd, voice actor Stephanie Cannon, and my publicist Noelle Holten for their commitment and brilliance. The entire team at Bookouture has been very kind and supportive.

My parents for their love. My sister and friend Dhriti, for always being in our hearts and looking after us. Sasha for being my rock and inspiring me. All my friends especially Rachel Drisdelle, Michelle Feigis, Dafni Giannari, Scott Proulx, Kaushik Raj, and Sheida Stephens for their excitement, humor, and support.

Most of all, I'm grateful to the readers. Thank you so much for taking the time! I appreciate each and every one of you and would love to hear what you thought of the book.

PUBLISHING TEAM

Turning a manuscript into a book requires the efforts of many people. The publishing team at Bookouture would like to acknowledge everyone who contributed to this publication.

Audio
Alba Proko
Sinead O'Connor
Melissa Tran

Commercial
Lauren Morrissette
Hannah Richmond
Imogen Allport

Cover design
Head Design Ltd

Data and analysis
Mark Alder
Mohamed Bussuri

Editorial
Nina Winters
Sinead O'Connor

Copyeditor
Anna Paterson

Proofreader
Shirley Khan

Marketing
Alex Crow
Melanie Price
Occy Carr
Cíara Rosney
Martyna Młynarska

Operations and distribution
Marina Valles
Stephanie Straub
Joe Morris

Production
Hannah Snetsinger
Mandy Kullar
Ria Clare
Nadia Michael

Publicity
Kim Nash
Noelle Holten
Jess Readett
Sarah Hardy

Rights and contracts
Peta Nightingale
Richard King
Saidah Graham

www.ingramcontent.com/pod-product-compliance
Ingram Content Group UK Ltd.
Pitfield, Milton Keynes, MK11 3LW, UK
UKHW040718290725
7121UKWH00029B/204